Nice Girls
Finish Last

Also by Sparkle Hayter

What's a Girl Gotta Do?

Nice Girls
Finish Last

Sparkle Hayter

VIKING

VIKING
Published by the Penguin Group
Penguin Books USA Inc., 375 Hudson Street,
New York, New York 10014, U.S.A.
Penguin Books Ltd, 27 Wrights Lane,
London W8 5TZ, England
Penguin Books Australia Ltd, Ringwood,
Victoria, Australia
Penguin Books Canada Ltd, 10 Alcorn Avenue,
Toronto, Ontario, Canada M4V 3B2
Penguin Books (N.Z.) Ltd, 182–190 Wairau Road,
Auckland 10, New Zealand

Penguin Books Ltd, Registered Offices:
Harmondsworth, Middlesex, England

First published in 1996 by Viking Penguin,
a division of Penguin Books USA Inc.

1 3 5 7 9 10 8 6 4 2

PUBLISHER'S NOTE
This is a work of fiction. Names, characters, places, and incidents
either are the product of the author's imagination or are used fictitiously,
and any resemblance to actual persons, living or dead, events, or
locales is entirely coincidental.

LIBRARY OF CONGRESS CATALOGING IN PUBLICATION DATA
Hayter, Sparkle
p. cm.
ISBN 0-670-86039-5
1. Women journalists—New York (N.Y.)—Fiction.
2. New York (N.Y.)—Fiction. I. Title.
PS3558.A879N53   1996
813'.54—dc20   95-21679

This book is printed on acid-free paper.
∞

Printed in the United States of America
Set in Minion
Designed by Virginia Norey

for Diana, Sandra, Nevin
and an eighteen-pound turtle named Henri

ANNOUNCER: Mr. Question Man, why is it that people walking on the bottom of the earth don't fall off?

ERNIE KOVACS: That's a popular misconception. Actually, people are falling off all the time.

—*The Ernie Kovacs Show*

Nice Girls
Finish Last

1

Someone had left a guillotine in front of my building.

It was a Tuesday night, and I'd just come from picking up my cat, Louise Bryant, at her agent's office, where I received a lecture about her bad attitude, how she refused to eat the sponsor's cat food, fell asleep under the hot lights whenever she felt like it, and kept clawing the Teamsters, one of whom had come down with rather a bad case of cat-scratch fever. We had one more shoot before our contractual obligation was fulfilled and I could retire the old girl.

She was whiny and I was tired when the cab let us off on Avenue B at Tenth Street, in a part of Manhattan known variously as Loisaida, Alphabet City, and the East Village. Con Ed was venting steam through a big orange and white striped tube, sending big, misty clouds into the air. Because the city had recently installed new streetlamps with a pinkish glow, the steam was pink, and gave the street a sinister, demimondaine cast. A slow wind blew the pink fog my way, enveloping me, and I had one of those chills, you know, the kind they say you get when someone is walking over your grave.

That's when I saw the guillotine, wedged between two garbage cans in front of my stoop as if someone had thrown it out with the trash. The absence of severed heads in the vicinity told me this was not a working guillotine, as the practicality of such an item in a neighborhood crawling with youth gangs known for dispensing summary justice would not have gone untested. Closer inspection showed the blade to be rubber and firmly bolted in place.

"Now that's what I call a deterrent," I said to Louise Bryant, who was growling softly in her carrier.

Pink mist swirled around the guillotine. When the mist cleared, I saw the telltale signature CHAOS REIGNS in red spray paint on the sidewalk. CHAOS REIGNS is a guerrilla art movement that drops its work randomly throughout New York's Lower East Side.

As my head was on the company chopping block at the moment, this seemed anything but random to me. No, this was an omen if ever I saw one.

My name is Robin Jean Hudson and I am a reporter in the sleazy Special Reports unit at the prestigious All News Network, where I have an ironclad contract that binds me to them, and them to me. And no, I am not one of those faces you see set before the hills of Sarajevo or the august halls of government or the wreckage of a natural disaster. You see me, trying very hard not to look embarrassed, in those four-minute reports on shoddy sperm banks, UFO abductees, and the shady side of the hairpiece industry.

Things were not good at the All News Network. Ratings and advertising revenue were down across the board—except for the two fat cash cows, Special Reports and the Kerwin Shutz show. Rumors of cutbacks, shakeups, and reshuffles were rampant. Morale was abysmal. The company mandarins were in intensive meetings and the place was crawling with high-powered talent flown in for these meetings. Something was brewing, the air was heavy with it. And it would happen soon.

The most persistent rumor was that older, third-string reporters would be taken off the air and put in other jobs to make way for the peppy, attractive reporterlings coming up through the ranks, kids who would kill to get even my crappy on-air job.

Well, I just happened to be an older, third-string reporter. I'm only thirty-seven, but that's a lot in TV years, which are rather like dog years.

I'll be honest, the report card on me for the previous year and a half would be pretty mixed. On the plus side, there was the award-winning series on vigilantism I had done while my boss Jerry Spurdle was overseas filling in for the Berlin bureau chief, and there was Nicky Vassar, a fraud I'd helped nail. Of course, my boss Jerry Spurdle took credit for both those things, which was His Lordship's right as executive producer of Special Reports. But the people in the know knew who had done the real work.

On the minus side, there were several threatened lawsuits that had come out of my ill-fated special report, "Death in Modern America." However, I had redeemed myself somewhat by taking full responsibility for that disaster, writing long, eloquent letters of apology to the Hackensack widow and to avant-garde undertaker Max Guffy. Only the cryogenics people were still threatening to sue.

So things were very uncertain. Each day I went in wondering if it might be my last day on the air. A guillotine on a dark sidewalk, therefore, was fraught with significance for me, and definitely not conducive to a Positive Mental Attitude.

I was, you see, a new woman with a new attitude. A good attitude. Yes, I was singing in the rain, walking on the sunny side of the street, making lemonade out of lemons. Life was just a box of chocolates. Or something that kind of looked like chocolate anyway.

So when my boss Jerry Spurdle marched into my office two months earlier, flashed me his evil "I control your economic destiny" smile, and said, "Get the crew. You're going out to Long Island City. I've got six bald guys with brain abscesses from a faulty hair replacement system who want to talk to you," I smiled and nodded, got the crew, and did the interview.

And when Jerry handed me my most recent script on UFO abductees and I saw that he had changed most of it and loaded it with sensationalism and clichés, I took it, looked at it, and smiled the sweetest smile I could muster, which was not like me at all.

Or, rather, not like the *old* me.

The *old* Robin Hudson would have fought long and hard with Jerry Spurdle, fought to the last sacrosanct semicolon. The *old* Robin Hudson would have taken that mutilated script to the tracking booth and ignored it, read her original script instead. She would have complained vociferously to her mentor, Bob McGravy. She would have anonymously called a half dozen funeral homes and arranged for their representatives to drop in on Jerry unannounced to discuss his final arrangements.

(This last option in particular was tempting me, as I had recently received a publicity package for a new service—"Parting Glance Funeral and Memorial Service Consultants—and had toyed with the idea of signing Jerry up for the customized Cage aux Folles service.)

But I took no revenge. What had brought about this radical change in my pathological behavior? Had I mellowed with age? Perhaps I had mellowed, a little. Perhaps I had come to the mature realization that there are times in life when one must compromise and play the game if one wants to get ahead, especially if one has an ironclad contract and one's professional redemption is largely dependent on the beneficence of Jerry Spurdle.

(Well, those lawsuits and the rumors about a major reshuffle probably had a bit more to do with it than maturity did.)

I always say it takes seven major muscle groups just to hold my tongue, so you can imagine the strain on me of having a good attitude under these conditions. Let me tell you, even with all the incentives I had, it was hard to be a goddamned ray of sunshine all the goddamned time.

If it wasn't for one final, important factor, I couldn't have pulled it off at all. I didn't have the fight in me anymore after my postdivorce boyfriend Eric and I split up. It just seemed easier to take the path of least resistance, you know what I mean? If I just played by the rules, for a change, what could go wrong?

I keep forgetting that my life is ruled by no law but Murphy's. What could go wrong? Only everything.

The guillotine had me spooked but, as part of my new positive attitude, I shrugged it off. Bloody guerrilla artists, disturbing my peace of mind that way. I kicked the guillotine. It made me feel better.

Very gingerly, I inserted my key into the thick steel door of my apartment building, a prewar on East Tenth street, slowly opened it, and peeked into the foyer, dimly lit by a yellow bug light. The coast was clear. My downstairs neighbor Mrs. Ramirez was *not* waiting by the mailboxes, as she often was.

This was a good omen. Mrs. Ramirez is eighty-one years old, has a hyperactive hearing aid, reportedly hasn't had a man since 1942, and imagines I am having all kinds of sinful fun she never had. I only wish I were. Lately, she had been *off* my back a little, ever since Sally moved in next door to her. Sally is a painter, a tarot reader, and a witch. Really. She's a good witch, though. She casts good spells only, because she believes good and evil deeds both come back to you threefold, and she's still trying to clear her karma for that spell she put on Brooke Shields when they were both freshmen at Princeton.

Sally's beliefs are no wackier or more harmful than those of any other religion. But Mrs. Ramirez saw in Sally an agent of the devil sent to deliver a curse unto her and was convinced the witch was making her hair fall out, her bowels shut down, and her feet swell. All I knew was, since Sally moved in, opening the way for an influx of other odd characters, such as the mysterious guitar-playing man who lived above me, Mrs. Ramirez had been spread a little thin and hadn't had as much time to trash my reputation.

As usual, the elevator was out of order, which meant I had to climb four flights while schlepping Louise in her carrier. Louise is a big, heavy cat, it was a long climb, and I had had a very long day. When I dragged my sorry carcass through the door of my apartment, I was exhausted. Even my face was tired, stiff, and sore from smiling so much, which took a lot of energy. Not to mention the energy it took to keep from barfing whenever my boss, Jerry Spurdle, said something crude or stupid, which was often. For example, that day he asserted that self-control came much easier to his gender than to mine. The temptation to remind him how he had nearly bankrupted himself recently in pursuit of an eighteen-year-old exotic dancer was powerful indeed. But I kept mum, because my desire to disprove Jerry's self-control hypothesis was even more powerful.

All I wanted in the world at that point was eight hours of solid z's—harder and harder to come by lately. Physically, psychologically, and emotionally exhausted, I could have dropped onto my bed in my clothes and high heels. But Louise Bryant was howling for her dinner and she hates to be kept waiting, so I fed her her regular dinner of cat food sautéed with bok choy and oyster sauce, cooled to lukewarm. Ignore her or try something new at your peril.

After brushing my teeth and checking myself for signs of necrotic fascitis, I put on my flannel pajamas and cued up a CD of lullabies and chants sung by monks in a rain forest. I picked up my sated cat and got into bed with her, petting her until she started to purr. Well, petting is probably an understatement. Every night, I gave the old girl the kitty equivalent of a shiatsu massage, just to get her to sleep with me so I wouldn't have to sleep alone.

Once she fell asleep, I curled up next to her, listening to

my soothing CD and reciting the Serenity Prayer, putting the day safely behind me. Just as I was about to close my eyes, the phone rang and my answering machine picked up.

"Robin, this is your mother," I heard.

"Yes, Mom, I recognize your voice," I said softly, but I didn't pick up the phone. I was too tired.

"I just called to remind you that your Aunt Maureen is arriving in New York today for two weeks," Mom said, in her guileless voice. "Something to do with her church."

Now, correct me if I'm wrong, but I thought that in order to "remind" someone of something, you had to have told them about it previously. And my mother had not mentioned it. I would have remembered. You meet my Aunt Maureen once, you never forget, no matter how hard you try. Aunt Mo is a force of nature. Think Mussolini in a corset and a wig, and you won't be too far off the mark.

No, she did not expect to stay with me, *thank God*. Instead, Mom said, she was staying in a hotel just a few blocks from my place of employment.

Well, this was not good news. I know, I know. Blood is thicker—and stickier—than water and I should have picked up the phone and called Aunt Maureen and asked about her plans, but I didn't. My plan was to avoid her at all costs. If my Aunt Minnie, who lives with Mom, or Aunt Flo, or my father's black-sheep sister Aunt Lucille came to town, I'd sleep on my fire escape so they could sleep in my bed and I'd show them all around town.

But Aunt Mo—no way.

Among her special talents—which had once included rooting out communists in the public libraries and Girl Scout troops of northern Minnesota in the 1950s—was that Aunt Mo knew how to reduce me to my insecurities, so I couldn't risk seeing her. Ironically, I was trying hard to be the kind of polite and obedient young lady she'd wanted me to be, and her presence would be a threat to my Positive Mental Attitude because something about her brought out my rebellious instincts. Maybe it was those monthly letters chastising me for getting divorced and telling me what I could have done to save my marriage, if I wasn't such a pigheaded fool agnostic. Maybe it was the fact that because of Aunt Mo I hate the taste of Tabasco. When I was a kid staying with Aunt Mo, she'd put Tabasco on my tongue whenever I said a bad word or told a lie. In fact, she put Tabasco on my tongue just as often when I told the truth. This is the part that gets me. She put Tabasco on my tongue even when *she* knew I was telling the truth, if it was an uncomfortable truth she wanted me to keep to myself. It was an early experience in censorship. To this day, when I taste Tabasco, I taste hypocrisy.

I guess that sounds like a petty thing, Tabasco, but all my complaints against Aunt Mo are not petty. After my Dad died when I was ten, Aunt Mo tried to get custody of me, citing my mother's mental illness. (My mother believes she's a member of the British royal family, which, even if true, is nothing you want to boast about to the neighbors.)

My mother had forgiven her for the custody fight. I hadn't.

Thinking about Aunt Mo, I couldn't sleep for shuddering. It took me fifteen minutes just to will away the image of her that appeared every time I closed my eyes. I was able to relax only after replaying my CD twice and imagining myself in a beautiful place with a handsome man I used to love once, a long time ago.

So there I was, perched on the edge of the gentle abyss, when, suddenly, the low-pitched siren of a car alarm went off on the street below, sending me bolt upright.

I hate those fucking car alarms.

Another went off, emitting intermittent shrieks, then another, and another. I opened my window, stuck my head out, and saw a man running through the Con Ed mist, grabbing the handles of car doors and setting off all their alarms, including one that activated a car horn, which in this instance played the first few bars of the *Godfather* theme over and over.

The man ran away. Up and down the dark steamy street, lights turned on and heads appeared in windows.

The insane symphony of car alarms was soon joined by a chorus of loud cursing that rained down on the heads of embarrassed car owners as they went out and turned off their alarms. After fifteen minutes only one alarm remained, the one with the intermittent shriek. Another fifteen minutes and someone started shooting at the offending car until the alarm stopped.

Jesus, there were guns everywhere. Well, this answered one of Life's big questions: Is the whole world nuts, or is it just me?

The car owners were all gone, windows went dark again. The street was quiet now. All I could hear was some man's laughter, increasingly distant and hollow, like someone laughing into a wide-mouthed jar.

When would this day ever end? Louise was awake too, and looking like she might go sleep elsewhere, so I closed the window and went back to bed, giving her another rubdown, playing my CD again, re-reciting the Serenity Prayer, and, finally, gently, falling to sleep.

I was in that comfortable, swimmy limbo, the hypnagogic space between consciousness and unconsciousness, when the phone again rang and I heard my machine pick up.

"Ms. Hudson, this is Detective Mack Ferber of Manhattan South—Homicide Division . . ."

I reached for the phone.

"Robin Hudson," I said.

"Oh, Ms. Hudson. Is this Robin Hudson or her machine?" He sounded young.

"This is Robin Hudson. What's your name again?"

"Detective Mack Ferber . . . Homicide . . ."

"And what do you want?"

"Um, Ms. Hudson . . . did you know Dr. Herman Kanengiser?"

"Um." I reached past my snoring cat for my alarm clock. Louise Bryant sleeps like an old man, with drooling and little raspy snores, and she gave a full-bodied snort when I moved her.

"Ms. Hudson?"

"Yeah, I know him, kind of," I said, studying the glow-in-the-dark clock face intently. It was twelve thirty a.m.

Actually, I hardly knew Dr. Herman Kanengiser, which is ironic when you think that I almost let the guy see me naked. Dr. Herman Kanengiser was my gynecologist, sort of. He leased space in the building I worked in, the Jackson Broadcasting building. That, direct insurance billing, and the fact that he took evening appointments made him ideal for a working woman, like me.

It also made it hard to get an appointment. I had finally got in to see him, about six weeks earlier, only to get beeped for an undercover shoot before we even got to the examining table. It took over a month more to schedule a second appointment, which was canceled that day.

"What happened? I mean . . ." I began to say.

"I'd rather discuss it in person."

"Well, why do you want to talk to me?"

"Are you up? Can I stop by? I *really* don't want to talk about this on the phone," he said.

I have a saying. My door is always open to men with warrants and/or badges. Legitimate badges, that is. After getting his badge number and calling him back at Manhattan South to confirm, I told him to come on over.

I was physically awake but mentally groggy, and had called him back on autopilot. But once I got off the phone, I realized what Ferber had said. He was a homicide cop and he had spoken of Kanengiser in the past tense. That meant Kanengiser was dead. Murdered.

Because I am a tad self-absorbed, my first thought was entirely selfish: whatever had happened, I wasn't going to get into trouble for it. My whereabouts all evening long could be attested to by witnesses. After leaving work, I had a meeting with Kerwin Shutz about some vigilante videotape, then drinks with my associate producer Tamayo and my new cameraman Mike. From there I went to my cat's agent's office and waited for the Teamsters to bring Louise back from her shoot, which had gone into overtime because of her bad behavior. It's just the nature of my life that I sleep better at night if I have a good alibi, since this wasn't the first time I'd had an appointment with someone who later ended up dead. It's like, my karma or something.

2

Call it vanity, but because there was a man coming over, I felt I had to fix myself up a bit, get out of the flannel nightshirt and into something respectable, touch up my thick red hair, put on some lipstick. I am not particularly proud of this side of myself, but that's the way it is. The cop might be cute.

Thank God the maid service had been in that day and the place was relatively tidy. The maid service was an important step on my road to maturity. Left to my own devices, I live amid clutter. Okay, clutter is another understatement. Left to my own devices, my apartment looks like the scene of a thorough Gestapo ransacking, or perhaps a small soccer riot.

Tidy as my apartment was, it did look like a bookstore's self-help section had exploded inside it, as I had plastered uplifting, inspirational sayings all over the place. Cut from books, magazines, articles, or comic strips, or handwritten, they were everywhere. My refrigerator exhorted me to THINK POSITIVE. On a lampshade was the message CHOOSE HAPPINESS! My toothbrush cup preached KEEP THE FAITH, while above my telephone was this from Confucius: TO GO BEYOND IS AS WRONG AS TO FALL SHORT.

Rather than have to explain this to unexpected company, I took a few of these more conspicuous bromides down.

A half hour later, Detective Mack Ferber knocked on my door. I was glad I'd preened, because he *was* good-looking, in a slightly goofy and very appealing way, a bit jowly with droopy brown eyes and curly brown hair. Unfortunately, he was also a lot younger than me. He looked at least fifteen years younger, but I realized he couldn't possibly be that young and be a full detective.

"Get you something to drink?" I asked, trying not to sound too Anne Bancroft. "A soft drink, I mean. I know you're on duty."

"No thank you. I'm sorry to have to tell you this way . . . ," he began, then stopped.

Ferber apparently wasn't very good at breaking bad news to people yet. Probably hadn't been in Homicide long. He sat down on my old blue armchair, perching himself on the edge of the cushion. I shoved a hatbox off the faux-leopard love seat across from him and sat down.

"Mind if I tape this?" I said, pulling out my microcassette recorder. I always think it's a good idea to have a record of encounters with authority figures.

"No . . . I guess not."

"So what happened to the guy? Is he dead?"

"Yes," he said.

"I figured, because you've been talking about him in the past tense. Gee, that's too bad. God. What happened?"

"He was murdered, in his office, some time between seven p.m., when he made a call to reserve a table at Brasserie Bleu for ten, and ten-thirty p.m. when the body was discovered by a cleaning person."

"Wow."

"You were the last appointment in his book last night. Did you keep that appointment?"

"No. That appointment was canceled," I said, and before he could ask for my alibi, I presented him with the minute-by-minute accounting of my whereabouts that evening, just to get it out of the way.

"Who canceled the appointment?" he asked.

"He did. Or his office. I got a message canceling it."

"That's interesting. It seems the night nurse got a call that took her away from the office on a false emergency, and your security people were called away on a false alarm elsewhere in your building. Someone wanted to get Kanengiser alone."

"Premeditated," I said, nodding. "How was he killed?"

"Shot in the heart."

"Poor slob. Damn shame. Seemed like a nice guy too. Did you get the guy who did it? Or the woman who did it?"

"Not yet," he said, looking at me strangely. "You're very calm about this."

Now it was my turn to sigh. "Well, I used to be a crime and justice reporter, a few years ago, and . . . I dunno. I'm hard to surprise."

Ferber looked at me and smiled. He was starting to grow on me a little, so I crossed my legs, bounced my foot slightly, and reminded myself of my new rule about not dating younger men.

"Did you know him well?" Ferber asked.

"No. I'd seen him once about six weeks earlier for maybe ten minutes when my boss beeped me. This was the rescheduled appointment," I said. "Any idea why he was killed?"

"Not sure. It was made to look like a robbery. Some files were pulled out, papers scattered on the floor . . ."

"What did he have worth stealing? He told me he bills insurance directly, so he couldn't have much money around, and it couldn't be a junkie looking for drugs because Dr. Kanengiser was a gynecologist, and there aren't too many crazed Ortho-Novum junkies out there."

Ferber cleared his throat.

Before he could say anything, I said, "Of course. He had confidential medical files."

Ferber didn't say anything.

"Were any files missing?" I said.

"We don't know yet."

"But that's one theory."

"I have several theories. Was there . . . anything in your file someone might have been after?" Ferber asked.

"I don't think I even had a file yet," I said.

"So, you didn't know him well."

"No. I didn't know him at all. I spoke to him for maybe ten minutes that first appointment, so . . . although, he did mention that he was divorced."

"In what context?"

"He asked me if I was married. I told him I was divorced, and he said he was divorced himself. Have you talked to his ex-wife? That's where I'd look."

"Yes, both his ex-wives," Ferber said. "One's in Miami. She's been there for the last two months. The other one was at the movies with her boyfriend."

"You know Kanengiser was really good-looking, don't you?" I said.

"You think that had something to do with his murder?"

"Good-looking guy like that, divorced, shot in the heart? To me, it says jealous ex-lover or jealous husband."

Files schmiles. This was a crime of passion. First of all, Kanengiser was shot in the heart, not the head. That, I felt, was significant.

Second, as I said, Dr. Kanengiser was really good-looking. In fact, if you ask me, he was far too good-looking for his job. The first—and only—time I went to see him, one of the other women in the waiting room said, "Your first time with Dr. Kanengiser? You are in for a treat. Wait until you see those blue eyes. Like Paul Newman's."

Do I care? I thought. The man's a doctor, not an underwear model. But she was right. He *was* very good-looking. A gynecological examination is awkward in the best of times, but it's really awkward, even unnerving, when your gynecologist is good-looking.

(I must admit that while I sat in his office soaking up his chiseled beauty, I speculated about dating him later. But how weird would it be to go out on a first date with a guy who had already stared into your sex organs with a flashlight?)

Because of this, a part of me was relieved when Jerry beeped me before Kanengiser could insert his forearm up me, and even more relieved when my second appointment was canceled. As my friend Dillon Flinder, silver-haired medical correspondent and pansexual adventurer, put it later, "When a guy is that good-looking, it's a fine line between a gynecological exam and what is known on the street as a good fisting." Dillon has such a way with words.

It was at this point that I realized things could get really ugly, because there's something inherently salacious about Dr. Kanengiser's specialty, and I figured I wasn't the only TV personality to see the guy, as he leased office space in my building. That could give the newspapers and the tabloid TV shows a celeb angle: GYNO TO TV NEWS STARS GUNNED DOWN.

I mentioned this to Ferber and he said, "We've sealed the patient files. We won't be telling the news media who his patients were unless one of them becomes a suspect."

"That's wise."

"So you weren't there and you didn't see anything," Ferber said, disappointed.

"I'm sorry. I really wish I could help you. You look so let down."

"That's okay," he said. "Yesterday was an unusually bad day, a record homicide day. My partner's in the hospital, she has to have some tests, and I've been working solo since six this morning. . . . I think I will have that soft drink."

We were bonding. I blew some dust out of a glass and poured him some seltzer. "So what are we up to so far this year, for homicides. We're over seven hundred, aren't we?"

"Last figure I heard was seven hundred seventy-two," he said.

"Did they ever catch that ninety-four-year-old man who killed his ninety-two-year-old brother in the Bronx?"

"No."

"The guy is ninety-four and he has arthritis, how far could he go?"

"I don't know."

"What about the drifter who killed the woman who took him in? Her name was Felice something, she met him in Madison Square Park and it was love at first sight . . ."

"Yeah, I know that case. Haven't caught him yet either."

"You probably already know this, but there was a very similar case a few years ago, same MO. That victim was also killed with selenium in her coffee."

"Yeah, the Freddy the Freeloader case," Ferber said. "You know your murders."

"Well, as I said, I used to be a crime and justice reporter and I've had other brushes with murder . . ."

"You'd be surprised," he said. "It's not that common to meet women who like to talk about murder."

Boy, he was adorable. He reminded me very much of this guy I had a crush on back in high school, a guy with the same dogged, doe-eyed good looks. With that fresh face, he couldn't have been more than twenty-seven or twenty-eight, which is young for a detective, I think. But then, they seem to get a touch younger every year, which worries me a little. I work in television, and it ages you quickly.

By now I was feeling more Blanche DuBois than Mrs. Robinson. It was all I could do not to offer him some milk and cookies and ask him if he'd ever seen a grown-up woman naked. I was going to invite him to look at my scrapbooks—I'd kept scrapbooks of unusual murders for years—but I figured he had other places to go and people to see.

In fact, he had. As soon as he finished his seltzer, he got up and thanked me for my time.

I walked him to the door and when we exchanged cards I

noted he didn't wear a wedding ring. Man, I was getting bad. When the moon was full, I was like a she-wolf with her nose in the wind. Maybe it was because the only man in months who had come close to touching me in an intimate manner was now dead, shot in the heart in his office.

"Hope you catch the killer," I said.

"Yeah, me too," he said. "By the way, you know there's a guillotine in front of your building?"

"Guerrilla art. We get a lot of it down here."

"Weird," he said.

Yeah, that's what I thought when I saw the guillotine, but now it seemed like the least weird thing about my day. What a day. It had just been one thing after another, culminating with news of the murder of someone I knew oh so slightly. Well, where's the bright side to murder, smart girl? I asked myself. That's a toughie, but you know, I found a bright side. At least I wasn't the one who was dead.

When I spoke to my friend Claire Thibodeaux later, she found another bright side. I often fall in love during murder cases. I'd never thought of it before, but she was right. I'd met my ex-husband during the murder trial of mobster Lonnie Katz. I'd fallen for my ex-boyfriend Eric, who always insisted on calling himself my "transitional" man, during the Griff murder case. In fact, shortly after a big murder case in my hometown, when I was a kid, I kissed my first boy.

I don't know why that is. My karma, I guess. Anyway, given my record in things romantic, I wasn't sure falling in love was much of a bright side given the down side, one dead doctor.

When I finally got back to bed, I lay there for a while, awake, thinking about Kanengiser. Whoever had killed him had planned it in advance, and had had the foresight to get the night nurse out of the office and cancel my appointment. So it was someone who had had access to his office and had seen the appointment book somehow, perhaps on a previous visit. Possibly a jealous husband or lover who had come by to pick up his wife or girlfriend at the office, but more likely a woman, a girlfriend and/or a patient of Dr. Kanengiser, I thought.

Then I caught myself. It wasn't any of my business—I barely knew the guy. The cops were on the job. Who did I think I was anyway, Bat Girl? The last thing I needed at the moment was to get mixed up in a messy murder. Sure, it had been fun to chew the fat on old homicides with a young cop. But those days were behind me now. I was a grown-up. In fact, I hadn't looked through my murder scrapbooks in months, since I had decided that my interest in the subject might be unhealthy and abnormal.

Curiosity, I remembered, always got me into trouble. It was curiosity that cost me my coveted interview with avant-garde undertaker Max Guffy, which killed my series, "Death in Modern America," no pun intended. Well, it wasn't just curiosity. Vodka was also involved. But it was mostly curiosity. The two, vodka and curiosity, were to be avoided, because, you see, my troublemaking days were over.

3

It was a sign of my deep state of denial, combined with temporary post-sleep amnesia, that when I woke up the next morning to the sight of the parchment Desiderata poster on the ceiling above my bed, I had forgotten about Kanengiser.

"The headlines at this hour: After years of decline, the murder rate is up in New York," intoned the very serious voice of the announcer on 1010 WINS All-News Radio. "But air pollution levels are down, and the forecast says, rain all day."

"Well, there's a mixed message for you," I said to Louise Bryant. "My chances of being killed immediately and violently are up, my chances of being killed slowly by lung disease are down, and either way, it's going to rain all day."

Louise didn't even open her eyes. The cat responds to only two sounds, that of the can opener and that of my singing (any song, as long as the lyrics are her name sung over and over).

It was raining all right. Through the water-smeared window, the street was a blur of gray people going to work, moving like blobs of mercury on glass, rushing past the guillotine on the sidewalk without even seeing it. What a great day to stay at home and be unconscious, I thought, but I couldn't call in sick. A bad flu season had eaten up my sick days for the year by February. If I took another day, especially for mental health reasons, it would end up as another black mark on my permanent record.

"Dr. Herman Kanengiser, gynecologist and member of the District 27 community board, was found dead of a gunshot wound in his midtown office last night. Police say they have no suspects at the moment," said the guy on WINS.

Oh yeah, I thought. Dr. Kanengiser.

I'd been feeling all right, but being reminded of the murder brought me down. I turned off the news—too depressing—and put on a tape of bouncy, pick-me-up tunes to fortify me as I showered, checked myself for signs of necrotic fascitis, and worked myself back into that excellent state of denial.

Perhaps my bathroom mirror said it best when it sloganeered: AVOID UNPLEASANTNESS.

There would, however, be no avoiding the Kanengiser murder. When I got to work, the whole place was buzzing with it. Normally, the murder of a nonfamous doctor would cause barely a ripple in the ANN newsroom. Oh, it might attract some prurient interest and inspire a few sick "dead gynecologist" jokes among the dark-humored newsroom drones, but otherwise no one would notice. When you're trafficking in news from places like Sarajevo, one dead doctor in New York doesn't mean much. Life is cheap in Casablanca. Unless of course it happens in your building.

MURDER ON 27, screamed a poster on Democracy Wall, the ten-foot-long employee bulletin board in the hallway leading to the newsroom. Democracy Wall is where we post employee news, gossip, jokes, weird letters from fans, and odd but true news stories. It "belongs" to the workers.

I skipped the terse bulletin about the murder and scanned the wall instead for news of the executive meetings, rumors about the reshuffle. There was nothing.

"Did you hear about the murder . . . ," producer Susan Brave said, coming up beside me at the wall.

"Can't talk now," I said. "I'm late."

I was, in fact, running late for a mandatory security meeting that morning.

"You've probably already heard that a doctor on the twenty-seventh floor was shot and killed last night," Pete Huculak was saying when I walked into the conference room and took a seat in the back next to Dillon Flinder.

Pete was the security chief for Jackson Broadcasting and its affiliated enterprises, which included ANN and the JBS building itself.

"I don't want you to be alarmed. Our security is very good. The security for the commercial floors was pretty relaxed—the tenants wanted it that way so their customers could come and go freely—but something like this couldn't happen in the broadcast facilities," Pete said.

A skeptical murmur swept the room. True, after the World Trade Center bombing, our founder, Georgia Jack Jackson, had installed *Star Trek* airlock doors leading into and out of the broadcast facilities, as well as a vast system of video surveillance cameras, all of which gave the place a combination biosphere–prison farm atmosphere.

Despite this, there had been a number of security breaches and other disturbing incidents that put everyone a bit on edge. First, shortly after the new security force came aboard, someone had taken advantage of the transition to swipe a bunch of purses, including mine. Our TV psychologist, Solange Stevenson, had been menaced by an elderly Kansas widower who showed up at ANN, waved an unloaded hunting rifle, and complained that Solange was sending him secret messages (on that special frequency they shared) accusing him of homosexuality. Someone had broken into anchorwoman Bianca de Woody's dressing room and stolen her wig, two pairs of her shoes, and her spare underwear. And Kerwin Shutz, ANN's right-wing talk-show host, had been getting these perplexing phone calls that sounded distinctly like someone farting for about a minute before hanging up.

(Contrary to a popular rumor, I did not make those calls.)

As if that weren't bad enough, ANN's senior war correspondent, Reb "Rambo" Ryan, recently "grounded" after a disturbing incident in Haiti, claimed someone had taken a potshot at him as he was walking down Eighty-fourth Street.

Pete couldn't do much about that, but we all felt he could do more about building security, which was why the on-air "Talent" had got together and demanded this meeting. The death of the doctor the night before gave it added urgency.

Pete and his personally assembled army of fifty company cops marked the third step in the year-long fortification. Keeping nutty fans and nutty terrorists out, not to mention busting cigarette sneaks who defied the company-wide ban on smoking, was a tough job.

It was the opinion of the masses that Pete was not up to it. Before Pete took over our security a few months earlier, he had done bodyguard and security work for a few celebrities in Hollywood, including Georgia Jack, when Jack was out there trying to buy another movie studio.

Jack had hired Pete capriciously. Jack did that sometimes. Met someone at a cocktail party, got drunk with him, and the next thing you know, he's head of security, or of the Documentary unit, or, in the case of my boss, Jerry Spurdle, of the Special Reports unit. Jack stood by his capricious hires to the bitter end, too damn proud to admit to making mistakes. That meant we were stuck with Pete for a long time.

So Pete's reassurances rang hollow.

"We all have to be aware and keep an eye out for each other. If you see anyone suspicious lurking around, you have to let us know immediately. Hector, get the lights," Pete said, and one of Pete's deputies, the one we knew as Barney Fife, flicked the switch.

What followed was a slide show of some of our most dangerous known fans. Most of these we knew by name, like

Donald Forcus, an ex-con who was carrying a very big torch for Bianca de Woody (a bad bit of luck, him being an arsonist and all). Donald had what my Aunt Maureen would call an "unfortunate" face, reminiscent of a cartoon duck, which made his given name all the crueler.

Also easily recognizable was Hank, the fan who was stalking Dillon Flinder. Hank was an unemployed drifter who had lost a series of jobs because he would only walk backward.

"How does he stalk you?" I whispered to Dillon. "With a mirror? Or does he just walk backward until he bumps into you?"

"I'll see Hank coming a mile away," Flinder conceded. "By the way, I hear you're going out with Fenn Corker when he comes to town."

"Who told you that?"

"I don't remember. Is it true?"

"Yeah."

"Why, Robin? He's such an ass. Yet you won't go out with me."

"I know too much about you, Dillon," I said.

Dillon was known for his admitted sexual adventures with large fleshy fruits, and it was just too weird to me, dating a man who had dated a watermelon.

After the slides and a short film on self-defense, the lights came up and Pete went to the blackboard and began writing platitudes down for us. An ounce of prevention is worth a pound of cure. Be alert!

"Better safe than sorry," he said about six times during his little lecture. Afterward, he asked for questions and I was so tempted to put up my hand and say, "Duh, is it better to be safe? Or sorry?"

What a waste of time this was, not that I had anything against wasting time. The more time I spent in this boring meeting, the less I spent with my boss, Jerry Spurdle, who was living proof that the people inside television are just about as nutty as those outside television, maybe more so.

Some of the biggest nuts in the business were, in fact, inside this very room. In the front row, Sawyer Lash, fresh off his overnight shift, was nodding earnestly at Pete's every salient point and taking notes. Known as the network's dumbest anchorman and biggest goody-goody, Sawyer's star had risen for a while during our Time of Troubles at ANN a year earlier. But it had fallen again quickly, and now he was back in the netherworld of overnight news updates, where viewers were less likely to notice if he confused Liberian rebels with librarian rebels.

A few weeks earlier, someone had sent Sawyer a sick gift— a dead sparrow in a plastic hosiery egg. And that was from someone who claimed to like him.

Just in front of Dillon and me, Dave Kona was talking softly to Solange Stevenson. Solange was a huge security headache, not only because as a TV psychologist she attracted a deeply disturbed viewership, but also because she actually invited clearly insane people onto her TV show, with bad results on more than one occasion. Like the time she reunited all those adopted people with their birth parents on her show and a fistfight broke out. Or the time two rival girlfriends of an imprisoned serial killer got into a hair-pulling catfight on the show and gave Solange a bloody nose when she tried to intervene.

As for Dave Kona, he was just twenty-three, hadn't been on air long, and so hadn't really had time to attract a cadre of deranged fans.

Too bad. The supercilious pip-squeak was after my job.

"When I was guarding Barbra . . . ," Pete said, seguing into one of his war stories.

My attention wandered further. Pete's other deputy, Franco, had just come into the conference room and was hulking by the door. He was bigger and stronger than Hector, but he didn't inspire much confidence either. Franco was famous for getting lost while on patrol.

I'd never noticed it before, but Franco sure had a lot of

hair in his ears. Big tufts of brown hair stuck out of his ears. I'd never seen that much hair in someone's ears before. Where did it come from? It looked like it was growing out of his brain. His head must be full of hair, I decided. I hadn't noticed his hairy ears before because he'd worn his hair over his ears, apparently for a reason. But Pete had ordered haircuts for all the company cops the day before and Franco, being a good Boy Scout, complied.

Maybe he didn't get his hair cut, I thought. Maybe he just grabbed on to those tufts and pulled his hair down through his ears.

"Are you paying attention, Robin?" Pete asked suddenly, and I jerked my head and nodded guiltily. "We all have to be alert."

"Yes sir."

"These common household items can aid in your self-defense," Pete said, listing a fine-toothed comb (run tooth-side under an assailant's nose, it could slice right through the septum and cause a massive nose bleed), an umbrella, and a can of hair spray.

Kid stuff, I thought. I have a self-defense system that makes the DEW line look like a spite fence. In addition to the poison ivy I grow in my window boxes as a kind of burglary disincentive program, I keep a bottle of cayenne-spiked cologne, an automatic umbrella, and a number of small weaponlike appliances around, such as an Epilady hair removal system and a high-velocity glue gun with two settings, stream and spray, so I could give an attacker a face full of hot glue at ten feet. This last marked an escalation of the arms race for me. I wasn't ready to join the masses and get a real gun.

"Be careful," Pete said, dismissing us.

Wish I'd thought of that.

"Did you hear about the murder on the twenty-seventh floor?" Louis Levin asked me as I passed through the giant human pinball game that is the ANN newsroom. I was on my way to Special Reports.

Louis, a disgruntled news producer, was sitting in his wheelchair at the afternoon producer pod, a stationary island amid streams of people carrying armfuls of videotapes and news copy, pencils clenched in their teeth, rushing to get the news on the air.

"Yeah, I heard. I just came from the security meeting."

"What was the mood of the room?"

"Scared," I said.

"You know who's really scared? Reb Ryan. He's been on a tear about this murder for the last hour," Louis said. "He thinks he's a sitting duck here."

"I wouldn't believe anything he said."

"Well, Reb's crazy, but he has a point," Louis said. "If someone has been able to get in to kill a gynecologist, what's to prevent a crazy fan from getting in to shoot an anchorman, or a methodical terrorist group from getting in and taking over a broadcast beamed around the planet?"

"Don't say that too loud. You know management is looking for ways to boost our ratings."

I didn't tell him that I was one of Kanengiser's patients, or near-patients. Louis ran the oldest established permanent floating rumor file in New York—a locked file known as Radio Free Babylon, with constantly changing passwords—which moved around within the ANN computer system. Why invite controversy and sick jokes?

Besides, I wanted to avoid the whole subject of the murder as much as I could without arousing suspicion.

I changed the subject. "Any news from the executive suite?"

"Not yet," he said, as an intern handed him some wire copy. He scanned it quickly and then said, "The meetings are very hush-hush."

"Louis, here's the AOA on the new school prayer bill," an edit assistant said, handing Louis a tape.

(AOA stands for "Any Old Asshole," known in more polite circles as MOS, "Man on the Street.")

Louis took the tape and popped it into the monitor on his pod while talking both to the edit assistant and to me. He has the amazing ability to conduct two or three conversations simultaneously without losing the narrative thread of any of them.

"My best source is on the job, though," Louis said, winking at me. Louis didn't know it, but his best source was my best source, Phil the omnipotent janitor. Louis didn't have any new information because Phil had been out with flu the day before.

The phone rang on Louis's desk. "I'm listenin'," he said when he answered. "No. Haven't seen her."

He hung up and turned to me. "That was Jerry. He wanted to know if you were in the newsroom. I lied."

"Thanks."

"Who'da thunk Jerry Spurdle would become such a big success? Great ratings, big moneymaker, and on top of everything else, he won that ACE award. Bet he really has a swelled head. How is it, working with him these days?" Louis asked.

"Oh . . . you know."

Louis was goading me, expecting me to say something like, "He's more fun than a flesh-eating virus." But I clammed up. If you can't say something nice and all that. Anything I said about Jerry was bound to end up in the rumor file, and I didn't need the trouble because, as you know, my trouble-making days were over.

Louis gave me a sad look and shook his head.

"You know," he said, "Jerry's been bragging that he broke Robin Hudson, the rogue filly."

"It's more complicated than that," I said.

"He says, like all women, you can be subdued by a strong hand, metaphorically speaking. I dunno, Robin. You gotta do what you gotta do, but your reputation is suffering with the troops. They think you've sold out to that sleazebag."

"Why do I have to hassle with Jerry? The job's being done without me. Tamayo drives him nuts and I can concentrate on my work. Besides, Dean Wormer has me on double-secret probation. Another mess-up and I could be working the cash register in the cafeteria for the duration of my contract."

"You were the rogue filly," Louis said, wistfully.

The Rogue Filly. I think he knew I'd like the sound of that.

4

The Special Reports offices are housed in an extraneous set of men's and ladies' rooms a couple of hallways off the newsroom. Although the swinging bathroom door from the outer office to the hallway has been replaced, we still have tiny, ceramic bathroom tiles on the floor and the suite retains a certain residual bathroom ambience, especially in the afternoon when the sun shines through the narrow, opaque glass windows placed high in the wall.

As the network's number-two moneymaker, behind Kerwin Shutz, Jerry Spurdle could have had the plushest offices in the building. But he was known as much for his low overhead as for his high advertising revenues. Having a spartan, utilitarian office was part of his image, one especially appreciated by ANN president George Dunbar, a man who expected his employees to provide their own pens and paper clips and once proposed letting corporations sponsor aircraft carriers, space shuttles, and national parks to reduce the deficit. How proud our fighting boys and girls would be, shipping off to war on the battleship *Pepsodent*.

"There's tobacco in the shredder," Jerry was screaming at our associate producer, Tamayo Scheinman, when I walked in.

"I'm quitting smoking," Tamayo said, as she says three or four times a week. I noticed she had a nicotine patch on her arm. "I shredded my cigarettes so I couldn't smoke them."

Tamayo came from Japan, where she grew up with dual citizenship, daughter of an American man and a Japanese woman. While her American father was a devoted Japano-phile, Tamayo loved all things American, especially unfiltered Camels.

Unfortunately for her, ANN and its affiliated networks un-der the Jackson Broadcasting umbrella, like many other com-panies, had become completely nonsmoking, and had banned smoking for employees even outside of work. As you can imagine, this just added to the jolly newsroom atmosphere.

So when they transferred Tamayo from the Tokyo bureau, they made her sign a pledge that she would quit smoking by the end of her three-month probationary period. She had ten days to go.

"*Guten Morgen*, Robin," Jerry said to me. He was studying German.

"Good morning."

Tamayo handed me a message and left me to absorb Jerry's loathsomeness singlehanded.

"You look like you put on a little weight, Robin," Jerry said, walking around me to size me up. "You know that's a sin in television."

One of Jerry's favorite old-style sexist ways to cut a woman down to size was to criticize her physical appearance. Ever since I had begun trying to adapt and mature and behave myself, Jerry had been milking it for all he could. He knew he could say anything to me and I would say nothing nasty back to him. So I couldn't, for example, point out to Jerry that he was pale, soft, and somewhat overweight and dressed like an aide in the Nixon White House. In fact, he looked like a Nixon White House aide who had swallowed another Nixon

White House aide whole. Claire, who used to work with me in Special Reports, called Jerry a "smug, dissipated white boy" with an ego so big you could tie a rope to it and fly it in the Macy's Thanksgiving Day parade. But Claire could talk that way. She was a rising general-assignment reporter who'd been trying out in Washington and was expected to be offered a full-time job there in the reshuffle. I, on the other hand, had to be a good girl.

So I just smiled.

"Gotta watch out. Lose your looks in this business and . . ." He made a slashing motion across his neck.

What an asshole. Quite honestly, losing my looks is the least of my worries. I am a five-nine, buxom, good-looking redhead, at least I think I am, and if you think you are, it's as good as true. Not to brag about it, because believe me, beauty can be a curse. I know it's not the sort of thing one should complain about, but you see, I'm also very clumsy. My looks draw attention to me, so that many more people are watching me when the spike heel buckles under me in a restaurant and I accidentally mow down a passing salad girl, who sends a giant bowl of iceberg lettuce flying, raining greens on a whole section of diners.

This is not a hypothetical example. This is my karma, beauty without grace. I am Jerry Lewis's nutty professor . . . in the body of Rita Hayworth.

"You need a haircut too. But that isn't what I wanted to talk to you about. Come into my office," Jerry said.

I followed him.

"Have a seat," he said, waving me in and slamming the door so the glass walls of his cubicle shook.

At that point, he put on his eyeglasses, a pure affectation. Tamayo and I had looked through them and found they were plain glass. Jerry wore them because he thought they made him look cerebral.

"We're going to shelve the Congressman Dreyer story," Jerry said and looked over his glasses at me for a response.

No argument here, I thought, since there wasn't any story as far as I was concerned. Jerry had it on "good information" that Dreyer, a staunch proponent of morality and traditional family values, was having an affair with his secretary, and was holed up with her somewhere in Manhattan. But when I looked into it, I couldn't find anything to substantiate the story. Despite the fact that I despised Dreyer's politics and would have loved to have proven him a hypocrite, I learned nothing except good things. He spent a lot of time with his family, he worked hard, and colleagues past and present said his word was his bond. All we had to go on was that his wife, an antiques collector, had gone to Belgium on a buying trip, the kids were with her parents, and the congressman had gone off on some hush-hush fact-finding trip with his secretary and personal assistant, Lizbeth Greyfarm.

Personally, I think Jerry wanted to fry Dreyer because Dreyer was rigidly anti-porn and anti–strip club, and Jerry was rigidly pro-porn and pro–strip club.

"I still think there's a story there," Jerry said. "But you're unable to find it for some reason. And we need a story for next Monday night's slot, thanks to your death series bombing out, which threw the whole Special Reports sked out of whack for the year."

"There's that blind tap-dancing troupe," I began.

"It's for our adult viewing slot. We need something sexy. Did you hear about the murder on the twenty-seventh floor? A gynecologist?"

"Yes," I said, feeling a clammy dread flush down my body.

"I was talking to Pete Huculak in security about it and . . . I think we have a special report here."

"It's kind of . . . local, isn't it?" I said politely.

"As a single murder, yes. But wait, there's more. This guy's a gynecologist, right? He's good-looking. Someone handcuffs him to a chair and shoots—"

"Handcuffs him to a chair?"

"He was handcuffed to a chair, then shot in the heart."

"How do you know this?"

"The cleaning guy who found the body, he called our security before he called the cops. Security shot a videotape of the murder scene. *Exclusive* tape of the murder scene, in other words, and we're going to get a dub."

That was the clincher for him, because we hate to waste good videotape in Special Reports, especially exclusive videotape.

"There's more. Know what they found on the floor, among other things? A matchbook from Anya's."

Anya's was an S&M club on the West Side.

"This is a perfect angle," Jerry said, and his porous, flaccid face could barely contain his glee. I'd worked with him long enough to see the neon signs flashing before his eyes. GYNECOLOGIST. HANDCUFFS. MURDER. EXCLUSIVE VIDEOTAPE!

"S&M is big in the nineties. Remember that cover story *New York* magazine did? And it's not just kooks, it's your doctor, your dentist, the guy who does your tax return, the sweet-faced girl who teaches your kids to read, a guy like Dr. Kanengiser. Is the murder linked to this dark world? It doesn't even matter. The victim is linked to it."

You know, it's not that I'm against exploring the totality of human experience, the human condition, as a reporter. After all, in the past year I'd done "Co-ed Call Girls," "Transvestite Daddies," and "Over-Thirty Virgins." But, having learned the dark lessons of the ill-fated "Death in Modern America" series, I was trying to look on the bright side, become a better person, and do a nice series for a change, one that didn't involve kinky sex, dead people, deranged people, and/or criminals. I wanted to do a series that might endear me to the viewers, help redeem my past sins, and hoist me firmly onto the New Niceness bandwagon. Good news is also part of the totality of human experience.

"What about that blind tap-dance troupe? I could shoot an interview with them tomorrow. Or the deaf bass player . . . ," I offered.

"Robin, all bass players are deaf, eventually."

"Well, the matchbook might not come directly from Anya's. Those sex clubs and phone-sex lines advertise on matchbooks given out in delis and stuff. It could come from . . ."

"Anya's matches are only available at Anya's. I called and asked."

I'd been debating whether to tell Jerry that I'd seen Dr. Kanengiser, as I didn't want to inspire any jokes or summon up any images of my genitalia in his mind. But he'd left me no choice. I had to play that card.

"I might not be the best reporter for this piece," I said. "I had an appointment with him last night. I didn't keep it, but I did see him once."

"And so? You knew him well or something?"

"I didn't know the guy at all. He never examined me. But it still makes me uncomfor—"

"And you're not a suspect?"

"Of course not."

"Good, wouldn't want any more of that Griff trouble we had. So he didn't examine you and you're not a suspect. Nice try, Robin, but you can't get out of this on some ethical loophole. The word around here is, he was a busy boy up there on the twenty-seventh floor. Not all the women who came to visit him were patients."

"But rumors don't—"

"Robin, he's just a really grabby example of someone who may have been involved in the S&M lifestyle. We don't need a lot on him."

"I don't mean to be impertinent . . . ," I began.

Jerry pulled out the lower left drawer of his desk. The drawer stuck slightly, causing his coffee mug, which reads CHIEF MELON INSPECTOR—WTNA TV & RADIO, and the ACE award for the vigilantism series—the series I did despite the fact that the trophy bore Jerry's name only—to rattle.

"See these?" he said, motioning to a drawer full of papers. "These are the résumés of all the reporters who want to replace you. You don't seem to get that what's good for Special Reports is good for all of us. I've carried you a long time in this unit, Robin. You know I have."

"But Jerry, just hear me out—"

"Robin, it seems whenever I listen to you we get into trouble. Do I have to remind you that, because of you, the cryogenics people are suing us . . ."

"That wasn't my fault!" I said. "Besides, the heads were saved."

This referred to an incident at the Cryogenics East center, where the heads of some thirty-five people were kept frozen in hopes of being brought back to life some day with bionic bodies. While we were shooting, on an unseasonably muggy day I might add, there was a power failure compounded by the breakdown of the backup generator. Meltdown. The place exploded in panic as the proprietor tried to get LILCO and an emergency electrician on the line and his assistants ran out to the gas station next door to get ice to keep the frozen heads frozen.

It turns out our lighting equipment shorted out the system, which was the fault of our new cameraman, Mike. He wasn't used to operating with American voltage. In any event, as I said, the heads were saved, thus saving my conscience from the added burden of thirty-five rotting human heads.

"Your fault or not, these things always seem to happen when you're around. And I still don't know what you said to offend Max Guffy," Jerry continued.

"You know how touchy morticians are . . ."

"The point is, I think you know what side your bread is buttered on, Robin."

Just for emphasis, he opened that big drawer full of résumés again.

What an asshole, I thought, even as I smiled at him. Try as I might to be like Atticus Finch, to walk in Jerry's shoes a mile before judging him, to understand why he was the scum-sucking ass-kissing sewer-sniffing son-of-a-bitch he was, I just couldn't quite manage it. All I could manage was the fake smile.

"Get on the horn and call Mistress Anya. Set up an interview. Then try to get one of the ex-wives," he said, grabbing his suit jacket off the coat hook and walking me out of his office. "I'll be in executive meetings all day."

Grumbling, I returned to my office, where this Confucian gem stared out at me from my blotter: THE RELATION BE-TWEEN SUPERIORS AND INFERIORS IS LIKE THAT BETWEEN THE WIND AND THE GRASS. THE GRASS MUST BEND WHEN THE WIND BLOWS UPON IT. Of course, how one defines superiority might be a matter of dispute, but if you think too long about things like that, pretty soon you have a bad attitude and all your hard work is wasted.

So Dr. Kanengiser had a matchbook from Mistress Anya's club, I thought. That was something we kind of had in common. Because I had her card, in my Rolodex, in two places, under Dominatrices and under Sadism. (Since coming to Special Reports, I had put together a very strange Rolodex, full of Virgins, Sadists, Victims, Embalmers, and, of course, UFO Abductees—listed by both their Earth names and their alien names.) About a year before, we'd interviewed Mistress Anya and five other dominatrices for a quickie report we put together after a New York judge ruled that S&M for money was not considered prostitution under New York law, since intercourse was rarely involved (although, if the dominatrix is feeling charitable, she lets the guy jerk off).

In New York, Anya was the unofficial queen of the professional whip-snappers. In addition to her club, which bore her name, and a leased-access S&M talk show on cable, Anya was the self-proclaimed head of the Marquis de Sade Society, whose mandate is "to promote sadomasochism," since apparently there isn't enough pain and suffering in the world already. She was, as they say, a media slut, who'd go on the air anytime, for any reason, to promulgate her philosophy and attract like-minded souls to her club. Positive publicity, negative publicity, it was all the same to her.

"I'd be delighted to talk to you tomorrow," she said when I called her, and the way she said "delighted" made it sound like a four-letter word.

I penciled her into my new Filofax date organizer.

Five phone calls later I tracked down both of Kanengiser's ex-wives. Ex-wife number two, Gail Perlmutter-Kanengiser, who was staying with a friend in Miami, had only one question for me.

"How much will you pay me?"

We call this the *Hard Copy* effect. Thanks to tabloid TV's liberal use of checkbook journalism, it was getting increasingly hard to get people to talk on television for free, unless of course they had a book, a movie, or a political agenda to promote, or an axe to grind. Special Reports may have been sensationalistic, even sleazy at times, but we did not practice checkbook journalism.

When I told her this, in much nicer language, she hung up on me.

Next, I called Detective Ferber at Manhattan South, but he was out so they put me through to another detective just assigned to the case, who was also out: Detective Richard Bigger.

Shit. Well, there was no point leaving a message for Bigger. I knew him from a previous investigation. At that time, he had been paired with Detective Joe Tewfik, who had since retired to become an upstate restaurateur.

There are good cops and bad cops. Tewfik was a good cop. Although much decorated, Bigger was a weasely, officious, stick-up-the-ass control freak with the sharpest teeth and sorriest mustache I'd ever seen on a *Homo sapiens*. We had instantly, instinctively disliked each other. It was as if my very existence insulted Bigger. He saw me as some kind of wild-eyed antiauthoritarian bohemian, which is so unfair. That was the *old* me.

If Bigger was now on this case, that meant it was going to be even harder to get information, as Detective Richard Bigger was not media-friendly. He hated the media, but he especially hated me. Maybe because he had once been in my apartment on police business and had come in contact with my poison ivy plants. How was I to know he had a poison ivy allergy that made him suffer doubly the effects of the plant?

By the time I came back from lunch, the Kanengiser murder had been eclipsed by breaking news, company rumors, and other urgent things, such as Franco's hairy ears, which everyone was now starting to notice.

The "exclusive" videotape that security had shot at the murder scene was on my desk with a note. Jerry wanted a tape log on his desk by the end of the day. The last thing I wanted to do at that point was look at a murdered man, but it was my job, so I popped the tape into the deck and sat back in my chair, a yellow legal pad propped in my lap.

The tape had been shot from the doorway into Kanengiser's inner office, where the body was found.

"Don't go in," said a voice off-camera. It sounded like Pete Huculak.

"Why not?" said another voice, that of Hector.

"Don't disturb the crime scene."

The camera panned around the room, fixing on Kanengiser's body, a side view. Sure enough, Kanengiser's hands were cuffed behind his back, and he was fully clothed. Hector panned around the room some more, zooming in on some papers scattered around, a tipped-over paper-clip dispenser, some litter on the floor.

The camera was still rolling when the police arrived—Detective Ferber, two uniformed officers who both looked old enough to be his father, and a doctor, who said, "He's dead."

Ferber put on rubber gloves and began picking stuff up with

tweezers, dropping items into plastic and paper evidence bags held by one of the uniforms, while the other tried to pick the lock on Kanengiser's handcuffs.

"One nickel, one dime, one matchbook—a place called Anya's," Ferber said. He was behind the chair when he said it, so I didn't get a clear view.

A few minutes later, the tape ended.

The connection to Anya's seemed pretty tenuous at best. Kanengiser might have bummed those matches off of someone else—although, in connection with the handcuffs, it did look bad. On the other hand, the biographical information faxed over by the American Gynecological Association made him sound like citizen of the year. He had graduated from Harvard Med, did his residency at Columbia-Presbyterian, was active in independent politics on the district level, and had served a term on his community board. At first, I thought that community board thing might lead somewhere, but it turned out the most controversial proposal the board had passed was a rezoning initiative to open certain residential buildings to on-site day-care centers.

A Lexis-Nexis search turned up a few brief mentions of Kanengiser in local stories about district zoning meetings and the institution of a beefed-up neighborhood watch program. There were a lot of stories about doctor killings, however. I weeded through them and came up with three other unsolved homicides: a neurosurgeon killed in a Seattle mugging, a doctor who performed abortions killed in Kansas, and a doctor of physics killed in a carjacking in California. None of them seemed connected to Kanengiser, unless Kanengiser had performed abortions at one time, although nothing in the AGA information indicated that was the case.

So much for my serial killer theory. But the Lexis-Nexis search wasn't completely fruitless. Under the slug "Doc-Killing" was a story that was completely unrelated to Kanengiser, and yet extremely significant to me.

It was the story of Cecile Le Doc of Nice, France.

"A lovely woman," was the unanimous opinion of her neighbors. "A sweet, submissive, and devoted wife."

Sweet, submissive, and devoted—until one night after an argument, when Cecile Le Doc beat her husband to death with their eighteen-pound turtle, Henri.

Poor husband.

Poor turtle.

I couldn't resist putting this one aside for the murder scrapbook I entitled "Unusual Weapons."

Just as I was about to leave for the day, Kanengiser's night nurse-slash-receptionist, Vicki Burchill, returned my call.

The night Kanengiser was killed, she said, a strange man had called, saying that her apartment was on fire. Only there was no fire. Someone had wanted Vicki out of the office. No doubt the same someone who had called the ANN office and left a message with Tamayo to cancel my appointment.

"Were any files missing?" I asked. In that case, it might not be S&M at all, it might be blackmail. Secretly, I hoped it was. Don't get me wrong. Blackmail isn't pretty and because Kanengiser was in the JBS building it could hit pretty close to home. But there was a bright side to it, since blackmail is a touchy subject for any public personality, but more so at ANN, as we'd been stung in the past. That angle alone could be enough to kill this story and get me back onto some good news.

But Ms. Burchill dashed these hopes when she said, "No. We did a complete inventory. Just finished it about an hour ago. So far, nothing's missing."

That ruled out blackmail. A blackmailer might photocopy things, but for credibility he, or she, needed the original. Damn.

Beyond that, Vicki Burchill had little to offer. She hadn't worked for him long, had no idea if Kanengiser was into S&M, and couldn't for the life of her imagine who would kill him.

"But the person who called you on the false fire story was a man," I said.

"It *sounded* like a man," she said. "But the police detective says there are gadgets people can use to disguise their voices on the phone, so I can't even tell the gender of the caller with confidence."

Or it could be the killer just paid some bum to make the call.

It was a dead end.

All I'd found were dead ends. After a day of dead ends, it's Miller Time. I put the tape log on Jerry's desk, and went to meet McGravy.

5

"It's good to see you, Robin," Bob McGravy said.

"It's good to see you too, Bob." I ordered a light beer and slid onto a barstool next to him.

Bob is the vice president in charge of editorial content at the network, a man with sterling journalistic credentials. He worked for Edward R. Murrow and CBS during their golden era. He's also the guy who hired me and, with legendary assignment editor Lanny Cane, taught me television news, or at least tried.

More importantly, McGravy had been largely responsible for building ANN's reputation from laughingstock to network of record. But ratings were replacing reputation on a number of fronts, and McGravy had declining influence over the network at large. Nowadays, they used him mainly as a fireman, flying him from bureau to bureau to solve one problem or another.

"I don't see enough of you these days. I'm so busy. Been too long."

"Even longer since we came to Buddy's," I said.

This place took me back. Great place, Buddy's, an authentic, unpretentious New York bar Bob had introduced me to years before, back when he still drank and I was a young, promising reporterling who figured she'd be the Moscow correspondent by the time she was thirty-seven. Here, McGravy and his old newshound friends had turned me on to vodka stingers and whetted my appetite for the roguish nature of the business with their bawdy newsroom stories.

Buddy's has been around since World War II and, judging by the photos of the original establishment, the decor hasn't changed much since 1944. The hardwood floors are worn down and the red vinyl in the semicircular banquettes has been patched over a few times. McGravy and I like it for its old New York flavor, for its habitués with red carbuncular noses, lots of tattoos, and names like Billy One-Eye, Spider, and Fat Pat, for its two kinds of wine, Mountain Chablis Red and Mountain Chablis White, which come in cardboard boxes with spigots.

"Can't stay long, Robin. I have a date with Candy and then I have to pack for another road trip tomorrow," McGravy said, taking a judicious sip of his soda with lime.

In the past few years, he had given up drinking and smoking, although he held on to his red meat, refined sugar, saturated fats, and love of forty-ish former chorines named Candy and Frosty, grande dames of the lash-fluttering class. What can I say? Some men just like those real girly girls, you know, the kind with the feather-fringed dressing gowns and little fluffy dogs they carry around like handbags. McGravy loved 'em, and they loved him back, and they took good care of each other. It's nice when it works out, you know?

"It's good to have you back, Bob," I said. "Even if you're only in town briefly."

"I wish I could say it's good to be back. I leave for two weeks," he said, "and the place goes wacky. Someone is shooting at my anchormen, ratings are down twenty percent, and cutbacks are coming."

"Maybe they'll shoot enough anchormen and you won't

need to make any cutbacks," I said. "Sorry. My sick sense of humor."

Bob didn't even smile. Instead, he took off his horn-rimmed glasses and rubbed his eyes in a fatigued, battle-weary way.

"Listen Robin," he said after putting his glasses back on and nervously patting the white comb-over that hid his bald spot. "I asked you to meet me for a reason."

All the good nostalgic feeling left me suddenly and I felt a sick chill. He asked me here for a *reason*. This was it, the talk I'd been dreading, the one where I'm told the company appreciates my years of service, but their needs have changed and there's no room left for me in the new order, that I'd be "happier elsewhere" but they'd keep me on the payroll in some blow-job position until my contract expired. Naturally, this delicate task would be entrusted to McGravy, because he knew how to handle me.

I took a gulp of my light beer and, fortified, said, "What is it?"

"There are people who think you're unstable. I'm sorry to . . ."

"What 'people'?"

"It's not important. I was asked to speak to you because someone has been playing pranks on some of the executives, and your name came up when they were making their list of suspects."

No doubt my name was near the top of their list, along with Louis Levin's. I'd heard about these pranks and was insulted anyone would suspect me of perpetrating them, since they were so amateurish. For example, someone sent away for Rogaine information on behalf of our less hirsute executives, and someone dropped VD pamphlets into the mailbox of an executive who had recently left his wife. Pathetic and downright mean.

"It isn't just the pranks, Robin. It's a history of behavior the executives think is . . . odd and insubordinate."

"Bob, everyone is odd, some people just hide it better than

others. And I have been on my best behavior the last couple of months. I did most of the work on that vigilantism series . . . I nailed Nicky Vassar . . ."

"And all that is taken into account. God love ya, Robin. I'm sorry about this. I didn't want to bring it up at all, but . . ."

"It's okay." Actually, I was relieved it wasn't the "happier elsewhere" speech—yet.

"I just want you to keep up that good behavior, okay?" he said, and I nodded.

"Seriously."

"I'm taking you seriously."

I had planned to complain to McGravy about the sensational, gratuitous, and spurious story Jerry was making me do, but this didn't seem a propitious time to whine.

"Bob, am I going to be affected in the reshuffle?" I asked. "Is that why I have to be on my best behavior?"

"I can't tell you that, Robin," he said. "You know I can't."

"I am going to be affected, aren't I?"

"I can't tell you."

"Please don't let them send me to Nutrition News, Bob. Or take me off the air."

"Robin, I can't discuss the content of our editorial meetings. Don't ask me again," he said. "So how's life with Jerry? Are you behaving yourself?"

"I'm trying to behave myself, but Jerry gets worse every day. He goes out of his way to provoke me—"

"Yeah. But the guy knows how to get ratings, that's for sure."

McGravy said this with a kind of grudging respect for ratings I'd never seen in him before. If anything, he had always disdained ratings, and felt that the network's mandate was the story first. For years, he had waged a one-man crusade against the tabloidization of broadcast news, a Sisyphean mission in the age of Amy, Tonya, and O.J. Although ANN was not nearly as tainted as some of the networks, it had fed at the trough too often and too noisily for McGravy's tastes.

Special Reports was always the first hog at the trough. Yet, despite that, Jerry's star was rising at ANN. While the rest of the network struggled for ratings and ad revenue, Special Reports was effortlessly generating huge piles of money for our fearless leader, Georgia Jack Jackson, who greatly appreciated this moneymaking. Jackson was fighting off a slow, persistent takeover attempt by televangelist Paul Mangecet and needed all the cash he could raise. The pressure was on.

"It makes you wonder what we'll do for ratings," McGravy said. "How much is the media unconsciously manipulating events in order to get the best possible story? How are we influencing the outcome in order to grab viewers? To what depths will we lower ourselves to ensure our economic survival?"

I took that last rhetorical question rather personally, as I had done some pretty sleazy stories for Jerry and so knew a little about the depths to which one might stoop.

"This is me you're talking to, Bob," I said. "The woman who once posed as a sperm-bank customer. The woman who broke the exploding cheek-implant story. Who kept a straight face when a timid church secretary from Kansas told me she'd been gang-banged by aliens who got her drunk aboard their spaceship."

Things are apparently pretty much the same all over the universe.

"I know you didn't want to do those stories. I wasn't passing judgment on you."

Wearily, Bob sighed and punched me lightly in the shoulder. He had bigger problems on his mind.

"Are you learning to roll with the punches a little bit, Robin?"

"I'm being a very good girl," I said. "Thanks for the Cab Calloway tape, by the way."

"It's a real pick-me-up in the morning, isn't it? 'Jumpin' Jive, makes you nine foot tall when you're four-foot-five,' " he sang. He emptied his glass. "Always cheers me up. I gotta go, Robin. Just remember, whatever happens, it could be a blessing in disguise."

"Wait! What does that mean? Is that some sort of . . . warning?"

"Robin, nothing's set in stone yet. Just remember, a blessing in disguise."

Inspirational saying number 246: It's a blessing in disguise.

Naturally, this worried me. If it was already a done deal and they just weren't ready to tell me yet, then I wanted to know in time to, as Tamayo put it, "take the short sword"—quit before they bounced me off the air.

On the other hand, I didn't want to make it any easier for them by quitting prematurely, not if there was a chance I could stay in television a while longer. I don't know why. It wasn't like television had been bery, bery good to me. But it certainly had its high points, like the vigilantism series, and it was kind of like a home to me. I'd been with ANN since the beginning, and if I made it to my next anniversary I'd get a silver-plated satellite pin and a signed certificate from Georgia Jack Jackson.

"I'm flying down to Miami late tomorrow," Bob said, putting on his coat. "I'm going to miss a few of the meetings."

Now I suddenly saw the whole picture. It could go any way for me, and McGravy wouldn't be here to stand up for me in the executive meetings, so I had to be extra good and make an extra-swell impression on the higher-ups.

Bad news indeed. The Stoly bottle behind the oak bar was glinting at me most invitingly. But before I could consider the temptation further, McGravy said, "Don't do it, Robin, re-member Max Guffy."

The door into Buddy's opened and the resulting draft blew Bob's comb-over up, so it stood almost on end, exposing his bald spot. He didn't notice and was about to go when I pulled him back and gently pushed the hair back over his bald spot. "Look nice for your date," I said.

Bob smiled at me, kissed my cheek, and said again, "Remember Max Guffy." Then he left me to finish my beer alone.

Max Guffy was a good reason not to give in to the vodka goddess. It was such a good reason that I pulled out my reporter's notebook and wrote it down, inspirational saying number 247: Remember Max Guffy.

As if I could forget him. Getting avant-garde undertaker Max Guffy had been a real coup for me, as he'd never done a television interview before and he'd never allowed cameras into his operation. For months I'd schmoozed him, and finally he had agreed to talk to me, without cameras, in preparation for an on-air interview that would set the tone for my special report on death in modern America.

The meeting began well and we established what I thought was an immediate rapport. Then Guffy showed me around the embalming, makeup, and hair facilities, where I had the dubious privilege of watching three dead people sitting side by-side, strapped into chairs under hair dryers while a stylist coiffed a fourth corpse in front of a mirror. Afterward, we sat in Guffy's eerily quiet office and I confessed I felt uncomfortable, knowing that most of the people in the building were dead, that we were outnumbered, so he poured us both shots of vodka from the full bar he kept in his office for the bereaved.

Now, it wasn't just vodka, it was Zubrowska, a beautiful, hard-to-find Polish vodka that goes down like water and leaves a light honey aftertaste in the mouth. As you can imagine, a swift shot of Zubrowska really loosened us up. Before long we were laughing together like old friends and exchanging mordant undertaker jokes. When he offered another shot, I was feeling rather warm and convivial, and took it. I hadn't had vodka for a while but I thought, hey, I'm in a funeral home. How much trouble can I get into here?

One slip of the tongue later, and an angry, red-faced Max Guffy was asking me to leave his office, saying he wouldn't speak to ANN if his life depended on it.

He called me "tabloidesque."

No more vodka, I resolved after that. As I said, that day with Guffy was the second-to-last time I had vodka, so clearly my resolve didn't last long. The last time I had vodka (and rather a lot of it) was with comic Howard Gollis, on our fourth date, the night we almost had sex.

Blessings in disguise, bright sides, silver linings . . . I wanted to believe in all that stuff, but it wasn't easy. Walking down Fifty-seventh Street to the subway, I passed five or six homeless people. Could they look at their lives and say, well, this is a blessing in disguise?

On the subway ride home I read the evening papers. Not having much information, they played the Kanengiser murder pretty light, with brief stories. None of them knew about the handcuffs yet, and none of them made any mention of his patients except to note that the police had sealed his files.

As I folded up the newspapers and stuffed them into my valise, a tough, mustachioed guy next to me, smelling strongly of liquor and chewing tobacco, struck up a conversation, telling me just how attractive he thought I was.

I wanted to be nice, so I said, "Thank you, that's kind of you."

He took this as an invitation to proceed further. He asked me out on a date and confided he'd been recently paroled from prison.

Where I come from, this is a courtship killer. What is it about me and ex-convicts? I wondered, because this had happened to me before and, coincidentally, both men had been free for exactly five days. For some reason, I'm very popular in the freedom-impaired community and I look especially good to guys who've been free for five days. You know, I appreciate their honesty and all, but what is it about me that makes recently released felons think a criminal record wouldn't be a big thing with me? To be honest, it wasn't even the criminal record that bothered me so much. It was that Aryan Nations tattoo.

In order to cut off conversation with this stranger politely and safely, I pulled out a book, a special book I had bought just for this purpose, called *So You Have Lupus*. I'll take conversation-stoppers for 200, Alex. This can stop it cold, since most people don't know what lupus is and are not sure if it's contagious. If they do know, they aren't particularly interested in hearing about it in detail.

The man had distracted me from my train of thought. I'd been wondering how the killer got into the building without alerting security. If he—or she—had come after six p.m., he or she would be required to sign in before proceeding to the commercial floors. However, someone could have come into the building during the day, when no sign-in was required, and just hidden out somewhere. That would require hiding out after the murder and leaving the next day during regular business hours. Risky, to say the least, but not impossible.

I made a note in the margin of my book. Even as I did, I was thinking, don't sweat this story. Just do the minimum required by Jerry, slap the security tape onto a generic piece about S&M, and move on to nobler things. Do not let yourself get sucked too deeply into a sleazy murder. Avoid unpleasantness.

"So," said the guy next to me, after roughly clearing his throat. "You have lupus?"

I got off at the next stop and took a cab the rest of the way home.

6

When I got home the guillotine was gone, retrieved by the artist, and my building foyer was free of delusional neighbor ladies. Things were looking up, until I got into my apartment and saw my answering machine was blinking three times, each flash like a threat. Lately, I had looked on my answering machine as at best annoying, at worst a sinister tool that allowed people I was avoiding to reach beyond the constraints of time and space to invade my home. It made unpleasantness unavoidable.

I pushed the play button and went to fix dinner.

"Robin, guess who," said the voice of Daffy Duck.

"Howard Gollis, I'm ignoring you," I sang to the machine. It had to be Howard because who else would call me and leave a rude message as Daffy Duck? Also, I recognized his flair for words. Tonight, he called me a "vodka-swilling red-haired succubus."

Speaking of crazy people. A dark, twisted renaissance man —comic, artist, writer—Howard Gollis was really sexy, truly brilliant, and unbelievably needy. Although we hadn't dated in a while, he hadn't yet stopped calling me. Of course, he hadn't had the courtesy to leave his name—or use his real voice—since we had that big telephone blowout, the time he called me at three in the morning because he ran out of Prozac and needed to try some jokes out on somebody and have them laugh. I had a five a.m. crew call the next morning, so I told him he couldn't call me at three in the morning anymore and he got mad. Since then, I had been screening all my calls.

I don't mean to make it sound like I am some femme fatale who has hordes of muscular, well-oiled men panting after her every casual acknowledgment. I do see myself that way in my more grandiose moments, but as much as I like to think I'm Theda Bara, the truth is I am probably a little more like Fanny Brice (in the body of Rita Hayworth).

There were plenty of men I liked who weren't panting after me, who barely knew I was alive. Those men who were panting after me generally did so because they were (a) psychotic or (b) couldn't believe someone like me would turn down someone like them. We clearly weren't compatible, but they didn't see that. I wasn't good enough to turn them down. It was a vanity thing, they had to redeem their self-image and it had little to do with their genuine feelings for me, so it wasn't flattering. I say that with the knowledge that I, too, am just a tad self-absorbed.

Anyway, Howard fell into the redeem-his-vanity category, as did Reb Ryan, who, despite my best efforts to dodge him, had cornered me in the hallway earlier that day and invited me to go to his gun club with him the following Saturday to shoot a few rounds.

And they say romance is dead.

The answering machine beeped into a message from Gary Grivett, a nice, funny guy from Minnesota I went out with once on a blind date. He wanted to know where I was at lunch. Apparently, we'd had a second date and I'd stood him up. As he was just in town for the day, he said he'd take a rain check. This was the third time I'd missed an appointment since losing my old Filofax in the Great Purse Robbery.

Two down, one to go. Somehow I knew the last message would be the worst of all. Sure enough, the next voice I heard was one that has chilled me to the marrow since girlhood, the voice of my dreaded Aunt Maureen.

That voice of hers . . . What can I say? It was like a trauma time machine, wrenching me back to the past. I heard her voice, and I was fifteen again and everyone was over at the house for a potluck. All the aunts and uncles are sitting around talking, I walk in with a guy I want for a boyfriend, and Aunt Mo grabs my face and says, loudly, "How's your ACNE?"

Then she twists my head back and forth so she can examine it more closely before starting a major debate on my ACNE in front of a guy I was trying to impress. I would like him to look beyond my ACNE and see the whole me, but it's going to be hard for him to forget I have ACNE when my aunt is moderating a panel discussion on my ACNE and suggestions are whizzing back and forth—"oatmeal plasters," "witch hazel," "tetracycline." Aunt Mo interrogates me. How often are you washing your face? Are you eating chocolate? You're eating chocolate, aren't you? She's eating chocolate, that's what she's doing!

I'm completely humiliated. I've been exposed as an illicit chocolate-eating ACNE Girl. I hope I never see this guy again as long as I live.

"Aw, let her go, Mo," one of my uncles says. "You're embarrassing her in front of her boyfriend."

Which just makes it worse. I'm embarrassed to be embarrassed. I'm embarrassed because he isn't my boyfriend and never will be now and he probably thinks it's really funny that they presume he's the boyfriend of a Girl Who Has ACNE.

"I . . . I have to go," the boy says. He leaves, I burst into tears and flee the room only to hear Aunt Mo say, "That girl's oversensitive, isn't she?" Another panel discussion about my social skills ensues.

That's my Aunt Maureen. No ounce of body fat, no wrinkle,

no blemish, physical or psychological, can escape her keen all-knowing eye or sharp tongue. As I got older, her rebukes grew worse. Even after all these years, she could get at me in a way nobody else could, maybe because she was such a big part of my life before I moved to New York, maybe because she looks so much like my dad, although my dad's jolly personality made his features more Churchillian than Mussoliniesque.

"I'm in New York," she said to my answering machine. "Well, I have to say, I'm not impressed with this city you love so much. It's filthy! The whole place needs to be boiled."

Not everyone appreciates New York's gritty and chaotic beauty.

"And it's full of homosexuals and nuts!" she sniffed.

Well, jeez, Aunt Mo didn't have to go all the way to New York City to find homosexuals and nuts. Why, she could just look around our own family. Aunt Mo might be in denial about her sister Lucille and Rosalind, Lucille's truck-driving roommate of seventeen years. But she couldn't deny the nuts in the family, not only my mother but Aunt Mo's only offspring Raymond, my cousin, who was standing beside his unsmiling wife Vivian in the family photograph in my living room.

See, here was a key difference between our points of view: Aunt Mo thought Raymond and Vivian were the perfect respectable couple and was always holding them up to me as an example of stoic marital perseverance, whereas I saw them as a murder-suicide just waiting to happen.

Seriously, my cousin Raymond is even nuttier than Aunt Mo. As a child, for example, Raymond had been terrified by women in curlers. If he encountered one in the Safeway or Kresge's, in the street, in his own home, he'd run screaming in the opposite direction and it would take his mother a full hour to calm him down.

Aunt Mo, who often chastised me for being oversensitive, had no problem with Raymond's "frail nature," as she called it. Frail, my ass. He taunted me constantly and when I rushed to throttle him he screamed for his mother, who would come in, see me on the offensive, and whip my behind with a large wooden paddle on which the words GOD'S LITTLE HELPER were written in gold-painted macaroni. (It had been the arts and crafts project at Raymond's Bible camp the summer before. Imagine, they'd had the kids make their own instruments of punishment to present to their parents in a ceremony on pickup day. At my Bible camp we made plaster-of-paris plaques that said, THE FAMILY THAT PRAYS TOGETHER STAYS TOGETHER.)

Now, I could have forgiven poor Raymond everything, on account of his bad childhood and all, if he hadn't started tormenting three of the most important people in my life—my mother, my dog Ernie, and me—with a cap gun fired at point-blank range. I had to get even. So I would put my hair up in curlers and then jump out at him from behind doors and around corners. Until I got caught, that is, by Aunt Mo, and again tasted the swift and stinging wrath of God's Little Helper.

Raymond is now a very unhappy man with a miserable wife (albeit with naturally curly hair) and three lackluster offspring. The last time I spoke with him, he told me, without solicitation, that he and his wife only believed in having sex to procreate, which by my count meant they'd had sex successfully three times in fifteen years.

See what I mean? Aunt Mo should be more concerned about her own creepy kid, the boy voted most likely to have a body beneath the floorboards.

"I want you to call me!" was the last thing she barked into my machine.

That was the last thing I intended to do.

For the past three years, I'd managed to avoid Aunt Mo when I was back in Minnesota, by planning my visits around her annual Winnebago pilgrimage to the birthplace of Senator Joe McCarthy. But this was trickier. She was on my turf.

Very quickly, I devised my strategy. Avoid Aunt Maureen

at all costs. If I absolutely had to see her, do it near the end of her visit, in the company of complete strangers, to minimize the risk of psychological trauma.

The odd thing was, I had been thinking I could use a little more contact with Christianity so I could get a refresher course in forgiveness and tolerance and things of that nature. As the old warning goes, be careful what you pray for, you might just get it. What I got was a whole lot of Christianity, in the form of Aunt Maureen, who wasn't a real fun or forgiving sort of Christian.

I suddenly felt extremely pessimistic. It certainly did seem as though the planets were aligning against me. Kanengiser, Aunt Mo, Jerry Spurdle, Detective Bigger . . . but then I told myself, these are *not* the jackbooted forces of the cosmos converging on my house to kick the shit out of me. These are challenges, tests that separate the women from the girls.

"Hell, we gotta look on the bright side," I said to Louise Bryant, who, after eating enough to choke a bear, had climbed into my lap so I could massage her into a state of bliss no human could possibly achieve.

"The bright side," I whispered again to her, stroking her velvety gray ears.

Sure, I had alienated several segments of the funeral-services industry while working on the death series. Shit happens.

Yes, I had been divorced in an ugly, humiliating, and highly publicized split from my husband, followed by an abortive six-month sexual frenzy with a younger man who had since gone to our Moscow bureau. But while I hadn't yet figured out what went wrong in my marriage—I was still searching through the wreckage for the black box—I was out there dating, at least, back up on the horse as they say. But I wasn't having sex yet, so I guess I was riding sidesaddle.

Financially, I was in okay shape. Louise Bryant didn't like her work much, but she had a career in cat food endorsement and was bringing in a tidy sum that kept her in catnip and had allowed me a couple of great vacations in the last year.

(Trivia note: Louise Bryant gets ten times more fan mail than I do. The cat food company employs one whole person just to answer her fan mail.)

All I had to do was ride out the reshuffle, and I could get back on track with the Master Plan, which was: (a) escape Jerry Spurdle/Special Reports, and (b) get back to general news and real stories.

Aunt Mo? Well, if I was vigilant, I could avoid her.

Kanengiser? Nothing I could do for him, poor schmuck. As the Serenity Prayer said, "God grant me the serenity to accept the things I cannot change." So I tried to forget about him, turning on the television and flicking through the channels— a documentary about Polish motocross drivers, a show about Hindi film, stand-up comedy—settling on the Channel 3 news. I caught the end of it, a story about a couple in Co-op City who had adopted three brothers orphaned by a car accident. I was about to turn to the Channel 7 news when I saw a promo for the tabloid show *Backstreet Affair*. They were on the Kanengiser story.

"Kinky gynecologist's ex-wife speaks," said the bellowing and emotive announcer.

Backstreet Affair paid people to talk, and in exchange for a healthy check, the doctor's second ex-wife was only too willing to go on camera in Miami and say Kanengiser was into all sorts of weird stuff. I took it the divorce had not been amicable.

"Herm loved porn. The man was a sex fiend. He wanted me to watch porn with him, and he wanted to do things he saw in the movies. Once, he wanted to tie me up."

As convincing as she sounded, you just can't trust the ex-wife's version of things. I am an ex-wife, and there have been times when I've made my ex-husband sound like a total bastard, when in fact he is only a partial bastard and has many redeeming qualities.

You especially can't trust an ex-wife getting paid thousands of dollars to say bad stuff about her ex-husband.

Backstreet also talked to three of Kanengiser's ex-girlfriends, all of whom he had been seeing while he was married. All three had alibis. All three concurred that he was an emotionally crippled shit who had trouble making a commitment and trouble being honest. The words *priapic, liar,* and *woman-hating heterosexual* kept popping up in the interviews.

It is very unpleasant to hear one's gynecologist referred to as a priapic, lying, woman-hating heterosexual.

If all that wasn't bad enough, *Backstreet Affair* talked to *four* women who had been dating him just before he died, all with disguised faces, first names only, all of them with alibis (one poor thing had waited an hour for him at Brasserie Bleu), and all of them certain they were Ms. Right.

After the reporter's stand-up bridge outside Kanengiser's apartment, the report went into a low-quality home video of Kanengiser giving a speech to a state organization of conservative school board members on the need for double standards in school sex-education courses.

Using his expertise as a doctor, he said that "Unfortunately, the reality of the world is that women bear a much larger share of the moral burden. It isn't fair, but that's the way it is. Boys will always be boys, and so if we want to restrain sexually transmitted diseases and unwanted pregnancy and strengthen the family unit, young girls need to be taught to restrain themselves."

That's a fancy way of making an old argument: Men can't help themselves, but women can and should, because two wrongs don't make a right. Which is another way of saying: It's not my fault.

Yet, it seemed that Dr. Kanengiser had helped himself to whatever came his way. I guess he was speaking from experience about his own uncontrollable lust.

"Someone has to say it," this expert on women went on. "The female sex drive is not as strong as the male sex drive and so different rules must apply."

Obviously, this man had never been a thirty-seven-year-old

woman during a full moon with a good dirty book and a bag of Duracells.

What an asshole. If what Channel 3 reported was true, his was a level of promiscuity I hadn't seen in a while, not since the advent of AIDS. This wasn't just an odd romantic adventure, which I've come to believe is very human, for men and women. This was superhuman promiscuity. Boy, what levels of energy and organization were required to manage that? And what tremendous fear of intimacy must have fueled it? How did he keep from calling one girlfriend by the name of another? Kanengiser couldn't have been happy, with his emotional and physical energies dissipated like this.

Two ex-wives, at least three ex-girlfriends, at least four current girlfriends. He must have lived in constant fear of discovery. How did this guy sleep at night? But, of course, he had his alibi ready: I'm a man.

So maybe a better question was, when did this guy find time to sleep?

Poor bastard, I thought, before putting him out of my head for the night. Dr. Kanengiser found out the hard way that when you mess with a lot of women, sooner or later you mess with the wrong woman; that the more sexual partners you have, the higher the odds one of them will be a crazy person. That's the statistic I figure they should teach in sex-ed courses.

7

The Jackson Broadcasting System building is a pink and granite skyscraper that takes up a whole block in the East Fifties. In addition to the All News Network, the JBS building houses the Jackson Network Corporation, the Drive In Channel, an all-sports network, and four floors of commercial space rented to various professionals. Most of the ANN facilities and offices are in the basement, which we share with a subway stop and a bar-restaurant called Keggers. Below us are two levels of sub-basements and two levels of subway tracks. It is a world unto itself.

To get to the commercial floors, you had to go through a separate entrance, to a separate security desk, to an elevator that only stopped at floors twenty-four through twenty-seven. You could not access the Jackson floors from the commercial elevator, or vice versa, unless you were part of the security, maintenance, or executive staffs, whose key cards and access codes allowed them to override the elevators' master program.

There was just one security guard manning a small desk at the commercial entrance. During the day, all delivery people had to sign in and out, but others went freely up to floors twenty-four through twenty-seven. Only after six p.m. were all comers and goers required to sign in and out.

I went to work early in the morning so I could check out the security setup for the commercial floors before our interview with Mistress Anya. This was above and beyond the call of my described duty and I almost didn't bother, but I figured, what the hell, it's practically on my way. Jerry wouldn't care. He didn't even care about Kanengiser's ex-girlfriends unless they mentioned whips and black leather, which was a damn good thing since most of them wouldn't talk to us unless we paid them.

See, to me this story was now about bigger things like double standards and hypocrisy and the yawning chasm between men and women, which occasionally erupted into fight-to-the-death warfare. But Jerry had made it clear. This was not about Kanengiser, it was about the dangers of female-dominant S&M. Tamayo's theory was that Jerry saw it as a metaphor for the gender wars, feminism run amok, and this was his way of warning the rest of America. Personally, I thought that was rather too profound for Jerry.

As I got onto the elevator, I noted there was a video camera in it. The commercial elevator was pretty slow, giving me time to listen to a Muzak medley of big band music and scan the morning papers for Kanengiser stories. They were now playing it big. The *News-Journal* had it on the front page with the headline, GYNO GUNNED DOWN.

KINKY SEX INVOLVED? asked a smaller headline below it.

According to their story, Kanengiser was "eyed as a possible GOP state senatorial candidate in the next election," which was a typical *News-Journal* exaggeration. Mostly, the article was a sanctimonious rap about a prominent man and minor local politico allegedly caught in some weird sex murder. The sleazy *News-Journal* thought it was the voice of moral America and it never let a story like this pass without some puritanical thunder.

Yeah, I thought, like this is the first time a respectable man died during a sexual indiscretion. Jeez. This was chump change compared to some of the more famous examples, like when Nelson Rockefeller's ticker gave out in alleged flagrante delicto, or when that Conservative British MP was found dead while wearing black lace lingerie in an autoerotic asphyxiation.

Or how about the infamous case of Félix Faure, a president of France, who died of a massive stroke while clutching a woman's head to his lap during an act for which the French are famous. They say his hands had already started to stiffen with rigor mortis before his lover noticed he was dead. The poor woman, who happened to be the wife of his official portraitist, was trapped there until her rescuers cut away enough of her hair to enable her to escape from the dead man's grasp. She no doubt had a difficult time explaining that haircut—not to mention the lockjaw—to her husband when she got home.

I got out on twenty-seven. At this hour—it wasn't nine a.m. yet—the twenty-seventh floor was like a ghost town. I was the only person on the floor. As I approached Kanengiser's door, now crisscrossed with yellow police crime-scene tape, I heard the muffled sound of a phone ringing somewhere, plaintively, unanswered. Kanengiser's office was between that of Gordon Hurd, Podiatrist, and those of Lewisohn, Murray and Whitehall, Certified Public Accountants. Walking the length of the gold-flecked linoleum hallway, I counted two dentists, a pediatrician, a ladies' room, a men's room, a cleaning closet, and a freight elevator. There was an alarmed exit to the stairwell. There were no video cameras on the twenty-seventh floor.

It was so quiet I could hear the elevator whooshing up in its shaft.

I checked out the ladies' and, yes, men's rooms to see where someone might hide. At first, it looked impossible to hide in either of the bathrooms, but there were ventilation ducts big enough for a skinny person to squeeze into. Other than that, there wasn't anywhere to hide. Surely the police would have checked the other offices and the cleaning closet after the body was discovered.

When I was still in the men's room, I heard people getting off the elevator, their voices echoing through the hallway.

I heard them approach. I didn't want to be seen leaving the men's room—wouldn't help my reputation at all—so I ducked into a stall. The door opened and two men walked in. I crouched on top of the toilet.

"I didn't know the guy," said one of the men, unzipping himself. "But I'm not surprised. My office is right next door, and a couple of times I was working late, and I swear I heard him having sex in there."

"We're getting together a committee of lessees," said the other man. "We've got to have better security than this. Those television people have great security."

They zipped back up. Only one of them washed his hands. Eeuw. They left.

I was about to get down off my perch and sneak out when another man came in. I heard him unzip. He whistled a bit, then said, "Yeah, yeah, that's it" to himself and whistled some more. When he left, he held the door for another man coming in, who said "Thanks."

I heard heavy footsteps approaching on the tile. He tried my stall. The door shook and he went into the next stall. I saw his khakis and scuffed black shoes under the cubicle wall. This was too much. I had to get out of there before he dropped trou.

But he didn't drop trou. I heard a match, and smelled smoke as the man lit a cigarette. After taking a few quick puffs, he dropped the butt into the toilet. I heard two quick squirts of breath freshener, a flush.

I waited until he was safely gone and fled to the street.

When I got down to the crew car, Mike and Jim were arguing about who was going to drive to the shoot that morning.

Mike had just rotated back from five years overseas as cameraman for war correspondent Reb "Rambo" Ryan, among others. I wasn't sure how Special Reports had lucked out and got him, but I figured he was being punished for something, maybe those forty-seven different traffic warrants on four continents still outstanding against him and the company. Mike had the distinction of being the only person to get a speeding ticket in Sarajevo during the height of the fighting there.

Because of this, Jim was our designated driver.

"You don't mind if I drive, do you, Robin?" Mike asked. "I hate being a passenger."

"Rules are rules," I said.

"This is the whip lady we're interviewing, right?" Jim said, shifting into gear and heading into midtown traffic.

"Right," I replied.

"Jeez. Wait until I tell my wife about this one. Have you ever whipped a guy, Robin?"

"Only in self-defense."

"Have you ever been spanked?" Jim asked.

"Oh sure. And I've spanked. But I'm not into it. I have to know a guy really really well before I'll spank him," I said. "What about you?"

Jim shook his head violently. "No way."

We both looked at Mike.

"You wouldn't believe some of the things I've done," he said.

"This guy was your gynecologist?" Jim asked.

"Almost," I said. "Close enough that doing this story feels extra weird to me, know what I mean?"

Hanging out with Jim and Mike was the high point of my job. I felt like one of the guys because we talked pretty freely about stuff, and we all had different viewpoints and different opinions. Jim was very normal. He lived in Jersey, in a house, with his wife and kid. After eight years of doing sound for Special Reports, he still hadn't been jaded by the oddities we covered. Every story left him shaking his head in amazement. His was the conservative, family-values point of view.

Mike, on the other hand, was not normal. No normal person spends five years chasing wars, going from one hellhole to another. Mike was forty-three years old, came from Ireland originally, and had a nine-year-old daughter with his ex-wife, who was American. Mike's point of view was freewheeling and libertarian, sometimes outrageously so, but he got away with it because he had an Irish accent. When Mike was calm, he had only a trace of Ireland in his voice, but when he got excited, or had a bit to drink, or was talking about home, you could really hear it. "Dem Flynns, de whole fockin' family's bank robbers," he said, when describing some neighbors from County Cork to Tamayo and me at Keggers. He rolled his *r*'s and said words like *smuggler* as "smoogler." Jim and I imitated him a lot.

Because of my adventure in the men's room on twenty-seven, we were late getting to Anya's. Don't be late, she had emphasized on the phone. She had meant it. When we got there, the haughty maid informed us that Madame was not yet ready, and we would be required to wait in Madame's minimalist living room.

"Please set up and be ready to roll when Madame comes in," the maid said. "She'll be about ten more minutes."

Madame's living room was a cavern, really, with twenty-foot ceilings and huge floor-to-ceiling windows covered in gauzy white curtains sashed with red velvet. The whiteness of the room was relieved only by the red sashes and a wall of glass and teak cases displaying a lot of medieval iron torture implements.

"Guess she's going to make an entrance," Mike said, strolling over to get a better look at the torture devices. "Wow, look at this weaponry."

"Nice disembowler," I said.

"When was the last time you had a good evisceration, girl? I mean, a really good one."

(Mike was one of the few men who could get away with calling me a girl—although I often refer to myself that way —and that was because he said it with respect and with that great *r*-rolling lilt. Ask an Irish guy to say that word, *girl*, for you and you'll see what I mean.)

"You're sick."

The maid appeared and said, "Madame is coming," and we went back to position. I put in my earpiece, which wasn't necessary since we weren't going live. But Mike liked to be able to talk to me while we were shooting, and I went along with it because he had worked with correspondents much better than me and I had to trust his judgment.

When the maid was sure we were rolling, and only then, Mistress Anya came in, dressed like Kaiser Wilhelm and leading her "slave" Charles around on a leash. Charles, a white man, was dressed head-to-toe in black leather so that only his eyes, nose, and hands were visible. He was on all fours.

"Sit, Charles," Anya commanded, and he obediently sat on the floor by the white leather sofa.

Anya then sat down, took off her spiked Prussian helmet, and smoothed down her short blond hair. With a different personality, she would have been quite sweet-faced. Her face was round and catlike, with big brown eyes and a heart-shaped mouth, but the cold, controlling aura she projected removed all gentleness from her.

"I'm ready now," she said, imperiously.

I showed her the photograph and said, "Did you know this man, Dr. Herman Kanengiser?"

"No, I don't think so. I'm not sure. I don't recognize the name at all," she said. "At least, not by that name. But understand that people who aren't yet completely comfortable with their sexual identity take new names when they enter our world. And many come incognito, in leather masks, for instance. 'Put a mask on a man and he'll be honest.' That's Oscar Wilde. 'Put a whip in a woman's hand, and she'll be honest.' That's me.

"I will say that a great many physicians, lawyers, judges, and other professionals, even policemen, are members, unofficially, of our society. We have quite a few clients from Wall Street in particular. If this doctor had a matchbook from Anya's, it means he probably visited the club."

"He doesn't ring any bells?"

"No," she said, without even glancing a second time at the photo.

"None at all?"

"No."

"Just out of curiosity," I said. "Where were you the night before last?"

"At the club, as I am most nights," she said, with clear annoyance. "I understood from Mr. Spurdle that I was going to get a chance to talk about the society."

Well, if Mr. Spurdle said it was so, who was I to quibble? I didn't know what else to ask her, so after that I just let her roll with her spiel about the Marquis de Sade Society and S&M—also known as B&D, for bondage and discipline.

I already knew rather more than I wanted to about S&M. You see, my most devoted fan, Elroy, is a masochist who fantasizes about me hurting him. In his last letter, he had listed the many things he was willing to do to win my heart. For example, and I quote, "I would shave my body with a dull razor and then sit in a vinegar bath just to win the privilege of licking the sweat from your feet."

Creepy, yes. But what harm had he actually threatened to me, other than to give my feet a good licking, an idea more disgusting than dangerous?

"Love and sex and pain and punishment are all inextricably bound up together," Mistress Anya was saying. "We're just more honest about it than most people, and more economical in the way we express it. Love needs rules, it needs a leader and a follower. Our love is about trust. The slave trusts me and gives me complete control, and I love him and punish him accordingly."

"How long have you had Charles here?"

"A month and a bit," she said. "So far, he's been a very good boy."

If Charles had had a tail, it would have been wagging.

"Is there longevity in these sorts of relationships?"

"Of course. I was with my late husband for eight years, until he passed away. Before Charles, I had Werner for three years."

"What happened with Werner?"

"I had to ask him to leave," she said shortly.

The "slave" Charles was looking up at me with that same needy look a dog has. It was so weird that he was acting like a dog. Mike must have been thinking the same thing because he whispered in my earpiece, "Is he allowed up on the furniture?"

This was a challenge. Whatever turns your crank, as they say. It's not that I have anything against kinky in theory, if you know what I mean, but when I'm confronted with it in real life I have a hard time keeping a straight face.

"Why did you ask him to leave?" I didn't really care, but I sensed this subject bothered her and I felt like yanking *her* chain a bit.

"He drank from the toilet," Mike whispered in my ear.

"He violated my trust," Anya said, then expertly changed the subject.

"When we're role-playing," she went on. "Words like *no* and *stop* mean "yes" and "don't stop." So we have control words for when one really does want to stop, words that cannot be confused. Every master and slave have their own words. Charles and I use *blender* for "no" and *artichoke* for "stop." Another couple we know use *bassoon* and *Venice*."

She picked up a sturdy, oversize table-tennis paddle.

"Now, Charles likes to be paddled, as opposed to whipped," she said. "I must stress it is important that people *not try this at home* without proper instruction. At the society and at the club, we teach neophytes how to hit without leaving bruises or damaging internal organs."

"How erotic. Hose me down," Mike said in my ear.

"The best point for paddling is an area of the rump we know as the sweet spot. Shall I demonstrate?" she asked, and Charles got off his haunches and began unbuttoning the square leather flap that covered his butt.

"Oh please, *artichoke!*" Mike whispered.

"That's all right," I said, quickly. "We're more interested in the philosophical aspects of your relationship."

I couldn't get into this. I could barely handle the regular low-grade S&M all lovers enjoy/suffer. I just wanted to get the hell out of here before Fido started licking his own genitalia.

Mistress Anya stood, ordered Charles the slave to heel.

"Come to one of our meetings," she said to us. "And do come by the club. I'll make some inquiries about this doctor."

She led her crawling sycophant away.

Apparently, the interview was now over. I couldn't help but be awed, and somewhat frightened, by the control this woman had over everything in her life. It takes a tough bitch to promote sadomasochism, I guess.

"Jesus," I said, back in the crew car. "That is one scary woman. Was it just me, or did you get the feeling she was hiding something? Like, she's skinning dalmatians for their pelts in the back bedroom or something."

"I thought she was almost attractive," Mike said. "But that slave gave me the cold quivers."

"That's because he was so doglike," I said. "And you hate dogs."

This I learned one day when we returned from a shoot and had to fight our way through a phalanx of animal-rights activists with their gonch in a knot because an anchorman had eaten a live oyster during a morning cooking segment.

"Bloody animal fascists," Mike said. No animal lover he; Mike had told me then that he'd run over twenty-seven stray dogs while he lived in Pakistan covering the Afghan war. By accident, he added, but I was skeptical. Twenty-seven dogs in two years is a lot, even in Pakistan.

Mike was good-looking in a pleasant, nonthreatening way: curly brown hair, freckles, twinkly eyes. He really knew how to make me laugh when I couldn't muster a laugh on my own, and, of course, he had that great accent. I'd just start to like him, as a *man* I mean, and then he would tell me about something like the twenty-seven dogs in Pakistan and it would turn me right off.

"Those control words . . . ," I said.

"All couples have control words, or phrases," Mike said. "One code word that means 'stop whatever you're doing.'"

"Good point," I agreed. "Burke used *London* on me if he thought I was acting crazy, and I used his real name on him. We had a lot of code words."

"My wife and I don't do that," Jim said. Jim either had the world's strongest, happiest marriage, or he was still in the denial phase.

The next person we interviewed, Kanengiser's first ex-wife, Hanna Qualls, was an expert on that phase. A petite and pretty management consultant, Qualls sat in her office and told us, "Herm had a problem being honest with women. Women loved him, and assumed a commitment on his part that he didn't intend. I can't blame him completely."

"Why not?" I asked.

"Because he didn't *intend* to hurt anyone, he was kind of helpless about it. He was never good at breaking off with women or telling them how he really felt about them. So he always had several women at a time, and he devoted a lot of energy to keeping them unaware of each other and keeping them from pressing for a commitment. In fact, I think Herm married me, and his second wife, to have some defense against other women, if that makes sense. You can't play that game for long without hurting a lot of people, and getting hurt yourself. I'm over the hurt now, have been for a while. But it took me a long time and a lot of therapy."

I understood completely. I too had been married to someone who was secretly polygamous, although not anywhere near Kanengiser levels.

"But, to be fair, I played a part in it too and so did every one of his other women. I let him get away with it for a long time. I even facilitated it in some ways because I loved him so much," she said.

I understood this as well. Getting away with long-term polygamy requires a certain amount of collaboration from the person, or persons, being cheated on. These are the signs of collaboration: you will accept any far-fetched excuse, you will overlook the most glaring clues, and in some cases, you'll save him the time and trouble of having to concoct a lie for himself by figuring out an explanation and presenting it to him on a silver platter when he walks in the door at three a.m. smelling of alien perfume.

I told her this, and she said, "Yes, it requires a lot of imagination. It's pretty easy to explain away lipstick on the collar. It's much tougher to explain away lipstick on the thigh. I kept denying it, until I found his black book and couldn't deny it any longer. The thing contained not only names of his women but sexual details about them! When he came home, I confronted him with it and then made him watch while I burned it in the fireplace. The next day, I saw a lawyer."

Media claims that Kanengiser was being scouted as a possible GOP state senate candidate were, Qualls said, "Nonsense. He sat on the community board because he wanted to preserve the neighborhood and his property from bad influences. He knew he had no hope of going beyond that because of all his women. I don't think he even wanted to, so the papers have completely distorted that."

"I saw a speech he made on television . . ."

"Yes, I know that speech. I heard that same argument when I finally confronted him. Men are not programmed to resist when beautiful women throw themselves at them. He is . . . was a very handsome man and successful and smart and charming and . . . he had a lot of genuinely good qualities too, and that attracted attractive women to him, you understand?"

"Oh yeah." That's why I had that new rule about not dating any more pretty boys.

In my opinion, this was the best stuff we had, although it wouldn't pass Jerry's muster since whips, chains, and tall, Teutonic women in black leather were not mentioned. The best I could elicit from Hanna Qualls on that subject was: "How do I know? There was so much I didn't know about the man that I can't even speculate about what he was or wasn't into."

The only one of the doctor's ex-girlfriends to talk to us, a glamorous model turned real estate broker named Susi Bure, offered no S&M link either, although she echoed what Hanna Qualls had said. "Did Herm mix up women's names? That was the least of it. I think the man had to have sex so much just to avoid having a conversation, because he could never remember my friends' names, my parents' names, where I worked. . . . One night in January he showed up at my place with a cake, flowers, and champagne for my birthday. My birthday's in September. There were other incidents too in our two years together. He wanted to be caught. Despite how much trouble he went to, to conceal things, another side of him was giving him away every step of the way.

"The thing that gets me now," she went on, "is that he always made me feel like it was my fault somehow, that I expected too much from him. Maybe I did expect more than he could give, but I didn't expect as much as I deserved. The thing I learned? If you don't expect much you don't get much."

Yeah, but if you expect too much, you just get disappointed, I thought.

"One other thing," Susi Bure said as we were wrapping up. "You know the matchbook that was found?"

"Yeah."

"I'm sure that wasn't Herm's. He didn't smoke."

So who smoked? I wondered.

Obviously, the killer. How had the matches come to be on Kanengiser's floor? Had they been in the killer's purse, or pocket, and fallen out when the killer took out the handcuffs or the gun? To me, this said that Kanengiser might have no direct connection to Anya's at all. The only connection might be the killer's connection.

8

After our interviews, I stopped off at security to get the elevator tapes from the day of the murder and to find out what, if anything, Pete knew (nothing so far, he told me). While I was waiting in Pete's office for Franco to get the dubs I requested, Kerwin Shutz rushed in, looking red-faced and very agitated. Kerwin always looked red-faced and agitated. Since taking over the eight p.m. talk-show slot, he had used it as a soapbox from which to rail against liberals, atheists, unionists, environmentalists, working mothers, welfare mothers, and single mothers, as well as to plug his book *I'm Right, They're Wrong* and its sequel, *I'm Still Right.*

Kerwin slapped something on Pete's desk. It was a bullet.

"Found this on my lawn this morning," he said. He turned to me, suddenly sweet. "Hello Robin. Sorry to interrupt. I'll just be a moment."

"I'm busy but I'll be right with you Ker . . ." Pete said.

"I need a bodyguard!" Kerwin screamed, and stomped out as Franco was coming in.

Kerwin was always claiming that people were shooting at

him, and he was most afraid of environmentalists, feminists, and gay activists, or as he referred to them on his show, "tree-huggers, ugly girls, and sissies." Not the first people I think of when I think of gun-toting nuts. In fact, gun-toting nuts were more likely to agree with Kerwin than to want to shoot him.

"Here," Franco said, handing me a box of tapes from the commercial elevator, along with a photocopy of a sheet from the sign-out log.

"Thanks," I said, without looking at him. Those hair-sprouting ears, you know.

Most people disliked talking to Franco because he hardly ever said anything back to you. When he first started at ANN, someone had floated the theory that Franco didn't understand English and was afraid to admit it, but he'd since spoken a couple of times and demonstrated that he understood the language, as long as you didn't use too many big words or non-literal expressions. He was part of the humorless horde. In fact, Louis Levin had put a kind of bounty on Franco, offering two hundred dollars to anyone who could make him laugh in front of witnesses. Tamayo, for one, was doing her level best to win that money. Whenever she ran into Franco, she assailed him with Gomer Pyle jokes she had learned from jarheads stationed at the Yakota base outside Tokyo. It was so bad that now when Franco saw Tamayo, he ran in the opposite direction. That one of our top-ranking Keystone Kops was afraid of a Japanese-American stand-up comic was not very confidence-inspiring.

Also not very confidence-inspiring: the day Hector patrolled the offices, with his typical affected law-enforcement swagger, one thumb hooked into his beltloop, the other hand on his gun, and a Kick Me sign on his back. Until Pete and Franco saw it, which showed you how much respect people had for our Barney Fife.

"These are only the tapes from the commercial elevator. What about the freight elevator?" I asked.

It turned out the other tapes had been sent over to the cop shop without anyone running dubs, so now I had to wait for the cops to dub them for me.

No matter. These were the tapes I was most interested in. They were grainy, black and white, but also time-coded, with hour, minute, and second, which would help match the names in the sign-out book to real people.

Back in my office, I scanned them on fast forward. You couldn't see much when the elevator was full except the tops of people's heads. After I did a quick log of the daytime tapes, I popped in the after-hours tape. Not many people went up and most who did got off on twenty-six or twenty-eight, where there were several accountants' offices. Nothing unusual about that, since it was tax season.

At 9:11:54, a man went up to the twenty-sixth floor. Oblivious to the security camera in the ceiling corner, he picked his nose, examined the result, then wiped it on the elevator wall. Eeuw.

As I was watching this unenlightening tape, Phil the enlightened janitor came by. He took priority in my eyes, so I paused the tape. Every day Phil came in to empty the trash, shoot the shit, and fill me in on the company gossip. An older guy, late sixties, early seventies, who had been in the States for only a few months, he claimed to have spent the last fifteen years working his way around the world as a janitor or handyman. During his life he had had all these near-death close calls, or so he said, starting when he was fifteen ("I looked eighteen") and served in the British army in North Africa. Rommel's Afrika Korps launched a surprise attack on Phil's unit and when it was over and Rommel had rolled past, Phil got up, looked around, and saw he was the only person still alive. "I felt dead sorry for me mates," he told me. "But me first thought was, 'Ha! Rommel, you missed one, you sorry bastard.' " He then made his way back to British lines. Later, he said, he was a fireman in Liverpool and had saved many babies and old women from fires.

Since then, it had been one adventure and close call after another.

I didn't really believe he'd been the only survivor of a ferry sinking in Bangladesh, or that he'd walked away from a small plane crash in the Himalayas, or that a cobra had come up the loo in Calcutta and tried to "bite me bum." (What a nightmare, huh?) I wanted to believe all his stories, though. They were entertaining and weirdly truthful, and I liked his philosophy. "I'm just too silly to die, I guess," he always said.

"Glad to see you back, Phil," I said. "Over that flu?"

"Oh yeah. It's tough on a man me age. Imagine, all the things I survived, to get nailed by a microbe or a virus."

"Heard anything from the executive suite?" I asked.

Since the recent custodial cutbacks, Phil had been emptying the poobah trash upstairs as well as that of some of the features offices at ANN.

"Madri Michaels is being taken off the air, pushed into a PR job," he said. "Bianca de Woody is to replace her."

An allergic reaction to having her lips cosmetically plumped had taken Madri off the air for a while. It took two weeks for the redness and swelling to go down, and in that time Bianca de Woody had made the seven p.m. slot her own. Anchorwoman Madri Michaels was no friend of mine. Still, I felt bad for her, and I felt bad for me. Madri was just a year older than me and she ranked slightly higher in the newsroom food chain.

"Heard anything about this murder on twenty-seven?"

"Spoke to the guy who found the body. A cleaning man. He's pretty shook up about it still," Phil said.

I'd spoken to the cleaning guy, Dom Lecastro, too, through an interpreter as Mr. Lecastro didn't speak much English. He'd only just started doing the twenty-seventh floor, didn't know anything about Kanengiser, and hadn't seen anything.

"I'm cleaning the north wing on thirty-five tonight," Phil said on his way out of my office. "All the Xerox rooms are on that side. Should be able to get something for you tomorrow."

"Thanks, Phil."

There was a commotion outside the door, and Tamayo's voice saying, "I'm going. You don't have to push."

I went out and saw her flanked by two security guards.

"We caught her smoking in a cleaning-supply closet near Sports," said one of the guards to Jerry, who was shaking his head.

There were few places you could still sneak a smoke at ANN. A couple of people had been caught on video smoking in the stairwells and one of them was fired because it was a third offense.

Okay, take a high-pressure place like a newsroom where people are staring at bad news for hours on end, add job insecurity, big egos, and troubled marriages, then ban smoking so the whole place is having a nic fit. And what do you have? Endless good cheer and camaraderie. You bet.

"I'll look after her," Jerry said, taking custody. He and Tamayo went into his office.

"Are you nuts!" he shouted at her. I pressed my ear to the glass. I heard him open that big drawer full of résumés.

"See these?" he said. "These are the résumés of all the people who want to replace you. . . ."

What an asshole.

After Jerry finished chewing her out, Tamayo brought me my mail and my faxes. She was such a startling presence. Maybe it was that shock of white-blond hair atop that semi-Japanese face, or maybe it was just her anarchic personality coming through.

"I can't remember what I did with your phone messages," she said. "Can I give them to you later?"

"Listen," I said. "This is really important. If a woman calling herself Maureen Hudson Soparlo, also known as 'Aunt Maureen' or 'Aunt Mo,' calls, I'm not here."

"Ever?"

"Ever. If she calls, I'm out on a story, won't be back until really really late, if at all."

"Got it," she said.

"Write it down, okay?"

Tamayo's heart wasn't really in her job—her dream was to be a full-time stand-up comic—and she didn't do a very good job in Special Reports (although she was a crack comic). Often absentminded, she'd wander off in midsentence. She'd take milk from the minifridge in our conference area and forget to close the door. By the time it was discovered, Jerry's liverwurst would be spoiled. She'd lose phone messages and forget to pick up tapes.

To make up for these shortcomings, I had to do a lot more work, and I did, because it was worth it just to have her around for comic relief and to harass Jerry, since I couldn't, due to my new Positive Mental Attitude.

"Someone told me to say hi to you. Who was it? Oh, Howard Gollis," Tamayo said.

"He's insane."

She gave me a pot-calling-the-kettle-black look.

"He's a creative personality," she said finally. "He goes to the edge. You thought it was attractive when you saw him perform."

She was right. When I saw him the first time, when I'd gone to see Tamayo perform at the Duplex, I thought he was very sexy, dark, handsome, and funny. Edgy. Lenny Bruce meets Mel Blanc with a soupçon of Leonard Cohen. His brand of humor was really out there, sick but very funny. More importantly, he was the first man I'd been sexually attracted to since Eric.

"You *begged* me to introduce you," Tamayo reminded me.

Again, she spoke the truth. I had begged her, and she had pointed out that he was a nutcase and I was a nutcase and we were both very vulnerable at the moment because of failed relationships and maybe we should steer clear of each other for the sake of innocent bystanders like herself.

So I begged her some more, and she introduced us. The first two dates were like a trip to Coney Island. Howard was really funny, we really hit it off. The third date he had a Fear of Intimacy attack. On the fourth date, we almost had sex, things went wrong, and the bloom was off the rose.

"I don't want to talk about Howard Gollis. He's history. What are you working on?" I said.

"The nomination forms for the Dumb-ass Foundation Awards."

"Dundas Foundation," I corrected.

"If Jerry's up for one, I stand by my pronunciation," she said. "He told me today not to bring my personal problems into the office. So I told him he had a few personal problems too, but nothing ten large lesbians with baseball bats couldn't handle. That's no idle threat, because you actually know ten large lesbians with baseball bats, don't you?"

"Indeed I do," I said.

You can find them in my Rolodex cross-indexed under Lesbian Justice and Vigilantism—Gays & Lesbians.

"Jerry's worse than that jackass Yamamoto I worked for on the Japanese game show," Tamayo said.

For someone in her mid-twenties, Tamayo had had quite a long and varied career. Before going to work for ANN in Tokyo, which had led to the job in New York, she had worked for a sleazy Japanese TV program called *Amazing True Stories*. They did features like "The True Living Gold Snake." Tamayo's job, as she summed it up, was "to paint the snake gold." Sometimes, when Jerry asked us to do something journalistically dubious, we would turn to each other and say, "It's time to paint the snake."

Before *Amazing True Stories* she had been a prize hostess for a Japanese game show she referred to as *Humiliate Me for Pennies*. What it entailed, I wasn't sure, but she once said that at ANN she finally had a job that didn't involve live tree slugs, styptic pencil, or welding glass.

Humiliate Me for Pennies. Exactly how was Special Reports different?

Just as she was about to leave my office, she turned around and said, "Did I mention that Bianca called, twice?"

"I'll call her."

"Call her now. It sounded urgent."

When I called Bianca back, she said, "Can you meet me? I'd like to talk to you."

"We can talk now on the phone."

"Oh, now's not a good time. It has to be done in person."

"Oh, all right," I said.

"Ladies' room near Sports, five minutes," she said, and hung up abruptly, without good-byes.

Bianca was waiting, and as soon as I got there she yanked me inside.

"What—" I started to say but she clasped one hand over my mouth.

"Ssssh," she said.

Bianca, blond and blue-eyed with a Varga girl figure, wasn't a bad news reader, although her appeal was perhaps best summed up by Dillon Flinder's involuntary comment, made somewhere between a grunt and a sigh, "That mouth! Oh God, that mouth." She had a great mouth—bee-stung, I think they call it—and she didn't require collagen to maintain it.

I'd already spent a considerable part of my day hiding out in bathrooms, including the ghost of a bathroom we now knew as Special Reports. Quietly, I watched as Bianca checked all the stalls to make sure we were alone. It was all pretty cloak-and-dagger, but I was nonchalant about it. Cloak-and-dagger was getting to be the normal atmosphere around ANN. Because I'm a tad self-absorbed and figure everything that happens somehow relates to me, I figured Bianca was acting strange because she'd heard something about my fate in the impending shakeup.

"Robin, isn't it awful about Dr. Kanengiser?" Bianca said finally, having ensured we were completely alone.

"You saw Dr. Kanengiser too?"

"Yeah. I referred you to him. A couple of months ago."

"You did?"

"Sure, when you and Tamayo and I had lunch with Solange and Susan Brave."

"Oh. Yeah."

"Yeah. Do you mind if I smoke? I mean, you wouldn't tell, would you?"

"No." I wasn't the type to call up the human resources office anonymously and rat on someone for smoking, despite HR's encouragement to snitch. HR had even set up a twenty-four-hour line you could call if you saw someone smoking at work, out on the street, even at a party after hours.

Bianca climbed atop the vanity and disabled the smoke alarm above the mirrors before peeling off her nicotine patch and lighting a cigarette.

"You wouldn't believe how hard it is to sneak a smoke when you've got a bodyguard shadowing you."

"Who?"

"Hector."

"Hector?"

"Pete's worried that one of my . . . fans is on his way to New York, so he assigned Hector to follow me around when I'm not on air. Hector is driving me crazy."

"Is that the reason for the cloak-and-dagger?"

She didn't answer that. "Robin, I want you to promise me that you won't tell anyone I saw Kanengiser."

"Why?"

"I went to him to have something embarrassing treated and I just don't want it to get around this rumor mill. Or worse even, into the newspapers."

"I understand," I said.

"I don't want Pete to know . . ."

Bianca was dating our security chief, Pete Huculak. Before settling into a steady relationship with Pete, she'd dated a lot of guys at ANN, including my cameraman, Mike. I mean, I'd dated a lot within the company too and she and I had dated a few of the same guys, but she'd dated more of them and much more seriously than I had. While I dated randomly and without any real relationship goals, she was a woman with a mission: Find a boyfriend. She was the type who always had to have a boyfriend. Once she told me she just felt safer with a man in her life.

It was understandable. In the last year she had leapt up the media-market ladder from a small station in her hometown of Cedar Rapids, Iowa, to a medium station in Cincinnati and then to ANN in New York. As Cincinnati had seemed a big, wild city to her, she'd naturally had some trouble adjusting to New York, so it was easy to see the attraction of a big, strong, take-charge kind of guy like Pete, who made her feel safe.

"He's old-fashioned and he wouldn't be very understanding about my . . . not that it's anything serious . . . I mean, it was cured before Pete and I . . . consummated," she said, with an odd note in her voice. The last time I had heard that coy, coded tone was when Dolores Savoy came up to me in the hallway of Hummer High School and asked for a tampon by whispering, "My friend just came to visit and she forgot her luggage. Do you have any?"

It was such a strain for Bianca, trying to be delicate about whatever it was she'd had treated, while at the same time trying to communicate her distress. Bianca seemed like a real nice young woman, and she could be very witty, but she was weird about sex and her own body. I mean if you can't talk about it openly with another woman in the ladies' room . . .

"I won't say anything," I said.

"I heard you were doing a special report on it, so I wanted to be sure."

"We're not trying to expose his patients," I said. Not as long as we had an even sleazier angle to exploit.

"Good," she said. "I know I can trust you."

She pulled a piece of paper from her purse and said, "You can't have this, you can only look at it. I think it might help you with your story."

But she didn't hand it over right away.

"I noticed this last night, as I was going through my medical records," she said. "I wanted to get rid of any traces of Kanengiser, because of Pete . . ."

Now she gave me the document, an insurance summary from our employee benefits department, showing a summary of her medical expenses for the first quarter of the year.

"Please note I was billed for six visits," she said.

"Noted."

"I only saw him three times."

"Wow. Bookkeeping error?"

"Maybe. But I thought it might mean something. I wanted you to have the tip."

"That's swell of you. Thanks."

"You think the tabloids will get hold of my name in this murder business?" she asked. "You know, 'Gynecologist to TV News Star Killed'?"

"The cops have sealed his files, so I wouldn't worry too much about it. Who else saw him?"

"I don't know. I referred him to you . . . I don't really know of anyone else. But he was in the building, and he saw patients evenings, so it wouldn't surprise me if other women here saw him . . ."

"What do you know about Kanengiser?"

"Not much."

"When did you see him last?"

"Two weeks ago, just for a follow-up."

"So you didn't see him the night he was killed?"

"No. I was anchoring all night."

"Did you date Kanengiser?"

"No, of course not. Did you?" she asked.

"No. I hardly knew him at all. You knew him a bit better. What do you think about this S&M connection?"

"I didn't get that vibe off him at all," she said. "But God, in New York, you never know, do you? A guy seems like a nice, normal professional, and he turns out to be into whips and chains. I've been on more strange dates with more strange guys in the short time I've been in New York . . ."

"In New York's defense, I've been on some weird dates too, but not all of them were native New Yorkers."

"Speaking of that, I hear you're going out with Fenn Corker," Bianca said, blowing a smoke ring in a way that would give Dillon Flinder a coronary.

"Who told you that?"

"He did."

"Why?"

"Oh, no reason. It just came up when I spoke to him on the phone last week," she said. She turned on the tap and ran her cigarette under it, then pitched it into the trash.

The PA system crackled. She was being paged.

"My master's voice. Gotta run. Thanks for keeping this quiet," Bianca said.

It wasn't much to go on, but it might lead this story away from S&M into something more prosaic, like an insurance scam, something boring that might convince Jerry to drop it altogether.

9

I caught Cyndi in employee benefits just as she was about to leave for the day. After she told me tersely that all benefits information was confidential, I said, "I'm reporting a possible rip-off to you. I'm helping you out. You don't have to tell me who he saw or why. All you have to do is check to see if other Jackson employees saw this guy, and if he was double-billing them too. All I need to know is yes or no."

"Oh, all right. I'll get back to you tomorrow."

"You can't do a quick search and beep me when . . ."

"Hey, I'm not one of you news moonies," she said. "I'm overworked, underpaid, and it's quitting time."

Quitting time, two words that did more for my state of mind than all the philosophy in the world. Time to put our work away and resume our real lives. There were places to go, people to see. Me, I was meeting Mike, Jim, and Claire at Keggers, the tacky but unassuming bar-restaurant-refuge in the basement of the JBS building.

Originally, Claire had wanted to meet at one of her noisy, twenty-something hangouts, but the older I get the less I like those places. Unless you're in full mating mode and the place is full of eligible men your own age, loud, crowded clubs are kind of a drag. You have to shout to have a conversation, people are always jostling past you, and you end up doing shots at the bar with some guy young enough to be your son (in one of those backward child-bride countries).

It had been over a month since I'd seen Claire Thibodeaux, longer since we'd been able to get together for more than five minutes, although we talked pretty regularly on the phone. She'd flown in from D.C. the day before to attend meetings and an all-star brunch on Saturday with Georgia Jack Jackson (to which I had not been invited). Her meeting that day was running late, fueling all sorts of speculation.

While I waited for her, Mike and Jim kept me company at a table near the bar and we had a wide-ranging discussion on male and female sexuality that began when Jim said that Kanengiser was right about one thing: Men had a much stronger sex drive than women.

I had to straighten him out.

"Women have strong sex drives too, I mean, who in their right mind doesn't like orgasms, and as many as possible? But we have fewer outlets and more penalties. That's why we're so pissed off."

"Still celibate?" Mike said to me, sympathetically.

"Well, yeah."

"See, most men would never be able to handle months of celibacy."

"It's not like I haven't been trying, Mike. I've been dating. But something always happens that makes me not want to have sex with my dates. That's the discrimination factor."

You know, after Eric and I split up, I had thought about being a libertine, and I hadn't, in fact, ruled it out yet. In theory, I was open to the idea of safe, dirty, noncommittal sex with several men I knew and admired until such time as I met someone I wanted to have a monogamous relationship with (who wanted to have one with me). In theory.

Of course, in theory, I'd be honest about it with the men involved and one thing I have noticed is that most men who want to be libertines don't want their girlfriends or lovers to be.

In any event, Kanengiser now stood to me as an example of where freewheeling ways could lead.

"I don't mean to be celibate but you know, whenever I end a relationship, I take a breather before entering another. It's my way to, in the words of Carrie Fisher, 'Find myself before someone bigger does,' " I said.

"You takes yer chances or you don't get laid," Mike said. "But I agree women have strong sex drives. I've known a lot of women with strong sex drives."

Jim said, "The thing is, once you have a baby, for example, the wife is tired all the time from all those three a.m. feedings, has no sex drive—"

I interrupted. "Or maybe just no energy."

"Whatever. But the guy still has the same sex drive he had before the baby was born. So what's a guy supposed to do? Not that I've ever cheated on my wife," Jim quickly added.

"Except for blow jobs at bachelor parties," Mike said.

"Well . . . ," Jim said. He wasn't willing to be as frank as Mike was, but he didn't argue with Mike, so Mike must have known something specific. I learned a lot from Mike and, through his prodding, from Jim. Like the unspoken fidelity loopholes: bachelor parties, "under ten minutes and out of town," and various scenarios involving being trapped in a life-or-death situation with an attractive member of the opposite sex. Mike assured me that a lot of women knew and took advantage of the latter two loopholes as well. He'd spent enough nights with married women in war zones, where normal rules are suspended, to know that under the right circumstances women can be as pagan as men. Not that Mike agreed with me all, or even most, of the time.

Jim had to go.

"Say hi to Claire for me," he said. "Tell her I'm sorry I couldn't stay till she got here. Have to get home to the wife and the baby."

Mike and I had Jim spooked about women and sex. He didn't want to leave his wife alone for too long these days.

"I'm always so tempted to lie to him," I said to Mike. "You know, for his peace of mind. He's been looking at me funny ever since we had that lunchtime conversation about vibrators."

"He wants to hear our points of view. That's why he always brings up the subject. Besides, don't you find as you get older it's more trouble to lie than to tell the truth?"

"Naw, I find that I get into a lot more trouble when I try to tell the truth," I said.

"You might be right," Mike said, taking a drink from his beer bottle and glancing around the joint. "There's a sinister vibration in this place tonight, isn't there?"

Now that he mentioned it, yeah, there was. It was busy at Keggers that night. Folks were two-deep at the bar and nearly every seat was taken in the dining room, with its faux Tiffany lamps, laminated wood tables, and malt-shop-style booths wallpapered with historic newspaper headlines. Rumors of reshuffles and cutbacks had everyone on edge, and the anchormen and male reporters were especially edgy, due to the reports of snipings. The place was crawling with on-air people looking for a little courage in a glass.

So far, the reported sniper had only shot at men, specifically Reb and Kerwin, but the women had things to worry about too, such as the reshuffle and, possibly, the repercussions of the Kanengiser murder. How many of them had seen Kanengiser? Most women find a gynecologist they like and stick with her or him, but news people move around to different markets, bureaus, companies so much that they jump from doctor to doctor, dentist to dentist.

That the files were intact must have been a huge relief, because Kanengiser's files would have contained highly personal information: records of pregnancies, abortions, infections, STDs, number of sexual partners, among other things. The kind of information that, thanks to the ol' double standard Kanengiser was so proud of, could be used to really hurt a woman.

As I was looking around, I caught Dillon Flinder's eye. Dillon, who believed in one very liberal standard for all, came over and asked if he could join us. Mike waved expansively at a chair.

"You heard about Kerwin?" Dillon said. "Someone took a shot at his house."

"Do you believe him?" I asked.

"I wouldn't, but after Reb got shot at . . ."

"Reb is notoriously paranoid too," I said.

"With reason," Dillon said. "He's been shot at in Afghanistan, knifed in Gaza, bombed in Sarajevo, escaped from kidnappers in Beirut, escaped from Tajik terrorists . . ."

I looked at Mike. I had been star-struck by Reb too, until I learned more about him from Mike, who had been Reb's cameraman for a while and had been kidnapped with him in Beirut. I sensed he was keeping a lot of secrets for Reb, but lately he'd broken down and exploded a few Reb "Rambo" Ryan myths.

For example, Reb claimed to have dated Kim Basinger when in reality they'd merely been tablemates at the White House correspondents' dinner. The "Tajik terrorists" who had tried to kidnap him in Dushanbe, according to Mike, were just touts trying to get them to buy carpets.

And then there was the Haiti incident, which Mike, loosened by a couple of beers, proceeded to describe to Dillon.

After a hairy tour of Chechnya that left Reb a bit shell-shocked, he had been sent to Haiti, where he really snapped his cap. According to Mike, Reb was with a bunch of other reporters on a bus, when the bus broke down outside Port-au-Prince. He panicked. After five minutes in the hot sun, Mr. Macho Hemingway Foreign Correspondent suddenly advised the others to start drinking their own urine to help conserve water, and then demonstrated, with a flourish, like a man doing a juicer demonstration in a department store.

(God, I hope he doesn't kiss Kim with that mouth, I commented.)

The other reporters watched him in shock but demurred when he suggested they all do it. Ten minutes later, they were rescued.

When ANN management heard this story, they decided Reb had been in the field a little too long. So they brought him back to headquarters to anchor and chill out.

I only wished Mike had told me this stuff *before* I'd gone out with Reb.

"Reb's been nuts for a long time," Mike said to Dillon. "He's happy in war zones, being threatened, at risk. He really gets off on it. He's miserable here, and he may be imagining threats because he's comfortable in an atmosphere of danger. That's normal for him. I told you this just to put Reb's sniper story in context. I'd appreciate it if you wouldn't mention it to anyone else."

"I'll try," Dillon vowed, which was the best he could promise. He was compulsively honest and not good at keeping secrets.

Neither was I. When Mike told me about the Haiti Incident, he had asked me not to repeat it, and in a loose moment I'd told both Claire and Louis Levin.

"I have to go, guys. Gotta date," Mike said, slapping some money down on the table. "Dillon, I'm sure these shootings, if they're real, are random. I wouldn't worry about being shot at, if I was you. See you tomorrow."

"I wouldn't worry about the sniper," Dillon said to me, "if it wasn't for that gynecologist being shot too."

"I'm working on that story. Stupid story but we have this exclusive security tape . . . ," I said.

"You know Solange was seeing him."

"Socially or professionally?"

"Professionally, I think," Dillon said. "What I'm wondering is, what if there's a connection between all these shootings? What if someone is shooting at people because they work in the JBS building?"

"What? As a vendetta against Jackson or something?"

"Yes. Perhaps a disgruntled ex-employee. Can't get into the broadcast facilities to shoot up the place, so he shoots a commercial tenant and takes potshots at ANN people on the streets."

"Hmm. You think this doctor wasn't killed because he was a priapic, lying, woman-hating heterosexual, but because of . . . geography?"

"I don't know. But it's a possibility, enough of one to make me nervous," he said.

"It's a stretch, Dillon. First of all, we don't know that a sniper exists. Second, the killer had to go to a lot of trouble to hide out in the building in order to kill a complete stranger."

Dillon wasn't listening. "Oh my God," he said.

"What?"

"There she is," he said.

I turned and followed his startled but adoring glance to Bianca de Woody, who had just come into Keggers with Deputy Hector.

"What's she doing with Hector?" he asked. "I thought she was dating that overpumped overtanned homunculus Pete Huculak."

"Well, they got an anonymous call that one of Bianca's fans has just been released from a mental health facility and may be headed this way in his grandmother's automobile," I said. "So Hector has been escorting his bossman's moll around when Pete's not available for the job. Kerwin's going to be pissed."

"And Reb. They both want bodyguards. Of course, Bianca's body is a body much worthier of guarding," Dillon said. "Dear heart, she's coming over."

This made him much more nervous than the idea of a sniper. He was even blushing a little, which is a state I'd never seen Dillon, a jaded, cynical old roué, in before.

"Hi Robin, Dillon," Bianca said.

"Hi Robin," Hector said. Whenever he saw me, he swallowed hard and his protruding Adam's apple went up and down his neck like an Otis elevator. I guess I had the same effect on him Bianca had on Dillon. I smiled politely.

"Bianca, you're looking just lovely tonight," Dillon gushed.

"Thank you," Bianca said. "That's so sweet."

They didn't stop, but greeted us in passing. Expertly, Bianca moved through the crowd, collecting compliments and dispensing sweet thank-yous without breaking pace.

After they'd gone to join Dave Kona and several other young reporters at a table near the jukebox, I turned to Dillon and said, "You can close your gaping maw now."

"That mouth," he said. "That mouth is worth three ratings points. I'm going to go over and ask her out."

Seeing my skeptical look, he said, "What?! I think I really have a shot with her. She went out with Kerwin so her taste can't be too refined."

"She went out with Kerwin? God, her taste is so much *worse* than mine."

"That's what I love, a beautiful woman with bad taste in men."

"Keep a safe distance, Dillon," I advised. "She's spoken for."

"Nothing ventured, nothing gained," he said, and left to pursue his quarry. Here was a man in his late fifties, and he still thrilled to the chase. I had a feeling Dillon was going to die at a ripe old age in the middle of a sexual indiscretion, just like that president of France. Just like Kanengiser. Maybe.

I wasn't alone at the table long. Louis came by and told me the rumors about Bianca replacing Madri, and that Turk Hammermill, an unbearable sports bore, was being extended in Beijing for the Amity games. Then Claire arrived. After shooting the shit a while, Louis motored away to spread the latest gossip.

"Kiss kiss," she said to me.

"Kiss kiss yourself."

As usual, Claire looked gorgeous, as one would expect from a woman who had worked her way through university as a model, but a year-plus of reporting had given her a more mature air, not to mention a shorter, anchorwomanish haircut.

"Sorry I'm late. I got back yesterday and it's been nuts since then," she said.

I raised my hand for the waitress, but put it down again when Claire said, "Nothing for me. I can't stay too long. The meeting ran late and I have to meet Tassy at Tabac for a drink. By the way, I was at Kafka's last night."

"Really?"

"Yeah. They said they were sorry I didn't make it last week. I wasn't sure what they were talking about as I was in Washington last week."

"Uh-oh."

I sometimes used Claire's name to get tables at good restaurants, because she is famous in New York and I'm not. I'd ask for a table for three, and ask to be seated while waiting for Claire. After ten minutes or so, I'd go to make a phone call, come back, and say Claire was called away on a news emergency and wouldn't be joining us. That's the upside of having famous friends. A lot of my friends and onetime friends have become rich and famous, like Joanne Armoire, my ex-husband Burke, and Claire, just to name a few. Me, I'm not afflicted with success. I'm just a carrier.

"Sorry. I only do that in emergencies," I said. "So what happened in the executive meetings?"

"They actually had some insightful comments about my reporting. That was mostly flattering. But this image consultant they brought in suggested I might want to change my last name to make it easier to pronounce and 'cleaner looking.' When I told him I wouldn't do that, he then suggested I merely change the spelling, spell it phonetically, T-i-b-a-d-o."

"And after you finished laughing your ass off, what did you say to him?"

"I just said no. I know other people have changed their names for television, but it isn't me to do that. Besides, instead of dumbing down my name, why don't we smarten up the viewers?"

"Yeah, why don't we? So, is it pretty certain now, the Washington job?"

"They'll announce it any day," she said, breathlessly. "I am dying waiting for the announcement. But the contracts are signed and I am starting to get excited about the move . . ."

Because I'm a good friend, I let Claire go on and on about how great her life was and how well she'd done in Washington. Her boyfriend lived there and she was so confident about the job that she and her beau Jess had gone apartment hunting.

I smiled as she described the fantastic apartment she'd found in Adams-Morgan, in a renovated townhouse that had been there since the McKinley presidency. I smiled bigger as she talked about the attached deck and two working fireplaces. This was a practiced smile by now, the smiling in the face of your friend's good fortune smile. I'd already used it plenty with Joanne Armoire, when she talked about the apartment she had her eye on, on Île Saint Louis in the heart of Paris.

In the last year and a half, Claire had hoisted herself from producer for Special Reports to general-assignment reporter to UN correspondent. Now, she was poised for a junior job in Washington, and from there—who knew? Claire made no bones about her desire to be a foreign correspondent and travel the world. I was happy for her, really I was. She was a good reporter and she worked hard and it couldn't happen to a better woman blah blah blah.

What made it hard for me was that once I was up for a similar job in Washington. Yup, I'd had my shot and I'd blown it by rising to ask the vice president a question and letting rip with a loud belch, an event that began a series of disasters in my life. If I could go back to that day and do things differently . . . For one thing, I wouldn't have had Mexican for lunch. And instead of sitting down in mortification, I would make a joke about it, try to eke some triumph out of the humiliation.

"So," she said, after sharing her happiness with me for fifteen minutes. "How are you?"

"I told you about the murder on twenty-seven?"

"Yeah."

Now it was my turn, and I let loose, how put-upon I was by Jerry Spurdle, how hard it was looking on the bright side when you're watching a middle-aged woman paddle a grown man who thinks he's a dog, how my Aunt Maureen was in town and how McGravy had warned me about blessings in disguise. But have you ever noticed how hard it is to get people to listen to your problems? Claire was hardly listening; she preferred to smile at herself in the mirror behind our table.

(I used to think it was pure vanity that made her do this, but it was something more profound. Her mother once told me that when Claire was three, she came in from the playground crying. Some white kids had called her ugly because of her dark skin. Mom Thibodeaux put Claire in front of a mirror and said, 'Look at yourself. You're beautiful.' She taught Claire to do this, praising her bone structure, her skin color, her eyes, her soul, and her mind. It was this kind of reinforcement that made Claire trust her own judgment of herself, not the judgment of others.)

"You know, I saw that guy once, Kanengiser, but I got a creepy vibe off him and didn't go back," Claire said.

"You saw him too? Hey, do me a favor."

"Yes."

"When you get home tonight, check your last benefits summary and see how many times you were billed for seeing him. Then call me."

She shrugged. "Okay," she said. "Sure. Hey, I'm sorry things are so tough for you now, Robin. But maybe things will change soon. I hear Jerry's in the running for the Berlin bureau chief job."

"Who told you that?"

"He did. That could get him off your back."

"He won't get it," I said. "But thanks for trying to cheer me up."

An internationalist wind was sweeping headquarters. Joanne Armoire had spent more and more time overseas before being offered a permanent job in Paris. Christine Muke had gone to Tel Aviv. Eric had gone to Moscow to field-produce. Turk Hammermill was in Beijing. Now, Jerry was jumping on the global bandwagon.

Although the company had let him fill in in Berlin for six weeks, his dream of getting that job full-time was rather quixotic, I thought, since there wasn't much chance ANN was going to let one of its biggest moneymakers go to a prestige post in Europe. But Jerry believed he was the right man for the job, and toward this end he had enrolled in Berlitz German, which he practiced on us all the time. He sounded like a man in desperate need of a Heimlich maneuver.

Some afternoons it got really bad. Tamayo, having a nic fit, would be in her office cussing in Japanese, Jerry would be in his office loudly practicing German, and there I'd be, trapped between the Axis powers.

It was not conducive to a Positive Mental Attitude.

Even less conducive was the sudden appearance of Reb Ryan in Keggers, at the bar, right by the door, wedged between Franco and Kerwin Shutz, who hit the bar every night as soon as his show was over. This meant I'd have to go past Reb when I left. There was another exit—an employee exit that required going through the kitchen—but I'd used it one too many times and the Keggers management had asked me to please refrain in the future.

I thought Reb was looking at me, but I couldn't be sure as he was wearing dark glasses. After one beer, he started compulsively taking them off and putting them back on at five-minute intervals.

"Why does he do that?" Claire said.

"I don't know. He also hums a lot. It's really annoying. I think the man is on the verge of a nervous breakdown."

"He wants to go back overseas and ANN won't send him," Claire said. "But they don't know what to do with him, at least that's what I've heard. Well, I should go so I can stop at home and shower before dinner."

I had to go too. I had to pick Louise Bryant up at the office of her agent, Dinah. But first I had to settle the bill, so Claire kissed my cheek and left without me.

I didn't want to walk by Reb alone, but fortunately a rejected Dillon was also leaving so we walked out together. As we passed Reb, I pretended I was totally engrossed in what Dillon was saying and even put my arm through his in an extra-friendly fashion.

That's when the fight broke out.

10

Eyewitnesses differed about what happened next. Franco, who was sitting next to Reb, was sure that Dillon had looked at Reb and then elbowed the beer mug out of his hand, sending it crashing to the floor. Kerwin Shutz thought that Reb had pushed his beer mug into Dillon's elbow.

I didn't see it. All I saw was the beer flying, and then Reb went ballistic.

"That's it," he shouted, jumping down from his bar stool and taking a swing at the significantly taller Dillon, who jerked his head away to dodge the blow. Reb's fist glanced off my forehead and sent me spinning to the ground. Using a chair as a crutch, I wobbled to my feet. Kerwin grabbed Reb by the arms and tried to restrain him.

"You hit a lady," he said. "Control yourself."

For his peacemaking efforts, Kerwin got an elbow in the kidneys. Reb wriggled free and turned away from Dillon to face Kerwin.

A crowd had gathered. People were shouting different things all at once. Mickey the barman was shouting, "Take it outside, for God's sake." Franco was shouting "Stop," but the loudest voices were shouting "Fight!"

Dillon moved away from the fighting and said to me, "Let's get out of here."

When we tried to leave, the crowd hemmed us in. The machismo meter was running high in this room and so were emotions. There was a powerful man smell in the room now, sweat and beer and a residual cigar-smoke smell that remained long after Keggers banned cigars from the place two years earlier. It was a heady smell, and I found myself falling under its spell. I was transfixed.

Reb and Kerwin circled. Kerwin jumped around awkwardly, like Ratso Rizzo, took a weak jab, missed, and quickly retreated. They circled some more.

Behind me, I heard Louis Levin and some of the writers giving play-by-play: "Battle of the Emmy winners, television titans, for the Bullshit Belt." "If Jack Jackson gets wind of this he'll wanna put it on the air." "That would solve our ratings problem for the nine p.m. time slot." Some people were betting: "Twenty bucks says Reb whips his ass."

Reb faked with his left and slugged Kerwin in the jaw with his right and Kerwin, dazed from the blow, swung wildly and smacked a sports cameraman right in the kisser. Kerwin and the cameraman exchanged blows and Reb, shut out, looked around for someone else to provoke, settling on Franco, who was trying to break up the fight.

"Don't fuck with me, security guard," Reb said, scornful, raising his fists. Franco was a big, hulking man, younger, stronger, and taller than the short, compact Ryan. Franco looked like he could squish the Napoleonic Reb Ryan between his thumb and forefinger.

Reb was trying to provoke Franco, Kerwin and the cameraman were jabbing wildly at each other, there was a lot of shoving around us. Everyone was angry, insecure, and frustrated, and half the people in the bar were probably having nic fits as well. I could easily see this turning into a full-fledged, bottle-breaking bar brawl as all these tense people gave vent to their emotions.

But at that point, Barney Fife arrived to save the day. Waving his gun above his head, Hector made his way to the fight scene to back up Franco, who was rather stoically taking Reb's insults.

"I'm not afraid to use this," Hector shouted, and the fighting ceased and the room again fell silent. Franco took his own gun out.

"You're behaving like a bunch of children," Hector said. "Now go back to your corners. And play nice from now on. Reb, Kerwin, I think Pete would like to have a few words with you guys."

"I have to tape a morning promo in a half hour," Reb said.

"That gives us plenty of time," Hector said. It was amazing the authority Hector had with a gun in his hand, and how he was able to delegate it. "Franco, take these guys to see Pete."

Hector, after all, had to make sure Bianca got home safely.

The crowd was starting to break up, disappointed that the fight hadn't drawn any blood or caused any injuries. Except mine. There was a small lump on my forehead, and the skin had been slightly broken, but it wasn't serious. After sterilizing the wound with vodka, the bartender gave me a Band-Aid and then Dillon and I left and got into separate cabs.

What was I thinking when I went out with Reb? Reb Ryan was a perfect example of my problem, which is that I tend to exaggerate wildly the fine human qualities of men I admire professionally. I confuse the man with his work. Reb was a dashing figure. During the Vietnam War he'd been in U.S. Army Intelligence, had been captured by the Cong and escaped from a POW camp, winning a slew of medals in the process. When he was discharged, he had put his investigative abilities to work as a war correspondent, and he'd won a ton of awards for his reporting. He had been one of my heroes.

But, once again, it was the control-freak thing. *He* picked the restaurant, Madras Jewel. When the waiter came over, *he* insisted on ordering for both of us—in fluent Tamil, which was so pretentious I wanted to barf. Despite my repeated pleas, he wouldn't tell me what he had ordered, which turned out to be squid curry, using whole squid.

I'm not a big squid fan. I don't mind the little chewy rings, but I'm always afraid the tentacles are going to sucker on to my lower intestine. I'm not a hot curry fan either. In fact, I do believe squid curry is the food they make you eat in Hell while a pompous ass like Reb Ryan sits across from you for eternity, taking his dark glasses off and then putting them on again every five minutes, telling you about all the beautiful women he's slept with and all the world leaders who tried to kill him.

I did not kiss him.

While the he-men of ANN were squabbling at Keggers, Louise Bryant had been squabbling with a Teamster. According to her agent, Dinah, Louise had been the aggressor.

"Without provocation," Dinah said. "He was just walking by and she stuck out her paw and dug her claws into his leg."

Dinah kept me in her office for an hour while she berated *me* because *Louise* was badly behaved. She suggested several courses of action to change Louise's behavior.

"Can we drug her? Can we declaw her?" Dinah asked.

"No and no," I said. Louise's bad temper and claws had saved my life once, indirectly, which is why the bloody cat food company had wanted her for their hero-cats campaign. Louise was very popular. She'd been in *People* magazine and on a bunch of television shows and she had hordes of fans, so it wasn't like they could fire her. On that set, Louise was an eight-hundred-pound gorilla.

"Positive Mental Attitude," I chastised Louise when we got back to East Tenth Street.

I had been thinking of retiring her, but because things were kind of insecure at work, I now felt it was best that she keep her career alive in case mine took another sharp turn south. How sleazy would that be, living off a dumb animal?

"Just hang on a couple of weeks," I said to her. "Until I find out where I stand in the reshuffle."

I opened the steel door to my building and there, standing next to the mailboxes, was my downstairs neighbor, Mrs. Ramirez, in a housecoat evidently made from the pelts of teddy bears. In the yellow bug light of the hall her normally blue hair glowed green. At her feet, her irritating, pop-eyed chihuahua Señor bared his ratlike teeth and growled his little sissy growl.

As I got my mail, I turned my back and tried ignoring her, whistling a bit, hoping she'd spare me a tongue- and/or cane-lashing. An absurdly futile effort. I heard the thump thump clunk of her cane behind me.

I always start out trying to be nice to her. So I turned and said, "Mrs. Ramirez. How lovely your hair looks tonight. Had your topknot tended today, did you?"

"Did the criminal and the transvestite whore find you?" Mrs. Ramirez shouted. Her hearing-aid batteries were a little low. She always shouted when her batteries were low. She usually keeps her hearing aid turned up high so she can hear what's going on in my apartment.

"What criminal? What transvestite?" I asked sweetly. Mrs. Ramirez mistakenly thinks I am running a transvestite call-girl ring in my spare time, and thinks every young woman, or man-woman, who comes into the building is a call girl coming to visit me.

"They came by tonight to see you. One right after another."

"To see Sally," I corrected. Sally, the witch, did psychic readings out of her apartment and did a brisk business with the demimonde. Young dog-collared rockers and their stripper girlfriends made up a big part of her client base.

"That woman put a curse on me," Mrs. Ramirez said, accusingly, as though I had something to do with it. Suddenly, she raised her cane.

Instinctively, I put a hand to my forehead to protect the bandaged lump where Reb had beaned me.

"Hit me," I warned her. "And *I'll* put a curse on you."

Just then, the mysterious, and insanely handsome, guitar-playing man who lived upstairs came around the hallway corner. We had eye contact for one suspended-outside-time moment and then he was out the door and the spell was broken. The guitar-playing man had moved in two weeks earlier, after Mr. Rybynski passed away. As there was no name on the mailbox and the super was in the hospital, I didn't know who he was. I could have asked the mysterious man himself, but we weren't yet on speaking terms. About all I knew was that he played the guitar, was about six feet tall and forty-ish, and was really handsome in an offbeat, kind of scary way, with long brown hair, intense brown eyes, and sharp, angular features.

And I knew I liked him.

It was that fabulous eye contact that made me so sure I liked him. It was intense. I mean, really intense, like a cold wind blowing across the moor. I had to force myself not to look back at him. One time I even caught myself involuntarily mouthing the word "hello" at him, and, simultaneously, he mouthed the word back.

Electrifying. Yet, despite my reputation for speaking without thinking, for some reason I couldn't bring myself to speak to him, maybe because of the flashing red lights and alarm bells that went off in the back of my head. Maybe because I was sure I had seen him somewhere before under unpleasant circumstances and until I figured out when and where, I didn't want to talk to him.

As soon as he was gone, I realized that he had probably heard me arguing with Mrs. Ramirez about whores and curses. What flattering picture of me would he cobble together based on that little exchange, not to mention the bandage on my forehead and my disheveled demeanor?

"I saw them, transvestites and criminals coming by all evening," Mrs. Ramirez continued. "And your aunt saw them too."

"My aunt?"

"Your Aunt Maureen. Such a good lady. Too bad you don't have more of that blood."

"My aunt was here?"

Mrs. Ramirez and Aunt Mo. This is a bad combination, like the meeting of matter and antimatter. As I've mentioned, Mrs. Ramirez erroneously believes that I am the Whore of Babylon, that my apartment is a nest of perverts awash in unsafe bodily fluids, and she insists on *telling* everyone she runs into about my immoral lifestyle.

And Aunt Mo insists on *believing* everything bad she hears about me.

I was being doubly menaced by evil old women. Two more and it was the apocalypse.

By this time, Louise Bryant was growling testily in her carrier, anxious for her dinner. I often accused her of letting success go to her head, but the truth is, Louise Bryant had always been arrogant and aristocratic, half pugilist, half princess, something I admire in an alley-bred cat.

Señor growled back at her and strained at his leash. I had half a mind to let Louise out of her carrier, as I figured she could take this anorexic gopher in a fair fight. She'd whip his ass. But Señor had a cane-wielding, cat-hating old woman on his side, so it wouldn't be a fair fight.

"Excuse us," I said, as politely as possible, and tried to push past her before she blocked my way with her cane. The woman was persistent and it took all my powers of evasion to avoid kicking the shit out of her in self-defense.

Don't get me wrong. I have a pretty firm policy about not beating the crap out of little old ladies. But in our ten years as neighbors, she'd landed a few blows with that hard oak cane of hers, and I'd had the stitches to prove it. One of these days, I was afraid, she was going to rap my head and I was going to snap.

Today might be that day, I thought.

There was only one way out, a trick I learned when I first moved to New York and was pretty innocent. Street creeps would sense my naïveté. Men were always trying to lure me into dubious situations. Pimps were always trying to recruit me.

Then I learned to scream. The moment I sensed a guy posed a threat, the very second I realized it, I'd turn, look at him, and abruptly scream like a demon from Hell, "Aaaaaagh! Aaaaaagh! Aaaaaagh!," scaring the shit out of him. Later, I refined it by looking just past him and screaming. He'd always look behind him, and I'd run away. It was a variation on an old Bob Hope gag.

So I looked beyond Mrs. Ramirez and screamed. Naturally, she turned to see what I was screaming at, and when she did I took off for the stairwell, running a whole flight of stairs with the loudly complaining Louise Bryant thumping in her carrier, before I felt I was out of the old bat's reach.

It took a lot out of me, but boy, that scream felt good.

"There has to be an easier way to live one's life," I said to Louise. I should move to a quieter neighborhood, I thought. I should get into another line of work.

Outside my apartment door I found a basket and a note left by Aunt Mo. The note said, "Hate the Sin, but Love the Sinner," which is Aunt Mo's way of saying she cares about me. The basket contained things manufactured by companies owned by Christian televangelist and takeover king Paul Mangecet. Aunt Mo had signed on with the Paul Mangecet people after she learned of his well-publicized attempt to take over ANN, which I considered yet another betrayal but Aunt Mo saw as a way to save me.

Aunt Mo's already high-pitched religious fervor had gotten a fresh shot of faith when she became an area sales rep for Paul Mangecet, Inc., weight-loss products, a program of high-protein shakes, vitamin supplements, prayer, and an exercise video sold under the name *Lose Weight with Jesus*, or *LWJ*.

Lose Weight with Jesus. This conjured up all sorts of blas-phemous images in my head, of Jesus in a leotard doing leg lifts and pec flexes on video. I dunno. It was my impression that Jesus loved you even if you were obese, and probably wouldn't want his name used to peddle 16.6 million bucks a year's worth of dubious weight-loss products. But Aunt Mo had made a small fortune on *LWJ,* and this had reconfirmed her long-held belief that God was on her side. Who could argue with profit?

While I knew this parcel of weight-loss products was a peace offering of sorts, I found it terribly insulting, more evidence that Aunt Mo was never going to get what I was all about, and that there was no use even trying with her.

Because I was expecting Claire to call, I eagerly played my messages as soon as I had popped my dinner and Louise's leftovers into the microwave. There was a message waiting from, I assumed, Howard Gollis.

"The last time I called, I forgot to ask: Did you enjoy the car-alarm concert the other night?" he said, as Ronald Reagan.

"What an asshole," I said to Louise.

The next message was from Aunt Mo. It wasn't enough that she had stopped by my building, she had to call as well. I couldn't bear to listen, and fast-forwarded through it.

Aunt Mo's message ate up almost my entire answering-machine tape. The next caller, a man, was only able to say, "I know something but I couldn't tell you when I saw you so I—"

And the tape ended and began to rewind.

I didn't recognize the voice. Goddammit, I thought. I could only hope that whoever it was, he'd call back. Unless it was Howard, in which case I didn't want him to call back.

The microwave timer dinged.

I'd programmed my VCR to tape *Backstreet Affair,* which I watched while I ate dinner—a bad idea because I almost choked on my manicotti when the first report came up. This time, the show wasn't led by the Kanengiser story.

Instead, *Backstreet* led with the Congressman Dreyer story.

Specifically, how Dreyer had been caught in an Upper East Side love nest with his personable secretary. They had some pretty compromising shots of the pair, thanks to long-range zoom lenses and sheer curtains. You could even tell that Dreyer wore boxer shorts with little gray elephants on them.

Wow. And all I'd been able to find was great stuff about Dreyer, what an upstanding, Dudley Do-Right kind of guy he was. Well, this made me question my own judgment. Maybe Jerry was right. Maybe I'd become too nice for my profession.

But how could that be? I'd been faking the good attitude, the positive outlook. I mean, I'd been trying, sincerely trying to be sincerely positive, but it just didn't come that naturally for me so I forced it a lot. Was I now doing it without even thinking about it?

While I was watching this, Claire called me.

"I know you're there. Pick up," she said on my machine. I did.

"I have some news for you. Bianca just called me. Guess what?"

"There was an anchorman fight at Keggers."

"Oh yeah, I heard about it. But that isn't what I was going to tell you. Someone took a shot at Dillon Flinder," Claire said.

"No! When? Where?"

"It just happened, like, in the last half hour. After he left Keggers, he went home and when he was walking his dog, someone took a shot at him."

"You're kidding!" I said. "He isn't hurt, is he?"

"No. He's shaken up. The cops are still trying to find the bullet. But he was walking on the East River promenade and the bullet may have ended up in the river."

"Maybe there is a sniper then," I said. "Dillon wouldn't make it up."

"No, he wouldn't. I'm thinking of starting a pool," Claire said. "Who will the sniper take a shot at next? I'm putting my money on Sawyer Lash."

"Put me down for Dave Kona . . . no." I stopped myself. It was bad karma to wish ill on my enemies. "Forget it. I'm supposed to have a good attitude."

"I don't like your good attitude as much as your old bad attitude."

"Thanks for your support. By the way, did you check your insurance . . ."

"Oh yeah. And you're right. I was billed twice," she said. "What does it mean? Fraud?"

"It could . . . for starters," I said.

What did it mean beyond that? That Kanengiser needed extra money? Maybe with two ex-wives, he did. Or maybe he was into drugs, or gambling. Maybe *he* was being blackmailed.

"It could be an accident, a computer glitch in Kanengiser's office," Claire said.

"Yeah. I'll find out tomorrow."

"That's something about the sniper, huh?" Claire said. "Well, at least he's not shooting at women."

After I got off with her, I called Dillon to express my concern about the sniping, left a soothing message on his machine, checked myself for signs of necrotic fascitis, got some ice for the lump on my forehead, and went to bed. For a long time, I lay there, reading the Desiderata on my ceiling, trying to believe its Zen words about how the universe was unfolding as it should and all that crap. After the day I'd had, I had a hard time making myself believe it. What part in the cosmic plan decreed a sniper?

Or, for that matter, this lump on my forehead? But maybe the lump was a kind of cosmic justice. I felt I probably deserved it for mishandling the whole Reb situation. I was sure Reb had, in fact, pushed his beer into Dillon's elbow in order to provoke an incident and have it out with Dillon because Dillon and I were acting so cozy.

I should have confronted Reb, been honest, just told him I wasn't interested in going out with him again rather than making excuses or playing these juvenile avoidance games, like shielding myself with Dillon at Keggers. I mean, wasn't I as bad as Kanengiser, to a lesser degree, unable to be honest and take my chances? But after all the stuff Mike had told me about Reb, I was afraid to talk to him, to say anything that might make him snap.

Kanengiser had been afraid to be honest too, I realized. I couldn't completely condemn him. Okay, I thought his speech to that association was a huge pile of retro crap. But as for his promiscuity, his dishonesty . . . he wanted to screw a lot of women, but the women kept demanding emotional commitment in return and because he didn't want to hurt their feelings, he implied an emotional connection. Maybe he didn't even imply it. Maybe he just didn't go out of his way to dissuade them of the idea. Possibly, he was killed because of his dishonesty. It was also possible that, after years of living his exhausting lifestyle, he'd come clean with someone and been killed for it. People don't like honesty any more than they like dishonesty.

While Kanengiser was an extreme example, I was familiar with that cowardice in my own way. When I was honest with Howard Gollis, he had started harassing me, and I was applying the lesson learned there with Reb, by not rejecting him outright whenever he asked me out, not making any sudden moves, not doing anything to alarm him or hurt his feelings.

I was trying to be nice.

11

The *Star Trek* airlock doors malfunctioned the next morning, trapping me between two of them for a very long five minutes while Hector tried to free me. Finally he did. As I was leaving the airlock zone, he started walking with me.

"Hi, Robin," he said nervously.

"Hi, Hector."

"Between you and me," he said.

"What? What's between you and me?"

"That doctor who was killed?"

"Yeah?"

"He had a lot of late-night visitors and we got a lot of calls about noise coming out of his office at night."

"What kind of noise?"

"You know, um, making, you know . . ."

"Sex noise."

"Yeah," he said nervously, dropping his eyes downward.

This just in. "Well, thanks, Hector," I said, humoring him, since I already knew way sleazier stuff about Kanengiser than that he'd had sex in his office. "Did you happen to see who the doctor was porking up there after hours?"

Now he blushed. I shouldn't play with him this way, I thought.

"No," he stammered. "But I thought you should know. Pete, Franco, and I, we think it was probably one of his lady friends who did him in."

"And you're in law enforcement, so you'd know. Thank you, Hector," I said. Thanks for narrowing it down. That left just about enough suspects to fill Yankee Stadium.

"I wanted to be helpful," he said, in full crimson flush by now.

"And you have been," I said, thinking, this boy needs to get laid. Can't even say the word *sex* to a woman without suffering a full-body embolism. Just like Bianca, talking in code.

What a relief it was to stop by Medical News and talk with someone who didn't have a big stick up the ass, in this case, Dillon Flinder, who, despite the close call of the night before, was strangely serene.

"I'm safe now that I've been shot at," he said. "The sniper hasn't done any repeat business yet. I feel like my name is crossed off his list now."

"Did you see the guy?"

"All I saw was a blur, dear heart," Dillon said. "I see the bump has gone down on your forehead. Sorry about that."

"It's not your fault, Dillon," I said.

"I was just about to go to the cafeteria for a decaf cap. Join me?"

"Can't. I have to call benefits and then meet the crew for another dominatrix interview. In fact," I said, checking my watch, "can I use your phone?"

"Please."

Cyndi in benefits was just starting to look for Kanengiser's billing.

"I'll get back to ya when I get back to ya," she said when I tried to nudge her a little. Jeez. Some people have such a bad attitude.

I had one more stop before I went to meet the crew for the Mistress Lina interview: Democracy Wall. There I paused briefly to see if there was any reshuffle news. None. There was a sniper warning prompted by the shot at Dillon, a schedule of executive meetings, and a few letters from fans and viewers, one of which said, "Dear ANN Commie liberals, You stink! You stink! You stink! You stink!" It went on for twenty-five "You stink"s, and was signed "Sincerely, Proud American." Well, who wouldn't be proud of a letter like that?

At the center of all this was a fake fight poster from the *Wrestling All-Stars* show on a sister network showing two grotesquely muscular wrestlers—with the heads of Reb Ryan and Kerwin Shutz.

THE BRUT CLASSIC MANLY MAN SHOWDOWN, said the poster. KERWIN 'I'M A FIGHTER NOT A LOVER' SHUTZ VS. REB 'THAT WASN'T BEER I WAS DRINKING' RYAN.

It was Louis Levin's work. I never should have told him about the Haiti incident.

Mistress Lina, an outcall dominatrix, did a lot of business in the medical community. I liked her much better than Anya because Lina had a sense of humor. On her business card, she included the quote "No Pain, No Gain," and she said she considered what she did a service to society because, "Do you know how many people out there are in desperate need of a good beating?"

Personally, I'm against beatings, but I thought that was a good answer all the same.

While Mistress Anya had been icy and plainly controlling, Mistress Lina was warmer, more down-to-earth, and more manipulative. For the interview she wore not dominatrix gear, but a generous floral caftan. She sat in her orange and brown kitchen sipping an herbal tea under a hanging spider plant slung so low the green, spidery extremities seemed to be growing out of her frizzy dark hair. Lina had a slave too, a smallish older man with a monkish fringe of brown hair and glasses, named Harvey, padding about—on two legs—in a crisp, pressed red flannel shirt carefully tucked into brown trousers. While Lina didn't feel compelled to make a big show of putting him in a leather bodysuit and parading him around like a contestant at the Westminister Dog Show, it was clear who was the boss here by the way Lina barked orders and Harvey mutely obeyed.

"Get Mama that list of bondage shops," she said to Harvey at one point, waving him with her finger to the fridge, where the list was held by a refrigerator magnet shaped like a chocolate-chip cookie next to a child's drawing of an airplane and a notice about a PTA meeting at I.S. 44.

Then, "Get Mama another cup of tea and a cigarette."

That "Mama" thing was pretty creepy, considering she was at least ten years younger than Harvey.

"This is the dead doctor from the news?" she asked, inhaling the smoke of her Benson & Hedges 100. "No, I've never done him and I don't remember seeing him at the clubs. What's his connection to B&D?"

"A matchbook from Anya's."

Lina flinched a little.

"You know her?"

"I used to work for her," Lina said, shortly.

"And?"

"I have nothing more to say on the subject of Anya," Lina said.

"What was she like to—"

"Nothing more to say," she said. "I'm calling the shots here. Now, let's talk about me. You wanna know how I got into S&M, right?"

According to Lina, she had found her calling pretty much by accident. At one time she'd been a New Jersey homemaker who carpooled and barbecued, did macramé, and sincerely cared about whether Tide did a better job with grass stains than Cheer. After her husband died in a car accident she had started dating again, and it was an old boyfriend who introduced her to the pleasures of pain.

"One night, as we were fooling around, he said, 'Would you be offended if I asked you to hurt me?' At first, I was offended, but then I got to know him better and I wasn't offended at all. In fact, after a while, I started to enjoy it. Before that, I was the masochist in relationships, emotionally. But that changed my whole life, my whole way of looking at things. It empowered me, gave me control."

"Do masochists often become sadists?" I asked.

"Some people are strict masochists, some are strict sadists, but most alternate between the two. I'm a sadist myself with Harvey and my customers, but not with my kids. I spoil 'em rotten, don't I, Harv?"

Harv laughed a little and nodded.

"I don't even spank my kids," she said, dropping a long ash into a brown ceramic ashtray.

"Why?"

"Because they're small and helpless. The guys I do, they're consenting adults. There's a big difference. Harvey, bring Mama another cigarette," she said, then turned back to me. "I'm trying to quit, so I keep the cigarettes in the living room."

Keeping the cigarettes in the living room didn't seem much of a disincentive when one had a flunky willing to ferry a single cigarette every few minutes.

"I turned pro," Lina said, "because some guy offered me money to spank him. It was so easy and, look, you make a helluva lot more this way than selling Avon. I make my own hours, support my whole family."

"Do you have your own control words?" I asked.

"*Goldfish* and *apple*," she said.

"How long have you and Harvey been together?"

"Two years. Two years, right, Harv?" she said, and smiled at him.

He smiled back and nodded. I guess what was most disturbing to me was that they seemed happy—happier, in fact, than most couples I knew. She liked to spank, he liked to be spanked, it worked out. It's nice when people find each other and it works out, I suppose.

We were about to wrap up, but I couldn't go without pressing her again about Anya.

"Please tell me anything about Anya," I said. "It could be important."

She sent Harvey for another cigarette, which she lit off the end of the previous butt, and after inhaling deeply said, "I didn't want to say this on camera. Who needs the lawsuit? But off the record?"

"Okay, off the record," I said. Off the record is like kissing your brother. "Turn off the camera, Mike."

"You can't trust Mistress Anya. I used to work for her, and the woman can't keep a slave. She's had seven or eight since her husband died, called them all Werner . . ."

"She's moved on to Charles now."

"So I've heard, but I never know what to believe about that woman. She's a notorious liar."

"How do you know this?"

"Harvey was Werner number one. He left her for me, and I then left her employ."

Harvey nodded. He opened his mouth to speak, then looked at Lina, who nodded. I was expecting a great revelation, but all he said was, "I was with her for three months."

"Can you describe it?" I asked him.

Again, he looked at Lina, and with her assent he said, "Terrible."

"See, Anya doesn't understand that discipline isn't enough. You also need love. I love Harvey, right, Harv?"

"Yes," the unbearably reticent Harvey said.

"Anya is incapable of love, you see. So her slaves never stay long, and the quality of her slaves keeps declining. One of them turned on her, gave her a black eye. Don't mention my name to her, she hates me."

"Is she vindictive?" It seemed a silly question to ask about a whip-wielding woman.

"You bet. When Harvey and I left, we got threatening calls for months and the following Christmas we got a parcel of roadkill, wrapped up like a present with a bow and everything. This is the sick part. It was addressed to one of my kids. I'm sure she's responsible. We can't go to the same functions within our community. We avoid each other."

"Is she violent?" Another silly question.

"Do you mean, would she kill someone? I don't know."

"What kind of men does she—"

"Listen, I just wanted you to be informed, okay? She's a liar. That's all you need to know."

Then she ended the interview, not abruptly, as Anya had done, but in a friendly, left-handed way.

"It's been a pleasure," she said. "Harv, after you've shown our guests out, run Mama a bath. I'm going to my room."

She left trailing orders. "Use the sea salts, not the oils, and unwrap a new loofah, Harv. The old one is starting to smell. . . ."

Lina had made a persuasive case against Anya's character, but I still suspected the answer to this lay elsewhere, with Cyndi in benefits.

Cyndi beeped me as we were packing up the car after the shoot. I called her on the car phone.

"You were absolutely right," she said. "Dr. Kanengiser was double-billing his clients. I checked with a few other insurance companies. He was ripping them—and us—off for at least fifty grand a year. And that's just what we've found so far."

Bingo, I thought. Confirmation that the overbilling of Claire and Bianca wasn't a mere bookkeeping error.

Well, that explained why Kanengiser billed insurance directly—not because he was such a great damn guy, but so he could double bill. It made it unlikely that his patients would notice discrepancies since they didn't have to file a receipt for reimbursement. I for one barely glanced at the quarterly summary of insurance claims the benefits department sent out, if I glanced at it at all. Usually, I just threw it in a drawer.

Back at the office, I called Vicki Burchill, the night nurse, and learned that Kanengiser had handled all the billing himself. She was sincerely stunned when I told her about the fraud, even more stunned when I asked her if Kanengiser did drugs or gambled, and claimed she had no knowledge of either.

Now that Kanengiser was dead, I knew so much about him, so much seamy and mundane personal stuff. He was an old-fashioned chauvinist Don Juan, a fraud, a connoisseur of fine wines, a superb raquetball player, a member of Mensa, and a sailing enthusiast.

It was weird. I mean, I had been willing to pay this man to stick his arm up me, a man who was a perfect stranger, just because he had a diploma on the wall. I don't know. You want your gynecologist to enjoy his work, I guess, but not too much.

While I was pondering this, the sun shifted in the sky outside the building, and the only sunlight we ever received in this office, the afternoon sun, came in through the high narrow windows and shone down in beamed slats that swirled with dust. I was alone in the office. It was quiet.

Someone came in. I was about to jump up and go out to see if it was Jerry when I heard a woman's voice saying, "It's very spartan."

It was Aunt Maureen.

"This is Special Reports. It isn't much, but we call it home. The highest-rated series come out of here."

It was Jerry.

"Well, I saw one my niece did and it didn't impress me. I never watch anymore."

Stealthily I crawled toward my door, so they wouldn't see

my shadow through the glass, and reached up to lock it. Just as quietly, I crept back and hid under my desk.

"Well, Robin has her own bad taste," Jerry said. "You know, I go to church every Sunday. I've been trying to convince Robin she could use a little religion . . ."

My office door rattled.

"It's locked," Jerry said. "Robin?"

I held my breath. Here I was, thirty-seven years old, an independent divorced woman, a taxpayer, and a professional, crouched under my desk like a four-year-old. I knew I should get up and go out there and face them like a Woman, but the two of them together, Jerry and Aunt Mo . . .

"She must be late, *again.* Would you like to wait?" Jerry asked.

No! I silently shrieked.

"I can't. I have a sales seminar and then a political action committee meeting."

"Oh, you're involved in politics."

"I'm thinking of running for school board next year," she said.

"Good luck to you. It was certainly nice having you visit."

"Well, it's nice to know everyone in the media isn't a counterculture McGovernik," she said. "Tell Robin it is urgent she call me. Absolutely urgent. I want to help her, to save her."

"Well, somebody certainly needs to," Jerry said.

When she was gone, I was left with a problem: How to come out of my office without letting Jerry know. Still under my desk, I reached up and pulled my phone down. I called Louis Levin and, whispering, asked him to call Jerry and get him out of the office for a few minutes.

"Welcome back, Robin," Louis said.

A minute later, the phone rang in Jerry's office and he took off like a shot.

(I asked Louis later that day what he'd said that sent Jerry running. "I told him I thought I saw strippers heading toward the Solange Stevenson studio for a show on implants," he said. "I decided against subtlety.")

When a disappointed Jerry came back, I was at my desk, smiling.

"*Guten Morgen, Fräulein,*" he said. He said something else in German that I didn't understand, something rude and/or filthy no doubt. I'm pretty sure I heard the word *Nacktheit,* which I think means "nakedness."

"Your aunt was here," he said. "You just missed her. She stopped in on her way to a seminar."

"My aunt was here?" I said, innocently.

"Yeah. Security called, said she was here to see you, so I went and got her."

"How did you know she wasn't an insane fan or something?"

"She had ID, and family pictures showing the two of you together."

"How long was she here?"

"Oh, about an hour," Jerry said. "I gave her a tour of the newsroom and chatted with her. A very nice lady. Told me a lot of stories about you. She seemed very concerned about what you were doing in your off-hours."

"Why? What did she say?"

"Just that she's very, very concerned and wants to talk to you. Oh, and she told me some stories about your childhood. About your fear of curlers. That's a new one on me, Robin."

"She has that wrong," I said, but I didn't elaborate.

"How was Lina?"

"Interesting but irrelevant, I think. Listen, I have a lead on this Kanengiser story."

"Something to do with Anya's?" Jerry said, eagerly.

"Actually no. Kanengiser may have had no connection to S&M at all. It turns out he was double-billing his patients' insurance companies, big-time. At least fifty grand in the last year."

"Insurance scam. *Yawn*," he said. "Mention it in the script, okay, but surely you aren't suggesting he was killed because he was padding his bills. If it had anything to do with it, it was just a symptom of what was wrong."

"He may have had gambling debts, a coke dealer to pay off . . . and I've even heard a theory that he was killed because he worked in the JBS building. It's possible it isn't S&M."

"Two words: Handcuffs, matchbook."

"But Kanengiser didn't smoke, which means probably the killer dropped those matches. So, yeah, it's possible the killer may have been involved in S&M, or has some remote connection to Anya's, but I don't think the murder has anything to do with it. The insurance fraud suggests Kanengiser had financial problems . . ."

"I think it ties it even more strongly to S&M," Jerry said. "Maybe he was feeling guilty because of all the women and/ or because of the insurance rip-off. Maybe he went to Anya's to get his punishment, to atone, to ease his conscience because women insist on making men feel badly for doing what comes naturally to them. It makes perfect sense to me."

Before I could think of a polite, nonconfrontational way to dispute this, he said, "You're not approaching this from the right point of view. I just have a feeling S&M is why he was killed. You women, you put faith in those things, right? Feelings, what do you call it, intuition?"

I call it enhanced right-left brain cooperative information processing, but I held my tongue.

"Saturday night, you go to Anya's and you get some juicy stuff. I'm sending Tamayo in too, undercover. Sunday you write, fax me the script at home, and then track and edit."

"She's going in undercover? Mistress Anya *invited* us to the club and you're going to . . ."

I stopped myself, upon hearing a tone of sarcasm creep into my voice. Bend with the wind, I reminded myself.

"Sure," I said. "But what if we don't have a stronger connection to Anya's? What if the murder isn't solved by Monday? Chances are it won't be."

I said all this as politely as possible, but Jerry wouldn't brook anything even resembling argument these days. I wasn't sure how much longer I could keep it up, trying to get along with him. But if I left there was nowhere to go but to infomercials. There I'd be, hawking Hair-in-a-Hurry or Rug-O-Rama Carpet Cleaning System for a living.

"Robin, that's your job! Get it? If you put as much energy into making this S&M link as you have trying to refute it, we wouldn't have to have this conversation. Your job isn't to find the killer. Your assignment is to find what connects him to Anya's. You understand? Then we go a little more in-depth, and take a look at others in that world. You'll do it as an unsolved murder. We don't need to claim a strong connection to Anya's, just a connection. Kanengiser, handcuffed, matchbook from sex club at scene, did it have something to do with S&M? Let's look at this shadowy world. It's a no-brainer, Robin. Earn your keep."

Once upon a time, Jerry had this twisted pseudo-crush on me. He was much nicer to me back then, relatively speaking. But he got over that sick infatuation and since then he'd been pretty merciless.

"But Jerry . . ."

"Do you understand the assignment now? Do I need to speak slower?"

Would anyone have blamed me if I'd suddenly jumped on his desk at that point, grabbed him by the lapels, and slapped him silly cartoon-style? But instead, I looked down at my feet and said, "Yes, I understand."

"This is Special Reports, not the crime and justice beat," Jerry went on. "We can look at any angle of a story. That's the beauty of it."

Defeated but seething, I nodded at him, lest he show me that drawer full of résumés again. The fact was, Jerry was golden, I was not, and he had the power to end my on-air career with a phone call.

In my office, I took inspiration from the saying taped to my pencil cup, A WISE (WO)MAN KNOWS IT IS BETTER TO LEAD BY FOLLOWING. No, that's not Confucius. This one came courtesy of a fortune cookie from the English No Problem restaurant. (Its real name is Kung Pao Kitchen, but the recent immigrants who own it have a big sign in the window that says, ENGLISH NO PROBLOM, so that's what everyone calls it.)

This adage had replaced a statement made by New York Rangers' captain Mark Messier after Messier and the Rangers won the Stanley Cup and removed a fifty-four-year curse from the city's head: YOU CAN'T BE AFRAID TO SLAY THE DRAGON. Fooling with dragons just gets you burned, I'd decided one day, and removed the Messier quote in favor of thousands of years of fortune-cookie wisdom on passive aggression.

12

Detective Mack Ferber finally called me back that afternoon.

"I'm not supposed to discuss this case with you, since you're doing a story on it," he said, but he said it most reluctantly.

"You're working with Detective Bigger on this case," I said.

"He volunteered for it."

"Do not believe anything he says about me," I said. "He hates me. It has to do with some poison ivy . . ."

"Don't worry," Ferber said. "I'm not interested in what he has to say about you. But he's declared a media blackout on the story to protect the privacy of the patients."

"Do you know Kanengiser was defrauding insurance companies through double billing?"

"Yes."

"You do know? Well, do you know if he had big drug or gambling debts . . . ?"

"I'm not supposed to discuss it but . . . okay, I'll give you five minutes to ask all your questions. Detective Bigger will be back in about five—"

"So he did have drug or gambling debts?"

"Neither."

"Well, where did the money go?"

"The insurance fraud doesn't seem to be related to the murder," Ferber said.

"You're sure?"

"Pretty sure."

"Do you have a suspect?"

"No, not yet."

"Leads?"

"Can't speak about that."

"You know, we've had this series of snipings at ANN people," I said. I told him Dillon's theory about the disgruntled ex-employee, and how Dillon, Reb, and Kerwin all said they'd been shot at. It was a long shot, I knew—why would a disgruntled ex-employee go to all that trouble to hide in the building to kill a stranger who had nothing to do with JBS? All the same, I was hoping with all my heart there would be a link, since that at least would spin the story away from S&M, now that the blackmail and insurance-fraud angles had fizzled out.

"Thanks," Ferber said.

"Any time."

As we talked, I frantically read over my notes, not wanting to leave out any important questions before the elusive Ferber got off the phone. Two words jumped out at me: *black book.*

"One of the doctor's ex-wives mentioned a little black book," I said. "She burned the one she found, but in all probability he replaced it. Have you recovered it?"

"I have to go," Ferber said, without answering my question.

"Is that a yes or a no."

"It means 'I have to go,'" he said, but he said it with an audible smile. "Listen, when you're finished this story, give me a call. We can talk homicides and stuff. I might have another story for you."

"A murder story?"

"Well, no. I coach a kids' softball team in the Police Athletic League. Are you familiar with PAL?"

"Sure." PAL is an organization run by cops for underprivileged kids.

"Nobody's done a story about PAL in a while. Do you ever do stories like that?"

"No, but I'm hoping to do some stories like that," I said, disappointed because I had mistaken grubbing for publicity, for a good cause of course, with flirting.

But I could use this. Two can play the you-scratch-my-back game. "I'll really think about it," I said. "In the meantime, if you learn anything about a suspect . . . you could call me. Any time."

"I'll do what I can," he said. I heard Detective Richard Bigger's voice in the background and Ferber hung up on me.

Franco was in my doorway with another box of tapes, these from the freight elevator, four six-hour tapes, starting from six a.m. the day Kanengiser was killed, ending at six a.m. the next day. He was about to say something when he heard Tamayo's voice in the outer foyer, and he beat a retreat to avoid her and her jarhead jokes.

These were far less useful than the tapes from the public elevator, where the floor was announced by a mechanical voice. In the freight elevators there was no way of knowing on which floor people got off. I could only guess. Maintenance and security people went up and down all day, but nothing jumped out at me, and nobody got on the freight elevator between seven forty-five p.m. and ten-twenty, when the poor janitor who found the body got on. He was followed by security and, a bit later, by the police.

It didn't tell me much, if anything. However, it was interesting to listen to people's conversations. These days, people are so inured to video cameras they don't even see them half the time. They talk freely, as though in private. Even Pete Huculak, who should have been more video-conscious, made

an indiscreet remark on tape two, saying to a security guard
I didn't know, "These reporters are soft, they're chickenshits."
The unidentified security guard got off and Pete rode up
alone.

An hour or so into the third tape, I heard Phil the janitor
tell Hymie, the blind guy from the lobby newsstand, some
gossip about Pete and Bianca.

"I was just about to empty the trash," he said. "And I hear
them screaming at each other, and then it gets quiet, and I
hear what sounds like those whale songs, you know? And then
I hear what sounds like a soprano caught in a bear trap and
I realize, they're having sex."

No wonder it took security so long to give me these tapes,
I thought.

"That Special Reports bloke, Jerry Spurdle? I'm pretty sure
I heard him having sex in his office too," Phil said.

Eeuw. Who did Jerry have sex with? I wondered. Maybe
that exotic dancer he was chasing for so long, the eighteen-
year-old with the "Kiss me, I'm Chesty" tattoo.

Phil got off first. As soon as Phil got off, Hymie said,
"Hello?" to make sure he was alone, farted loudly, and then
sighed with relief. Hymie got off a floor or two later and the
freight elevator was empty until it picked up a cleaning lady
a few floors up. From the way the cleaning lady wrinkled her
nose and said, "Holy Moses!" I guessed that Hymie's fart was
still in the elevator.

Why was Hymie using the freight elevator?

"Freight elevator? When did I ride up in the freight elevator?" Hymie said when I called him. "Oh yeah, when I took
my tax forms up to twenty-eight."

"Why were you using the freight elevator?"

"Well, I work for JBS, so I stopped in Accounting to get a
copy of my W-4. It's a pain in the rear to get to the commercial floors from JBS accounting . . ."

"You'd have to go down to the lobby and then up again
on a different elevator."

"Yeah, and this janitor . . ."

"Phil?"

"I didn't get his name," he said. "He let me ride up on the freight elevator with him."

Well, that made sense.

So—how could someone get in without being seen? That nailed it, I figured. It had to be someone already in the building, someone who had come during the day, when the place was busy, hid out somewhere on twenty-seven, killed the doctor, then hid out until the next morning, when he or she could leave pretty freely. And that could be anybody. It sure didn't seem random.

Someone from one of the insurance companies had tipped off All News Radio, and when I got home 1010 WINS was reporting Kanengiser's fraud.

WINS had gone one better, by managing to get hold of Kanengiser's computerized credit card records. What they found completely ruled out my gambling and drug debt theories. Apparently, most of that excess cash went to buying flowers, jewelry, perfume, and lingerie. His florist bills alone were out of this world. Seems he did a lot of "apology" shopping. One florist said most of his cards began with the words, "I'm sorry."

"So he ripped off the insurance company to finance his addiction to love, or sex, or both," I said to Louise, who was sitting on the windowsill above the toilet watching me put on fresh lipstick. "I bet he was sorry. I think he wasn't murdered so much as put out of his misery."

Jesus. The women increasing exponentially, the insurance company bound to get suspicious . . . Hunted by secrets and demons, maybe Kanengiser *had* been seeking punishment and atonement. Maybe he really was sorry.

In other words, maybe the murder really did have to do with S&M, with atonement. All the same, I had a hard time accepting it. I could accept the possibility that the doctor had seen a dominatrix once in a while for a therapeutic whipping. But I just couldn't stomach the idea that Jerry Spurdle had been right all along.

DON'T SWEAT THE SMALL STUFF, said a pink Post-it stuck to the sink. It caught my eye as I was reapplying my mascara.

I had a date that night. No big deal. I approached my post-Eric dating with a sense more of social obligation than of romantic adventure—like a school assignment, or a ticket I had to get punched x number of times before I would either meet a guy I really liked a lot or give up the game.

Lately, I'd been leaning toward giving up completely because I didn't have a good record in these things and I simply couldn't trust myself. I can't tell you how many times I've been absolutely convinced I was in love only to get my heart stomped with cleats.

And I can't tell you how many times I think back on guys I was absolutely moony for and cringe. Like Chuck Turner, a traditional lord and master back-home boy I thought I was going to marry. Until one night I looked up over his shoulder as we were having silent sex on the couch in his parents' rec room and I saw the novelty backward bar clock on the wall, and my future flashed before my eyes. I saw myself washing his boxers and serving food to him and his friends and spreading my legs for him on demand and keeping my big mouth shut, since every time I opened it Chuck accused me of trying to show him up. I realized that if I married Chuck I could never have an original thought and I would have to have bad sex for the rest of my days, and something roared to life in me and got me the hell out of there and on a plane for New York.

Clearly, we were incompatible, but I was going through a powerful conformity phase and didn't want to admit we were incompatible. Can't blame him because I didn't try very hard to show him who I really was, since I knew he would just reject me if he knew, not that he ever seemed that interested. I played my part pretty well for a while there. If I'd had my wits about me at the time, I would have broken up with him as soon as Aunt Mo met him and declared, "He's a wonderful young man." Yes, despite the fact that Aunt Mo liked him, I stayed with him for two years. Why?

He was a pretty boy. Just like men, women sometimes do not think with the right part of their anatomy. Also, he was a football hero at Hummer High School, and it was considered a real honor in town to be his chosen one. People treated me like I was Grace Fucking Kelly because the Turner boy had selected me as his lifelong sperm receptacle. Not that I would have been the only such receptacle—not that I ever was, in fact, as Chuck had a wandering eye—but I would have been the first string.

The point is, at one time I was madly in love with Chuck Turner. He'd walk into a room and I would feel like I had been kissed by God.

Man, did Kanengiser drive that pretty-boy problem home. During our initial consultation, I had sat in his office and fantasized about dating him! Why? He was a pretty boy. At the same time, I had felt very uncomfortable with him. Maybe I subconsciously sensed that, in his way, Kanengiser was just a high-IQ big-city version of Chuck Turner.

There are other horrendous examples, but I won't go into them.

And yet . . . I look back fondly on most of the guys I've known, even my ex-husband Burke. Eric and I had had a lot of fun too, but it had only been for fun as it turned out. We had both been gun-shy, and neither of us was comfortable being serious and having a "relationship." So once he had left for Moscow I was quite surprised to find out how much I missed him.

The memory of good times was all the hope I needed. So I was cautiously dating, back up on the horse and all that.

Fennell Corker, ANN film critic and my escort that evening, worked out of LA and was just in town for the meetings, so I figured there wasn't too much risk in one date. I didn't know him that well and he wasn't really my type—too tanned and moussed, with kind of an aging WASP chauvinist thing going. But since my "type" had only led me to heartbreak in the past, I thought it wise to date against type. Fenn wasn't too pretty or too ugly, too old or too young. He'd had an interesting career, from *Photoplay* and *Daily Variety* in the early sixties to the three broadcast networks, after which he landed in syndication for a few years before ANN picked him up. I figured he was good for a few bawdy stories about the Rat Pack, Marilyn, Annette, Frankie, you know. And it was better than being alone on a Friday night.

I'm not saying it isn't great to be a Free Woman on a great adventure, fraught with perils and dark princes, leading to fabulous rewards, as Tamayo puts it. I own my own life, outside of work that is. I do what I want, except at work. I don't have to put up with another person's annoying habits, or feel self-conscious about mine. Except at work. I enjoy my solitude immensely—but sometimes it's lonely. When you're lonely and someone semi-interesting asks you out, you don't worry too much about whether it's going to lead to a second date. Often, you don't want it to lead to a second date. You're just happy to have some decent company for the evening and hope you'll be decent company for them.

Admittedly, I was a bit worried because so many people had warned me about Fennell, but I figured as many others had warned him about me. Anyway, I wanted to form my own judgments instead of listening to office gossip, so I'd decided to go through with the Corker date. What was the worst that might happen? I might learn something?

Yeah, I learned something. I learned it sometimes pays to listen to office gossip. I learned it right after Corker picked me up in a taxi. Seems criticism wasn't just Fennell's livelihood, it was his life, his mission, and no area of the human condition was beyond his appraisal, from our taxi driver's earthy body odor ("Whew! I just got a whiff of fermented sink clog. My man, don't you bathe?") to my shoes ("Robin, do yourself a favor and buy some good shoes. Those just scream Florsheim").

"Maybe we should do this some other time," I said, trying to find a way to abort this date. "Aren't you afraid of the anchorman sniper?"

"Sniper," Fennell scoffed. "Listen, I've had some of Hollywood's biggest heavyweights threaten to break my arms and my legs. I'm not scared. Sniper probably doesn't even know I'm in town. Reb and Kerwin think they're so tough. Couple of pussies."

Ah, Fenn had the same endearing way with words that Jerry had.

"And Dillon is a nut," he said. "The guy once had sex with a watermelon for Chrissake."

True. But at least Dillon wasn't a hypocrite. Besides which, he was my friend. I was starting to get very annoyed, but I talked myself down, figuring Fenn hadn't been out of Betty Ford that long and he was sure to be crabby. I have to cut the guy some slack, I thought, as our taxi pulled up to the Doppelganger Cafe.

Doppelganger is a hepcat downtown bar with thematic staffing, the latest craze among avant eateries, like Lucky Cheng's, where all the waiters are Asian men in drag, and Skinny's, where all the waiters (male and female) are bald. That's in addition to all the restaurants with unofficial staffing themes, those that seem to hire only French chronic depressives, for example.

In the case of the Doppelganger Cafe, all the wait staff are twins. Not just twins, in fact, but good-looking twins. You'd think it would be hard to find so many good-looking sets of twins who wanted to work in the food service industry, but in fact Doppelganger isn't the only restaurant in New York that employs only twins. There's a place with a similar staffing policy on the Upper East Side, near Elaine's.

Me, I'm waiting for the restaurant that employs only Siamese twins.

Despite all of my attempts to be cheerful, dinner was a disaster. We got the Evil Twin as our waitperson, and there was much confusion about who was waiting on us, her or her sister. The food was mediocre, and Fennell complained about everything, then fell off the wagon and had two gin drinks. Between that and his seemingly endless repertoire of off-color jokes featuring talking parrots, it was turning into a very long date.

Maybe it was just like Claire said: I only dated guys I knew I wouldn't fall in love with, men who confirmed my desire to live alone. Not that my intentions were that overt. With the exception of Howard, I'd gone out with all these guys reluctantly, partly to get back up on the horse and partly because they were insistent and I thought it was better to be a nice guy and a good sport than to tell them to fuck off. I knew I was no day at the beach either and so had to make allowance for their personal quirks. It wasn't like there were long lines of stable, happy men waiting to ask me out.

After dinner, we went to a screening of a new comedy about heroin addicts. In the middle of it—mercifully before those hilarious needle scenes—my beeper went off.

Thank God, I was saved by the bell, I thought. The perfect excuse to cut short this date.

"Sorry about this," I whispered to Corker. "I've got to go."

"I'll go with you," he whispered.

"Sssssh," said the people behind us.

"That's okay, you stay," I said.

"I insist," Fennell said.

"Shut up!" said the man behind us.

Out in the lobby, I again tried to get rid of Fennell.

"I have to call this number and . . . why don't you just go back and enjoy the movie."

"Because it's a piece of derivative crap," Fennell said.

"Let me just call this number."

I went to a pay phone in the lobby and dialed while Fennell paced behind me. The place smelled like sour popcorn.

"Detective Mack Ferber."

"Detective Ferber, Robin Hudson. Did you just beep me?"

"Yeah. I'm afraid I am going to have to talk to you. Can you meet me at my office?"

13

"**W**e found the body tonight, in an abandoned building three blocks from your apartment," Ferber said, shoving mug shots in front of me. "The body's not in very good shape so we'll have to go with the pictures."

"You say his name is Joey Pinks?"

"Yeah. He's an ex-con," said Detective Richard Bigger, who was standing over me like a buzzard. "He did some time for trying to kill his mother ten years ago—she's dead now, natural causes—and he has a couple of forgery convictions, a transfer to a mental institution. He left there about a month ago."

I studied the mug shots carefully. It was hard to tell how old he was, thirties, forties maybe. His face was very white, roundish, ordinary. Another shot, taken by the cops, showed a red scar across the fingers of his right hand. That and a "Repent" tattoo were the only distinguishing marks.

"No, I don't think I've ever seen him before," I said.

"We found this on him," Ferber said, holding a baggie up for my examination.

It was my business card, with my home address written on the back.

"It's my address," I said.

"Your handwriting?"

"No."

"We found something else on this guy. An OTB slip for a horse called Robin's Troubles . . ."

"Shit . . ."

"And a joint, a few dollars, and a key for the Hotel Bastable," Bigger said. "Pinks was shot in the heart, same caliber bullet as the one that killed Kanengiser, and he had your card on him. So we think it has something to do with this Kanengiser murder. We won't know for sure until ballistics is finished."

"They're backed up," Ferber said.

"So I guess this guy was coming to see me," I said.

"And someone else got him first."

"Maybe he was coming to tell me something about Kanengiser. This is probably the key to the whole thing, and he's dead and what he knows has died with him."

There were cops all around me, most of them men, in this testosterone-choked office, young, fit guys in snappy blue uniforms and older, pudgier guys in plainclothes, jackets off and sidearms exposed. I found myself crossing my legs and remembering my rule about not dating cops, especially younger cops. Especially younger, pretty-boy cops.

Not that any cops had asked me out . . .

"A strange man called my answering machine," I said. "I don't know who he was, or why he was calling me because the message was cut off. But I wonder . . ."

A uniformed cop came up. "Sirs, ma'am, Ms. Hudson's escort wants to know how much longer she's going to be."

Fennell had *insisted* on coming down to Manhattan South, and he was waiting for me outside on a bench. He was probably out there insulting the cop-shop decor or making rude remarks about body odor.

"I guess we're through," Bigger said, although he said it suspiciously. He was just plain suspicious of me, but it was as if he couldn't figure out why and it was really bugging him. "We'll call you if we have any more questions."

When I got out, Fennell said, "You certainly are the most interesting date I've been out on recently," he said. "C'mon, let's go get a drink."

"Oh thanks, but I've had a really long, bad day," I said. "I just want to go home. Really."

For "safety reasons," Fennell *insisted* on seeing me home. Under normal circumstances I would have refused, but why take too many unnecessary risks? I told him he could drop me off on his way back to his hotel.

However, when we got to my place, Fennell didn't "drop me off." Despite my protests, he got out with me and sent the cab away. I knew then that his intentions were not honorable.

I said, "Well, thanks for a great time. See you on TV."

"Let me come up," he said.

"No thanks, I'm safe now."

"I'm not going to bite you. I thought we could talk. That's all."

"It's late. I don't think so. But thanks for a wonderful time," I said.

"You don't trust me!" he said, suddenly wounded. "I just thought a little company might be nice, that's all."

What? Did I just fall off a turnip truck? I was oh too familiar with this routine, which hadn't worked on me since the last college frat party I attended in 1981. Now I was supposed to soothe this fragile artist by assuring him that I did trust him and he could come up for coffee and conversation, and then we'd get upstairs and a new cycle of coercion would begin.

"I'm tired, so thanks anyway, but I need to call it a night," I said.

At this point, I usually got the "Think you're too good for me? Don't flatter yourself" speech from guys like this, or else a play would be made for sympathy sex by making me feel guilty for not liking him enough and thus hurting his feelings.

But Fenn tried an even more audacious approach.

As I started to turn he grabbed me, spun me around, took me in his arms, and started trying to kiss me. I say *trying* because I did not want to kiss him and I was twisting my head every which way, trying to wriggle out of his grasp, saying, "No, Fennell, stop."

Sometimes, you can be too nice. I knew how to get rid of this guy. What I didn't know was how to get rid of him NICELY.

So he didn't stop and his big fat lickered-up mouth finally suctioned onto mine.

My arms were pinned against my sides but my hands were free. There was a car behind me and I let myself fall backward onto it, which set off the car alarm, scaring the shit out of Fennell. I took the opportunity to run up to my building. Fennell stood there screaming at me. I don't know what he was screaming, because of the car alarm and all, but I could see his mouth wide open and his eyes bulging.

Jeez. Guy buys you dinner and he thinks he's entitled to stick his tongue in your mouth, no matter how much you protest. And I didn't even want him to buy me dinner. I wanted to buy my own to head off such an incident, but Fennell had INSISTED. After arguing for ten minutes, I had let him pay the damn bill. What an asshole.

He got off lucky. In my purse was my beloved high-velocity hot glue gun, with two settings, stream and spray. I could have turned Fennell's face into a giant hot glue ball, if I wasn't such a nice person.

Damn. Why did I have to be so irresistible? One thing I can't stand is a man who won't take no for an answer. I sure had dated a lot of them recently.

As I was going in, the insanely handsome man from upstairs was going out and we had another moment of heart-stopping eye contact. He mouthed the word *hi* to me, almost shyly, and

I felt myself mouthing the word back, before rushing past him.

I just couldn't decide: Run away from him or talk to him? He gave me such a charge that I was knocked a little senseless and walked smack dab into Sally at the mailboxes.

"Whoa! Your aura!" she said, recoiling slightly.

"What's the matter with it?"

"It's really heavy-duty, really dark."

"Sorry."

With her white Pan-Cake makeup, black-lined eyes, bright red lipstick, and black scorpion tattoo up the back of her shaved skull, she gave off a rather dusky aura herself. I sympathized a little with pious Mrs. Ramirez. I could understand how just looking at her made the old bat's bowels seize up. You had to talk to Sally a bit before you understood she was really a very sweet person. Weird, but nice. But I suppose she was quite frightening to an elderly, blue-haired lady who hadn't had a man since 1942.

"You ought to come by for a tarot reading," Sally said.

"I'll take a rain check," I said. "Have you seen Gladys Kravitz lately?"

"Ramirez? She was lurking about earlier, but then she got a visitor and she's been in her parlor ever since."

"Who was the visitor?"

"Some old woman."

"A big scary woman, with big, bouffy silver-blond hair?"

Sally nodded. "Don Rickles in drag."

"Listen, you didn't see me."

"Why . . ."

"I'm avoiding that woman," I said.

"Okay," Sally said. "By the way, I found out something about the guy upstairs, the one who plays the guitar?"

"What?"

"His name is Wim Young. He's an actor or an artist."

"How do you know? Did you talk to him?"

"I've only seen him twice and both times I was in a hurry. I asked Mrs. Fitkis on two. She's talked to him."

Mrs. Fitkis was a feisty unrepentant Communist and the widow of a longshoreman. I'd have to stop downstairs one of these days and have tea with her, talk about the workers' struggle and the insanely handsome man above me. Once I figured out whether I really wanted to know.

"I should warn you," Sally said. "I added up the numbers in Wim Young's address, street numbers plus apartment number. And you know what I came up with? 666."

"Thanks, Sally."

"It's a freebie," she said. "I'll do a spell for you if you like."

"No thanks."

What Sally does, it's just her religion, her attempt to find order in the universe and feel she has some control over it through the exercise of rituals, the uttering of chants, and the adherence to certain rules, the rules of good karma in her case. Just like Aunt Mo and the pope—and, in a way, Lina and Harv—she has a faith to stanch her fears of the great unknown.

I have a glue gun.

I became very aware that Aunt Mo was on the premises. I could *feel* her there. When I got to my apartment, I carefully inserted the key, turned the lock, and pushed the door open as quietly as possible, so as not to alert Mrs. Ramirez downstairs to my presence. I took off my heels so I could pad about stocking-footed, and slowly closed the door.

Louise Bryant wanted to be fed, so I stealthily stir-fried her dinner. The doorbell rang. With measured steps, I walked to the door and peered through the spyglass peephole.

There, corseted to within an inch of circulatory disaster, was my Aunt Maureen.

"Robin, are you in there?" she shouted.

I didn't answer.

"Robin, if you're in there, let me in. I want to help you, Robin. You need help!"

I held my breath. I could hear chained doors opening down the hall to see what the commotion was.

"She's not in there, Dulcinia," Aunt Mo said. Apparently, Mrs. Ramirez was in the hall with her. "That mustn't have been her. Well, you'd better call me that car service."

And she left.

Anxiously, I watched out the window for the car service to come and get her, partly out of concern—it wasn't safe for an elderly woman in my neighborhood after dark and I wanted to make sure she got into the car—but mostly because I wanted to see her leave. The car alarm had stopped.

There was a man standing on the street staring up at my window. I focused my eyes. It wasn't Fennell. It was . . . Howard Gollis, looking very handsome, I had to say, in black jeans and de rigueur black leather jacket. And just as I realized it was him, he saw my face in the window.

"Robin! Robin!" he shouted, doing his best Brando-as-Kowalski. "Let me in."

I turned out the lights, hoping Howard would take the hint.

Aunt Mo's car drove up.

"I'm sorry about the blindfold, okay?" he shouted.

He was referring to the time we almost had sex.

"I thought you'd be into it. I apologize!"

Aunt Maureen stepped out onto the stoop. I was afraid she'd talk to Howard and he'd mention he'd seen me in the window. I didn't want to show my face, so I was pressed against the wall, peeking out with my peripheral vision. I couldn't really see what was going on. But I heard Aunt Mo scream, "Get away from me," and then the car door closed and the car squealed away.

I peeked out. Howard was still there, staring up at my window. This was really ridiculous. I had no doubt that if Howard ever won my heart, he would immediately feel trapped and break same heart. I saw hints of this our first four dates, and enough other stuff to make me realize he and I were not compatible in the long term.

Stuff like his next little soliloquy.

"You *shrew!* You stupid, heartless bitch! Let me in *now!*"

he shouted. "You can run but you can't hide. You know you want me."

I moved away from the window and turned up my stereo really loud—Mrs. Ramirez be damned—in order to drown him out. Then I called Pete Huculak and left a message with Bianca about Joey Pinks, watered my poison ivy, checked myself for signs of necrotic fascitis, took a Valium, and went to bed.

14

When I looked out my window the next day, Saturday morning, the guillotine was back. What the hell did this mean? If Chaos Reigns was dropping it "randomly," how come it was back at this location? It was like lightning striking twice.

"Not a good sign," I said to Louise Bryant.

I called the ANN library and research department, and asked them to do a Lexis-Nexis on Joseph L. Pinks. They were kind of snippy with me, being overworked and underpaid, as most of us are. As a rule, I conduct my own searches, but it was Saturday, I'd had a shitty week, and I didn't feel like going in to work just to plug a name into the computer. The cops were on the job, et cetera et cetera.

Besides, I had a life that morning. I was supposed to meet Claire and Bianca for coffee. They'd both be coming from Jack Jackson's ANN All-Stars brunch, where I figured they would pick up a lot of inside info on the reshuffle.

On the way to meet Claire I bought the papers, which had lost interest in the Kanengiser murder in favor of more salacious news about the British royal family. The Joey Pinks angle wasn't covered at all, but that may have been because the cops ID'd him after the papers went to bed.

What I was most interested in at that point was the racing results from Belmont the previous day. Sure enough, Robin's Troubles had won her race by a length. Wow. Too cosmic. Of course, this racetrack triumph of Robin's Troubles could be interpreted in different ways, karmically speaking.

I place the occasional bet at OTB. I just wander in when I'm in a serendipitous mood and put five bucks on whichever long shot sounds lucky to me. One time, it was a horse named Hudson Queen, another time a horse named Eric's Chance. I had put five bucks to win on both those nags, who both trailed the pack in their respective races.

But then, I never expected them to win. I place bets just because I have a tendency to invest too much faith in omens and coincidences and stuff like that, and I need a quick, cheap reality check every now and then.

The point is, Joey Pinks bought that ticket for a reason. It sounded cosmic to him, because of what he knew or because of what he planned to do to me.

Thanks to Robin's Troubles, I got a lot of mileage out of my good news/bad news story when I met Claire and Bianca at Tofu or Not Tofu on Avenue A. This accomplished several tasks simultaneously, as it allowed me to tell, with humor and bravado, how close I'd come to danger for a story, gave me an anecdote, and let me laugh at the whole frightening thing.

"So the guy has my home address on him. And he's found dead three blocks from my building," I said.

"That's like one of those ghost stories they told at camp," Claire said, stopping to sip at her noncaffeinated herbal tea. "You know, the guy with the hook for a hand who escaped from an institution for the criminally insane and has been stalking young lovers and—"

"And they drive off and the hook's stuck in the car door," Bianca finished. Hector was parked in a car across the street, keeping an eye on Bianca.

"That's pretty much how I felt when I heard about it, like the punch line to a horror story," I said. "But it gets better. He had an OTB betting slip for a horse called Robin's Troubles, and this horse is a long shot. And it wins, pays fifty to one . . ."

"Joey probably thought it was his lucky day. And look what happened to him," Claire said.

"Not much of a bright side for him," I said. "The good news is, your horse finally came in, winning you a small fortune . . ."

"The bad news is, you're too dead to spend it. But you, you are so lucky."

"I dunno. I think this guy had something to tell me."

"Or he was coming to hurt you, Robin! The man tried to kill his mother, right?"

"Yeah, but this connects somehow to Kanengiser. I know it does."

Bianca, who had been sitting quietly during this, flinched visibly when I mentioned Kanengiser.

"Did you call security?" Bianca asked, looking into her cup.

"Yeah. They told me I was very lucky. Pete offered me Hector as a bodyguard when he's through looking after you."

"Maybe you should take him up on the offer," Claire said.

"Bianca, do you feel safe with Barney Fife as your bodyguard?"

"Not really," she said.

"See?" I said to Claire. "I could kick Hector's ass, easy. So what could some big dumb thug do to him? I could protect him better than he could protect me. But enough about Joey Pinks. Hear anything at the All-Stars brunch?"

"Yeah. A bunch of Jack Jackson's stories about how he started out with a small Sunday advertising insert business . . . ," Claire began.

"Anything about me?"

"About your job, you mean? No, sorry."

At that point Bianca's cellular phone rang and she took the call. It was Pete, telling her he was almost through at ANN and she should go back to her place and wait for him there. Her master's voice. She turned to me so Claire couldn't see and then mouthed the words, "Don't tell."

I smiled and nodded ever so slightly, but the result of her continued paranoia was that it incited my curiosity, which didn't need any more inciting these days, thank you very much. By now, I was wondering what deep dark thing she didn't want Pete to know about. With Bianca it could be anything from chlamydia to a past abortion to a yeast infection.

After making her hasty good-byes, she left.

"Man, Pete has her trained," I said.

"She's only twenty-three, twenty-four," Claire said. "She'll outgrow it."

"I hope so. She could end up rebelling like Mistress Lina, emotional doormat one day, dominatrix the next. Anyway," I continued, "I feel like I would have been in more danger if this Pinks guy had actually made contact with me, even if he wasn't after me, know what I mean?"

"Yes, I do," Claire said. "You think someone killed him before he could tell you something and now you're safe because of it. How is that story coming?"

"It's a piece of shit, but I don't care. Do it, get it over with, move on."

"So, the less you know about this murder, the less danger you're in," Claire said.

I didn't like the way that sounded.

"You think I'm trying not to find out what happened?"

"Don't get so defensive. I didn't say that. Whatever. You're very lucky anyway," Claire said.

Yeah, I thought positively, I was lucky the guy was killed. That was a bright side. But then I thought of what the IRA had said in a communiqué to Margaret Thatcher after she escaped unharmed from a bomb blast in her hotel in Brighton.

"You were lucky," the IRA said. "We were unlucky. But remember, we only have to be lucky once. You have to be lucky always."

"It's not just fear or whatever. There are so many leads away from the S&M angle, but Jerry insists on doing that angle. He has a 'hunch' . . ."

"And he has exclusive videotape."

"And several publicity-hungry dominatrices," I said. "But, Claire, what if he's right and I'm wrong? Maybe I'm the one who can't see the truth . . ."

"Without knowing all the particulars, between you and Jerry, I'd bet you're right ninety-nine percent of the time."

"It doesn't matter. Tomorrow I go in and edit a story, most of which will be devoted to spurious S&M demonstrations, and I have no idea who killed Kanengiser or why, and now I have a whole new corpse thrown into the works."

"Aw, sometimes I miss getting down and dirty in Special Reports," Claire said nostalgically.

Claire had changed the subject slightly. These murders loomed rather larger in my eyes than in hers. Hard to get people like Claire, who'd been to Rwanda, and Mike, who'd been to every major war zone in the last five years, worked up over a couple of dead guys in Manhattan.

"Yeah," I said. "It must be a drag, interviewing those pesky ambassadors and national leaders all the time."

"No, really. Special Reports was kind of fun in its way, because we didn't have to take what we did so seriously. We got a lot of laughs out of that sperm-bank story. And when we did the AOA on Satan? A classic."

"Yeah," I said softly. "But you got out. It's easy to look back on it and laugh, now that you don't have to do it anymore."

"You know, a friend of Jess's is looking for a speechwriter. It just occurred to me that—"

"What are you saying?"

"It'd be a great gig, a new city . . ."

"You think I should change careers? Have you heard something? I'm on my way out, aren't I? If you've heard something, Claire, you have to tell me. Why did—"

"God, Robin. Calm down. You mentioned earlier that you were thinking of changing careers and you were just bitching about how awful Special Reports was. . . . I remembered Senator Kiedis was looking for a speechwriter. The point is, there *is* life beyond television news, if that's what you're worried about."

Despite Claire's impassioned insistence that she knew nothing about my fate, I was not reassured. I felt that people were sending me veiled messages to prepare me for the blow, either because they were too polite to give it to me straight, or because they worried about my reaction if the news came at me full force.

"By the way, how was your date with Fennell?" Claire asked.

"Sheer hell. Didn't he tell you?"

"I didn't see him."

"Wasn't he at the ANN All-Stars brunch this morning?"

"No, he didn't show."

"Well, I'll tell you. He's a pig, an asshole, a boozer. He fell off the wagon last night. He criticized everything. He forced a kiss on me . . ."

"God, Robin. Why do you date these guys? There are lots of great guys out there."

Yeah, and Claire had dated all of them already. Claire was a serial monogamist. I think that's the popular term for someone who dates a lot of guys, but always one at a time. Mind you, she'd been with her current boyfriend, Jess, one of the few freshman Democrats in the House of Representatives, for a record seven months, so despite her checkered romantic record she felt qualified to give me advice.

"Why do you bother with people at ANN? You have to start dating outside the family," she said.

"When I started in television, Bob McGravy told me that it was going to turn my life upside-down and I'd never have regular hours. If I wanted a social life, he said, I had two choices: date within the company or date the short-order cook who works the night shift at International House of Pancakes. Besides, I did date outside ANN . . . I dated, and married, Burke Avery."

"Well, that's still within the news business, just a different network."

"And I dated this comic, Howard Gollis, and this guy in Seattle . . ."

"And you dated Eric Slansky, and you dated Reb Ryan . . ."

"You promised not to mention Reb Ryan. And in my defense, I didn't know about the Haiti incident when I dated him. You know, I'm not the only one overly impressed with Reb's awards and honors," I said testily. "Bianca dated him, and so did Susan Brave. Who knows who else succumbed to his overblown reputation."

"Okay, okay. Get a sense of humor," Claire said.

Claire was straining to be sympathetic. It was hard for her, since everything was coming up roses, more or less, in her life.

"Come on," Claire said. "Let's go shopping, look at men, and talk about me for a while."

It was a beautiful day, clear, brisk but not too cold. There were a lot of people out on Avenue A, which is a kind of bohemian-punk-anarchist-criminal main street. St. Mark's Place used to have that honor, but it became a bit too commercial. All manner of humanity drifted past us on the cracked sidewalk, old people, young people, white, hispanic, black, Asian people, people with green hair and pierced eyebrows and lips. Even the street people in mud-colored clothes who sold trinkets and old magazines on the sidewalk seemed benign.

It was good to be out.

"I love New York," Claire said. "I'm going to miss living here. . . . You'd be surprised how many people outside New York hear me say that and look at me like I'm crazy."

"My Aunt Maureen thinks it is the most wicked place on earth."

"What does she think about this neighborhood?"

"I don't know. I'm avoiding her. But I can imagine what she thinks. She'd look around this neighborhood and see only the disorder and the decay, the squats, the homeless."

I know how New York looks to people like Aunt Maureen, but I think it's the greatest city in the world. Not the center of the universe, but a microcosm of it. And I love my neighborhood, the mix of people, the guerrilla art and the weird folk art, the way kids string old sneakers up in trees in the spring. I don't know why they do it, and I never saw them doing it, but come spring and the trees are full of old shoes. On Ninth Street, the squatters adorn their buildings with odd but beautiful things, like upside-down mannequin legs painted in bright colors that form a fence around the roof of one building. I even love the vacant lots full of glinting colored glass and rusted automobile carcasses, and the peeling layers of posters on the walls of abandoned buildings, the homeless guys who sleep in Tompkins Square Park during the day because the city closed the park at night after the squatters' riots of 1988. I don't know why I love it all. It just moves me in ways I can't explain, that's all.

"What's this?" Claire asked, stopping to look at a graffitied wall, covered with symbol slang—little minimalist drawings almost impenetrable to grown-ups. This, and clothes with real bullet holes in them (factory-shot and shipped to the stores in this condition) were the two latest trends among our local youth.

"I love this wall," I said. Every week someone added to the hieroglyphs. I sensed a story was building on the wall and found it very frustrating not to be able to decipher it. I wondered if there was some inner-city Rosetta stone out there that would crack the code. I'd asked a couple of neighborhood kids, who had snickered and told me nothing. It was then I had realized I was part of the "older generation."

Even though I didn't understand what the wall said, it moved me, maybe because the only symbol I recognized was a heart.

"It's so odd," Claire said. "And strangely beautiful."

While we were standing at the wall, both charmed and puzzled, the mysterious and insanely handsome man walked by in the opposite direction. It sounds weird, but I felt him before I saw him out of the corner of my eye. I saw him see me looking at him, and I closed my eyes until he passed.

Even that moment of peripheral eye contact gave me a powerful charge, and when he was gone its absence made me feel suddenly exhausted, sleepy. This was ridiculous. Was this the so-called thunderbolt? Or a dangerous attraction?

Claire had been talking to me about the devolution of language, but I stopped hearing her. This guy had an effect on me. When he was around, all I saw was him, and all the noise around me turned to white noise.

"Wow," said Claire. "Who was that?"

"Huh? Oh. The guy who moved in upstairs."

"Whoa. You had excellent eye contact. Who is he?"

"Wim Young. He's an actor or artist or something like that. That's all I know. I don't know. He keeps to himself. But I keep running into him . . ."

"Haven't you talked to him?"

"No, I . . ."

"Honey, what is wrong with him? There's a guy for you."

"He makes me nervous. . . . He's . . . I don't know. I'm not ready for him. He plays the guitar a lot."

"So what? This could be true love."

There was a voice in my head that said that as well. But that voice had been famously wrong before and, fortunately, there was another voice too. You know, the voice of reason. Impossible, my brain finally said, when my cognitive cells had regrouped. You can't possibly be in love with a man you don't even know, even if you think you recognize him on some level.

Then I suddenly remembered where I had seen this man before, and that I had seen him many times, in fact. Oh, he looks a little different every time—he's very clever—but I'd know him anywhere. To paraphrase John O'Hara in *Butterfield-8,* I'd know him at the bottom of a coal shaft during a total eclipse. He was the sinuous and smoky Hungarian writer with the beautiful Oxford accent who had locked his dark eyes on me as we chugged out of Budapest on the *Orient Express* to Paris, many moons ago. He was the aqua-eyed rich Swiss-Italian guy backpacking around America in 1986, and the blond Teutonic god with the "Correspondent's Squint" whom I married.

He is the Devil.

I am only half-joking about this.

"A musician, Claire? At my age? Jeez. This isn't true love. This is a Margaret Trudeau Midlife Moment. This is me thinking with my genitalia again."

"I keep forgetting how elderly you are."

"Let's be realistic . . ."

"*Bock bock bock bock bock,*" she clucked like a chicken. It was the second "cowardice" reference of the day.

"Give me a break."

"Listen, I have to go to a matinee of a play this friend of mine is in. Why don't you come?" she said.

"Naw, I'm broke and anyway, I have an errand I want to run, but thanks for asking," I said.

Until Claire made that remark about how the less I knew the safer I was, I had planned on going home after seeing her. Maybe she didn't mean it the way I took it, which was as a dig about my courage. Maybe I was just being oversensitive. Whatever. It was enough to make me detour to the Hotel Bastable.

At one time, the Hotel Bastable, which was just eight or nine blocks from my place, had been a respectable lodging house catering to young immigrant men. Later it became a haven for poor, struggling artists and writers, like O. Henry, who lived there for a while before his fortunes took a healthy uptick and he was able to move into much finer lodgings at the Hotel Chelsea. Since then, the Bastable had steadily degenerated into one of the worst single room occupancy hotels in the city. Even Charles Bukowski wouldn't stay in this place now, and he's been dead for a couple of years.

The Bastable charged ten dollars and fifty cents a night or two hundred and fifty dollars a month, according to the stained rate card next to the desk in the "lobby." The smells of urine, disinfectant, and frying meat mingled in the dingy beige foyer where a guest was asleep, akimbo, in a chair. At least, I thought he was asleep. He might have been dead.

"I wanna know about a guy who stayed here, Joey Pinks," I said to the sneering man behind the small bulletproof window at the front desk.

"He's gone," he said, without emotion.

"I know. Can you tell me anything about him? When did he move in—"

"Can't tell you anything," he said. He was rubbing the palm of his hand suggestively. He'd talk for money. Well, I had two problems with this. First, I don't practice checkbook journalism, although because of my curiosity I would have compromised my strong moral convictions on this one. But the second problem made it irrelevant—I only had $3.47 on me, and I had a hunch Mr. Information would be insulted if I offered him three crumpled dollar bills and a handful of linty change.

I went back out on the stoop, stood for a moment, looking down the street, first one way and then the other. There were two men hanging out on the sidewalk, a black man wearing dark glasses and an elfish-looking white man who couldn't stop scratching himself, which he did as though he wasn't aware he was doing it. When he walked over to me, I leaned away slightly so that whatever was making him itch wouldn't jump on me.

"Smoke, smoke," he said, the traditional whispered come-on of the street pot seller.

"No thanks," I said.

"Ecstasy, cocaine."

"No thanks."

"You look lost," he said.

That struck me as a very existential statement.

"You live here?" I asked him.

"Yeah," he said. "You?"

"No."

"I didn't think so."

"Actually, I'm wondering about a guy named Joey Pinks."

"Yeah yeah, I know him," he said, scratching inside his ear with one hand and scratching his neck with the same hand that held his cigarette. The ember just missed his earlobe.

"Skinny guy, got here a couple of days ago. He was killed. Cops were by earlier."

The man did not stop scratching. It was amazing he had any skin left.

"Did you ever talk to him?"

"Are you a cop?"

"No."

"He bought some pot off me when he first got here. We talked a little then. He'd had some hard times, came back to New York looking for a pal, hooked up with some woman. Guess that didn't work out."

"Did he ever have visitors?"

"No. But I heard him on the pay phone in the lobby a couple of times."

"Did you hear what he said on the phone?"

"Something about a diary."

"A diary?"

"That's all I know."

A diary, I wondered, or a little black book?

While we were standing on the street talking, a dark blue sedan that had been parked at the far corner pulled out and drove slowly by. It stopped, hovering in the middle of the street in front of the Bastable. It was a chauffeur-driven car, but I couldn't see if there was a passenger, as the back windows were tinted.

I noticed it because of its suspicious creep. But I didn't take much more notice of it, figuring it to be some rich Yuppie looking for drugs, as this part of the Lower East Side was a pretty big drug marketplace. The scratching man thought so, too, and walked toward the car to make a pitch to the driver, who promptly rolled his window back up and took off like a shot.

"Damn tourists," he said when he came back.

"A lot of tourists come down here?" I said.

"Oh sure. In buses sometimes. Driving all the customers away."

"So about Joey Pinks . . ."

"Whaddya need him for, when you've got me?"

He was starting to flirt with me, winking (and scratching) to punctuate his remarks. Evidently, he went by the five-minute rule, i.e., if a woman spends more than five minutes with me she's attracted to me.

"You wanna go get a slice?" he asked.

Shooting the shit with street guys is a great skill to have, even if it doesn't look so great on a résumé, and I'm pretty good at it. If they flirt, I have two approaches, depending on the vibe I pick up. I humor them, but in a very tough and burlesquy "you couldn't handle me if you had me" sort of way. Or I act like I'm incredibly flattered. Not to be a snob or anything, but how very, very flattering it is to be asked out by a street dealer with no prospects who suffers from some sort of skin disease, probably contagious, that he picked up in his fleabag hotel. What a catch.

"No, but thanks for asking. Gosh, that's nice of you. But I have to run. Thanks for your help."

I started walking away. About halfway down the block, I

heard the scratching man calling after me. He was following me. I sped up, he sped up. Jesus. He wouldn't give up.

Why am I so irresistible?

When he got a little closer he called out, "You know, you have gum on your ass! I thought you'd want to know."

I looked behind me. Indeed, I did have gum on my ass. Not only that, but it had been there for some time, judging by the flotsam and jetsam it had picked up—black lint, a piece of toothpick, an orange Tic Tac.

Oh God, I thought. Did I have gum on my ass when the insanely handsome man walked by?

15

"**D**ress to blend in," Jerry had instructed us about the Anya's shoot Saturday night.

Now, what does one wear to a public flogging? My wardrobe just wasn't suitable, and I put together several feeble outfits before settling on my oldest pair of jeans, a ratty black sweatshirt, and a pair of ratty black boots, the boots to "blend in." I chose this ensemble after remembering what sexual adventurer Dillon Flinder had said. When going to a sex club, he had advised, wear clothes that won't stain.

Eeuw.

Dressing to blend in was somewhat easier for Tamayo because she had the wardrobe for it—lots of leather and a couple of cute black rubber numbers—right down to the accessories, the studded dog collar, the chain belt, the black streak of temporary dye that ran down the center of her bleached blond hair reverse Susan Sontag–style.

"What do you think?" she asked when she picked me up. "Too matronly?"

"No, you look great," I said. I looked up and saw Mrs.

Ramirez peeking out from behind her lace curtains. God only knew what she'd make of Tamayo.

"Well Robin, you look . . ." Tamayo didn't finish.

The cab was waiting. "Meter's running," said the cabbie.

We got in. As we were turning onto Fourteenth Street a big green tanker truck with the words D&L CESSPOOL on the side drove by. The guy in the D&L Cesspool truck beeped and waved at us.

"There goes a tragicomic accident waiting to happen," Tamayo said, as the cabbie pulled in behind the D&L Cesspool truck, following it, a little too closely for my taste, for several blocks.

"He's cute. Too bad he's a cesspool cleaner," I said.

"I didn't even know there still were cesspools. What would it be like to date a cesspool cleaner?"

"I dunno. If we went on a date, would he borrow the truck and pick me up in it? That alone would almost make it worth it. Anyway, we probably have more in common professionally than I want to admit."

"Cheer up. Maybe you'll meet Mr. Right tonight at Anya's," Tamayo said, as the cab pulled up around the corner from the club.

Anya's was located off Gansevoort and Little West Twelfth Street in the heart of New York's meatpacking district. The Meat Rack, as it is sometimes known, is a warren of cobblestone streets and squat buildings with iron awnings, a marketplace for dead animal carcasses by day and live animal carcasses by night. In addition to the meatpackers and the covert sex clubs, there are also apartments, bars, and restaurants like Hogs & Heifers, Kafka's, and Florent, and a number of abandoned warehouses. Regular folk mix here with the avant-garde and all manner of streetwalking prostitutes. It is a very visceral neighborhood, and spooky after dark. It's the kind of neighborhood where the streetlights do little but accentuate the shadows.

Jim and Mike were set up around the corner in the under-cover van. They calibrated Tamayo's purse-cam hidden camera for white balance and wired her for sound. Most of what she shot wouldn't be seen anyway—she had been instructed *not* to shoot faces, and the effects department would blur what Aunt Maureen would call the "naughty bits."

Outside Anya's, a couple of guys were negotiating some transaction with a woman on the sidewalk in front of a line of cabs and hired limos, waiting to whisk customers home.

"Well," Tamayo said. "It's time to paint the snake."

She and I went down the stairs to the door. Under a sign that said, CHECK ALL YOUR WEAPONS—EXCEPT THE ONE GOD GAVE YOU, we paid the $15 ladies' admission ($100 for men) and went through black curtains into a dungeonlike room with a no-alcohol bar. This was the public lounge part of the establishment, a creepy gray stone room with low ceilings and very low lighting.

Despite the sign outside, there was quite a lot of weaponry on display, paddles and small whips, racks, cages, spanking horses.

After checking our coats with the husky, whiskered, tartan-clad transvestite in the coat check, I went to the juice bar to wait for Anya, and Tamayo went her own way, undercover. Mike and Jim were going in a back entrance, so their camera gear wouldn't alarm the customers. Little did the customers know Tamayo was walking around filming them.

Gee, I hate undercover stuff.

Anya's is pretty middle-class sleaze. Although I hadn't been to an S&M club before, I knew from interviewing domina-trices for a previous series on S&M that there are darker, more wicked clubs where truly horrible things go on. At Anya's, the activities were basically role-playing, exhibitionism, and voyeurism. In the middle of the dungeon room, a man bent over a spanking horse was having his bare bottom paddled by a woman who, despite her black leather outfit, gave off a strong schoolteacher vibe. Others, mainly men, some wearing clothes, some naked, many wearing masks, watched.

Whatever turns your crank, Frank, but sex clubs just didn't do it for me. During our honeymoon, my ex-husband Burke and I, on a lark, went to an upscale, touristy live sex show in Amsterdam. We sat next to a lovely uptight couple from Essex, England, and watched one pair of bums after another bouncing in time to disco music. It struck me as joyless, mechanical, less a naughty erotic bacchanal than an aerobics routine. In and out, in and out, six more, in and out, in and out, four more.

A masked man had come up to me at the juice bar very casually, as if he wasn't completely naked except for the mask, scuffed black shoes, sport socks (you don't want to go barefoot in a place like this), and watch.

"May I lick your boots?" he asked.

"No, but thanks for asking," I said, ever polite, inching away. The cesspool cleaner was looking awfully good in my mind right about now. This guy next to me was probably a successful Wall Street analyst or something, I thought, a good catch. Anya had boasted that this was where Wall Street came to be whipped.

I consider myself a freethinker, but then, be a freethinker, and the next thing you know, you're making small talk with a naked investment banker from Massapequa. I dared not meet anyone's eyes, lest I burst out laughing. I have to really know someone well before I can do anything kinky with them, otherwise I just can't keep a straight face.

Take, for example, the time I almost had sex with Howard Gollis, which was also the last time I had vodka. Things were progressing smoothly. We were hot and heavy, panting, groping, about to tear our clothes off, when Howard stood back and smiled a wicked smile at me.

And he pulled out a blindfold.

"Is that for you or for me?" I asked.

"For you," he said.

"No, I don't think so," I said. I couldn't stop laughing for a half hour.

For a comedian, Howard didn't have a very good sense of humor about it and accused me of rank prudery, but jeez, what kind of guy wants to blindfold you the first time you have sex? Either a control freak or a man who is horribly disfigured, in my opinion. Or both.

So Anya's was a challenge. It was important not to laugh. As Dillon had informed me, "If you laugh at them, the masochists like you even more. If you tell them to get away, they adore you. If you call them bad names and try to kick them away, they'll worship you for life. It's like quicksand."

Anyway, I got the feeling after talking to Dillon that the biggest risk a woman faced at Anya's was being worshipped to death by a pack of slavering dog-men.

"Ah, you're here," Anya said. "I'll show you the place on our way up to the Sacher-Masoch Room. Your crew is up there, yes?"

"They should be."

"Come with Charles and me," she said, tugging on Charles's leather leash.

Above the public lounge was a couples-only room, which featured a free buffet, of which Anya was quite proud. "The baked ziti is excellent," she said. "Help yourself." I demurred.

I heard a mechanical grinding and gnashing through the wall.

"What's that?" I asked.

"The hamburger factory next door," Anya said, casually, seeing no irony in it. "Night shift."

Anya's seemed very banal for a den of iniquity. Maybe it was the ubiquitous naked, masked men in tennies and sport socks standing around eating white and yellow cheese cubes off floral paper picnicware.

On the third floor was the Justine Room, for male dominants and female submissives—closed tonight because of a

burst pipe—and the Sacher-Masoch Room for female dominants and male submissives. Anya's offices were on the top
floor.

"My late husband, Gus, he built this place. The spanking
horses, the racks, everything. Made it with his own hands."

"Quite a guy, Gus."

"He was, yes."

"Does Charles go with you everywhere?" I asked.

"More or less," she said, punching a code into the keypad
outside a large blue door, which then opened into the Sacher-
Masoch Room.

Inside, several women paraded their slaves around on
leashes for Mike and Jim, who were set up in a corner.

"If Hell had a kennel club . . . ," Mike whispered to me as
the slave-men went through their paces.

There were others in the room, a very large man in a harness with two dominatrices attending him and a lone woman
with a whip, who was introduced as Carlotta, Anya's "lieu-
tenant."

"These are our players," Anya said, introducing me to the
others, who gave their first names only. Some were masked,
some were not. All had signed releases, which are good things
to have when you're shooting sensitive material like this.

"Ms. Hudson has a few questions," Anya said, and gave me
the floor.

I passed a photocopied photo of Kanengiser around.

"Have you seen this man before, in this club or elsewhere?"
I asked. "His name is Herman Kanengiser."

"I've seen him before," one of the slaves said. I noticed his
mistress tightened his leash slightly when he did.

"Where did you see him?" his mistress asked, mockingly.

"Uh . . ."

"On television," said another slave. "He was on television
this past week, right?"

"Right," I said.

"That's probably where I saw him," the first slave said.

"Are you sure?" I asked.

"I'm sure," said the slave.

"Do you know anyone who knew him?" I persisted.

They all just stared at me so I moved on, passing the photo of Joey Pinks around.

"No, don't know him," said the slaves. It was so hard to tell if they were being truthful—they were so in the control of their woman masters, who betrayed nothing and were holding those leashes taut. You wouldn't want to play poker with this bunch of B-movie Amazons.

Maybe Tamayo was having better luck downstairs with her photos.

At that point, Anya took over. The woman had to control everything. We were required to stay through a paddling demonstration—or two—or three, and watch the man with two dominatrices be tied to a rack and stroked with a whip. We had to watch Anya put her spiked heel on the back of Charles's head and hold him down that way while she insulted him, calling him a lowdown worm, a dog, a poor excuse for a man, and several other charming endearments.

Mike was uncharacteristically silent.

So was I. I no longer felt like laughing. This was not harmless role-playing. I had a powerful urge to grab that whip from Anya's hand, break it in half, and punch her lights out for picking on the poor man. I wanted to hoist him to his feet and tell him to stand up for himself and rejoin the human race. I flashed back to a time when I was a kid, and I stood by and watched my schoolmates bully a new kid, and I did nothing because I was glad they weren't bullying me. I hated standing by now, even though they were all consenting adults and the slaves wanted to be treated this way for some reason.

My head was swimming. I felt nauseous. I felt myself swaying slightly and then heard Mike's comforting voice in my ear: "Artichoke, artichoke, artichoke. Let's wrap this up and get out of here. We've got more than enough."

Mistress Anya was pissed when we cut short the shoot. She

would no doubt call Jerry, who would no doubt chew me out for missing good tape opportunities. But so fucking what? I couldn't watch one more minute of it. I guess that makes me a prude.

Downstairs, I retrieved Tamayo.

"We're out of here," I said.

"Okay," she said, but she said it reluctantly. She was enjoying herself. Many men had asked to lick her boots, and she pretended she didn't understand English very well. "Oh, you *like* my boots," she said, and moved away, although, just for kicks, she had let one guy lick her boots.

"It was okay," she said. "I didn't mind."

"Did anyone recognize the picture?"

"A couple of people weren't sure, but most people said no outright."

"Well, we did our best," I said.

"My wife is not going to believe this," Jim said, as he loaded his sound deck into the back of the van.

"Let's get out of here," Mike said.

"Want to go for a drink?" Tamayo asked.

"Not tonight," I said.

"Well, I'm going over to Hogs & Heifers. Want to share a cab?"

"I'll drive you home, Robin," Mike said. "Jim's taking the van back to headquarters, and I have my car right here. I can drop you at the bar, Tamayo."

Before I could protest, Tamayo said, "Oh perfect."

I did *not* want to get into a car with Mike. I wasn't even sure he still had a license, since Jim did all the driving. But I didn't want to offend him, nor did I want to appear afraid, and Tamayo had already hopped in the back. I got in the front.

After we dropped Tamayo off at Hogs & Heifers, Mike said, "Sure you don't want to go have something to eat?"

"It's late."

"Okay. Thought I'd ask," Mike said.

"Thanks for asking," I said. "I just want to go home and take a one-hour bath in disinfectant."

Mike wasn't listening. He was staring into his rearview mirror.

"That car has been following us since West Street," he said.

I turned and looked out the back window. A dark sedan was behind us.

"Are you sure?"

"Positive. It was parked behind us, and when we pulled out, it pulled out. Some fucking pervert, we'll show him."

It looked like the car I'd seen in front of the Bastable.

Mike stopped abruptly and when the car behind stopped Mike suddenly floored it, right through a red light.

"Drive to a police station and see if it follows us," I suggested, brightly, as I scribbled the license plate number in my reporter's notebook.

But Michael O'Leary had other ideas.

"We'll lose 'em," he said, shifting into gear and squealing away at the next light.

"This isn't Sarajevo, Mike," I said. The car was still following us. "We have law enforcement here. Sort of."

"Reach under the front seat, will you, and give me my gun."

"Your gun? You have a gun? Jesus Christ. No, I won't get your gun."

Mike made a sharp, screeching turn onto Washington Street. He whipped around Tribeca's cobblestone streets, pulling a U-ie on West Broadway, where we lost the other car.

"Lost that bastard," Mike said.

"I changed my mind, Mike," I said. "Let's go for a drink. I need one."

We stopped off at the first bar we came to, a little hole in the wall on a narrow side street. There were three other people in the place, not counting the bartender, and none of them were talking to each other. You could tell by the litter on the floor that there'd been quite a crowd here earlier, probably

having a friendly old time, but then the party had gone elsewhere, leaving nothing but the misanthropes behind.

After I called Ferber and Huculak from the pay phone by
the bathroom and told them about the car, I thought again
about quitting my job: Maybe I should think seriously about
a career change. Even if I survived the reshuffle, I wasn't likely
to get back to general news anytime soon. That would mean
another year, maybe longer, of stalking call girls and fly-by-
night hairpiece moguls, another year of taking crap from Jerry
Spurdle. Then what? I'd be older and have sleazier and sleazier
pieces on my résumé. Maybe I'd be better off quitting before
they shoved me into some stupid off-air job for the duration
of my contract.

The problem was, I didn't know what else to do. Ever since
I was a little girl, I'd wanted to be a television reporter. I guess
it sounds sad, like wanting to grow up to be a congressman.
But it was my dream and I wasn't ready to give it up yet.

I joined Mike at the bar.

"You think you're being followed?" Mike said.

"I saw that car before. And last night or . . . two nights
ago. I don't even know what day it is now . . . Sunday? Anyway, the cops found a dead ex-con with my business card on
him and an OTB betting slip for a horse called Robin's
Troubles."

It was not conducive to a Positive Mental Attitude.

"What will you have?" the bartender asked.

"Vodka," I said immediately. Fuck Max Guffy. Fuck Howard Gollis. Then I changed my mind. "No, make it a Bud-
weiser."

"Grolsch," Mike said.

"I know it's all connected to the Kanengiser case, and I
think someone thinks I know something and is after me because of it. But I don't know anything! The cops have a lid
on the case, Jerry only wants me to use the murder to introduce S&M, every woman Kanengiser ever boinked is a suspect
and most of them won't talk to me anyway . . ."

"You should get a gun, Robin."

"I hate guns," I said. "But I feel like I might have to get one, because everyone else has one, you know? Why do you have a gun?"

"To protect myself."

Jesus. People were shooting at anchormen, and the anchormen wanted to arm themselves so they could shoot back. Dead felons turned up behind dumpsters, husbands and wives were blowing each other away, and people shot at the White House on a pretty regular basis. There were towns in the United States where every head of every household was *required* by law to own a gun. Chaos reigns.

I realized suddenly that I was talking in a very panicky fashion. Mike put his hand over mine and waved to the bartender for another beer for me.

"Didn't you want to help those slaves escape tonight? Wasn't it awful watching that?" I asked.

"They were all consenting adults and nobody was killed. You can't say that about wars. The thing I noticed was how odd the slave Charles was acting. Did you notice him twitching?"

"No."

"I'll show you the tape on Monday. He was nervous for some reason. There was something very strange about him. I have a sixth sense about this."

"Distemper?"

Mike smiled. He was a pretty good-looking guy, I thought. His face was kind of plain, but so animated by his wacky Irish personality that after you knew him a while, and had a bit to drink, he looked really handsome. But not pretty-boy handsome.

"They all seemed nervous, those slaves. What a concept that is, someone choosing to be a slave," I said. "I can see a little leather, a little role-playing for fun, but the humiliation . . ."

I stopped. Some current in the room changed and I suddenly became aware of Mike's smell. He smelled like a hardware store, an oiled rubber and brown paper smell, with just a touch of soap, no aftershave. I love the smell of men.

But now that I'd smelled him, I felt funny talking about sex.

"That was disturbing, I have to admit," Mike said. "I flashed back a bit to being a hostage in Lebanon."

Mike and Reb had been taken hostage in Beirut but they escaped after three weeks. Normally, Mike wouldn't talk about it, but he'd had a bit of beer, so I pressed him, because Reb had told me two different stories.

"How exactly did you guys escape?"

"Between you and me," Mike said, "we didn't exactly escape."

"Huh?"

"Have you ever read the O. Henry story 'Ransom of Red Chief'? These rogues kidnap a boy, try to get ransom from the parents, but the child is such a holy terror, the parents ignore the kidnappers. The child is drivin' them crazy, and he won't leave and the kidnappers can't get rid of him . . ."

"I love that story."

"It was kind of like that. Reb started compulsively singing and humming. It was something he learned in Nam, to clear his mind during interrogations. But in Beirut, he wouldn't stop, he couldn't stop, except when he was sleeping."

"What did he sing?"

"Oh, Reb sings it all. Sixties pop songs, operetta, Peggy Lee, English drinking songs, Irish drinking songs, the 'Marseillaise,' fifties advertising jingles. It got to be a bit much. The guards would come in, tell him to shut up, and beat him with sticks, but he wouldn't shut up. I thought they were going to hang us, but it wasn't a good time for them, strategically, to kill us.

"One night, after exercise, they put us back in our cell and forgot to manacle us, forgot to close the window. They even left a wooden crate so we could climb up to the window. We got outside, the night guard was mysteriously absent, and there was a taxi nearby. Don't tell anyone. Reb would kill me if I blew his story out of the water."

"Boy, Reb didn't tell me any of that. I heard the version where he chewed through his leather restraints, broke a window, helped you out and you walked miles, until a truck hauling melons gave you a lift. And the version where the truck was hauling Halal chickens."

"He really does believe we escaped, all the same. He thinks he's Irish too, or Irish American."

"He isn't? Reb Ryan? Sounds Irish."

"Nah, he changed his name years ago. Something East European, I think. But now he really believes he is Irish."

"Why didn't you let management know he was nuts before they heard about the Haiti Incident?"

"Because, I dunno. Code of the field. Everyone out there in the field is half-crazy, and Reb was a good reporter, in spite of everything else. It's funny, when he's on camera, he is the most incisive, truthful person I've ever met, but off-camera, he's delusional and you can't believe a word he says."

"How do you keep sane, Mike? I mean, you've seen much worse than this."

He laughed. "I rotated back to keep sane. Well, that wasn't the only reason I rotated back. I was in the doghouse for a couple of driving stunts in Rwanda. But the biggest reason I came back is my ex-wife, she's American, she moved back to the States, and she brought our daughter back. I wanted to be closer to Samantha."

His daughter, Samantha, was ten.

"I bet you're a great dad," I said.

He had another beer and showed me some of his pictures. Jim and Mike whip out their pictures at the drop of the hat. It's very endearing.

"You want to have more kids?" I asked.

"I don't know. I don't t'ink so," he said. A couple of beers and he got really Irish. "Not wit' dis job and dis lifestyle. I don't see enough of Sam now as it is. Besides, I come from seven kids, and I have truckloads of nieces and nephews. So many, I could unload 'em wit' a pitchfork. What about you?"

"Can't have 'em without a lot of costly medical treatment and risk and . . . well, it's just not practical for me. What happened between you and your wife?"

"Oh, we grew apart. She wanted a husband who was around more, someone to really look after her seven days a week. We've been divorced five years. I've spent five years dealing with it by jumping into one war after another. I t'ink, I don't know, but I t'ink I needed a big war outside me to take my mind off de war inside me. It was takin' too great a toll on me, my daughter, my job. So I declared a unilateral peace and came to America."

"What does your wife do?"

"She illustrates children's books."

"I've heard it's better if you mate with someone outside news."

"Who told you dat?"

"Claire says that. But I kinda knew that already. Relationships within the business don't fare very well, when both people are in news. Look at Elsie and Pat, Solange and Greg Browner, Reb and his ex-wife . . ."

"Your ex-husband is a reporter, isn't he?"

"Yeah."

"What happened wit' you two?"

"We were good in the short term, but we had different long-range visions. I guess we grew apart too."

"What drew you to him?"

Irish guys, most of them don't mind talking about love and romance, and they know how to do it without getting either wimpy or macho about it. Mike had a robust, healthy, slightly cynical interest in the subject, and wasn't afraid to ask questions.

"Burke is really good-looking. We met on a murder trial and we were seeing each other there every day. There was that sense of shared adventure, you know? He was looking for a little chaos and I was looking for a little order in my life. We both got a lot more of each than we bargained for."

"Be careful what you pray for . . ."

He squeezed my hand. I don't know if it was the sense of danger, or the beers, or that we had worked together so closely for the last couple of months, or the way he smelled, but I felt a deep pelvic twinge when he did that. Maybe it was the fact that he was sexy without being pretty, that he had that great Irish accent, that he told great stories, or that when I looked in his eyes at that moment I saw something kind of sweet and unprotected there. I completely forgot about the twenty-seven dogs in Pakistan.

"I think it's like this guy, Phil, says. He says, he's too crazy for love and too silly to die. I think I might be like that," I said. "I'm just tired of it all, the control games, the illusions."

"Ah, but you never know, do you? You t'ink you've smartened up and you can't fall in love and den, whammo, some fantastic creature walks into your line of vision."

Because I am a tad self-absorbed, I thought he was talking about me. I thought he was hitting on me because we'd been through a car chase together and had a few beers. I was about to cut the long evening short, tell him I was tired and would take a cab home, when he said, "Dere's dis great Afghan farewell. Have I told you dis before?"

"I don't think so."

"You should know it. 'Don't be tired.' When I want to give up the fight, I just tell myself dat. 'Don't be tired.' "

Don't be tired. I loved that.

Maybe that's why I invited myself back to his place.

16

Mike was still asleep when I woke up, dressed, and crept out of his Greenwich Village apartment, hungover and confused.

It was about six a.m. Sunday, a bright, bright day, and my eyes were stinging. After scanning the street to make sure there were no dark blue sedans lurking about, I pulled up the collar of my coat and began walking home.

There was almost nobody on the streets. I had a moment of déjà vu because this scene so closely resembled one in my nightmares. To wit, I wake up, and it's a beautiful day, but I'm the only person left on earth.

Oh God, I thought, I just went to bed with a man *before* our first date. That wasn't like me at all. How well did I really know this guy? Just because he's good-looking and tough and has a sense of humor . . .

This is always how it starts. I get close to someone through work and we end up in the sack and then we end up in some tempestuous relationship and we get our feelings hurt. I was repeating the same mistake I had made with Burke, with Eric.

Sure, the sex was good, but of course that had something to do with my long bout of celibacy. Sex, with another person, usually feels great after not having it for a while. It's like the old joke about the guy hitting himself with a hammer. When asked why he does it, he says, "Because it feels so good when I stop."

And yes, I had been the aggressor. I took full responsibility. But I had to stop getting involved with news guys, especially guys with whom I worked so closely.

I picked up *The New York Times* and hailed a cab on Sixth Avenue to take me home.

When I got home, the guillotine was still there but there was, thankfully, nobody waiting at the mailboxes. The stairway reeked of the sickly sweet smell of burning herbs and flowers. It is not wholly unpleasant, this smell, but kind of creepy and funereal. Sally was either entombing a pharaoh or casting some powerful spell, no doubt a love spell for some heartsick soul, or for herself. I held my breath to avoid getting a contact high, as about the last thing I needed at the moment was to fall in love.

There were two messages from Aunt Maureen, which I fast-forwarded through, and a message from Pete Huculak asking me to call him. His call I returned.

"I just heard from the police, they checked that license-plate number," Pete said.

"Yeah."

"It was a car service, hired for the day by Maureen Hudson Soparlo. Any relation?"

"Unfortunately," I said.

Jesus, Aunt Maureen was following me. Following me, hell. The woman was stalking me. That meant she'd seen me in front of the Hotel Bastable hanging out with drug dealers, as well as going into and coming out of a sex club.

Good God. It was going to confirm for her all the wild stories she'd heard from other people.

Of course, the good news was, I wasn't being followed by a killer, I thought, just Aunt Mo. There's a bright side. Maybe.

After I fed Louise Bryant I took a long, almost scaldingly

hot shower and checked myself for signs of necrotic fascitis. All I wanted to do was put on my flannel pajamas and watch *Four Weddings and a Funeral* for the thirty-seventh time. But I had to go into work and edit the stupid S&M doctor story.

Weekends were usually kind of fun at ANN. It was a blue-jean shop Saturday and Sunday, traditionally slow news days, so the atmosphere was more relaxed and playful.

Normally, the newsroom is a fine example of an orderly anarchy, with people at every pod, bodies streaming in every direction, and a lot of noise—rings and buzzes and "urgent story" alarms. But weekends were generally quiet—so quiet you could hear the soft, steady clattering of the old-fashioned Teletype machines we kept around just in case the computer system failed. And weekends were unsupervised, as the execs steered clear of the place, making it a fertile breeding ground for Nerf football games, spitball throwing, and the master-minding of pranks.

My first stop was the library, where I picked up two stories that mentioned Joey Pinks, old stories about how Joey, age thirty-four, after living quietly with his mother most of his life, had suddenly shot her.

"She was a terrible nag. You could hear her screaming all the time," said neighbors, who went on to say that the mother had driven two husbands into early graves and one other son, Joey's half-brother, into the nuthouse long before Joey grabbed the family firearm.

Joey, on the other hand, was "a devoted son, a good boy. Dutiful. Quiet." He was "completely distraught and remorseful about his mother's injury."

Other people had known a slightly different Joey Pinks, who snuck out of the house after his mother was asleep to hang out in California's S&M scene, where he was sometimes a "male lifestyle-submissive," and sometimes a "male lifestyle-dominant."

It did have something to do with Anya's, I thought.

I looked again at the tapes Tamayo had shot, but nothing jumped out at me. I popped in the tape Mike had shot the night before and looked at the scenes of Charles the slave, which Mike had mentioned. The slave did seem twitchy, but who wouldn't be, dressed in sweat-inducing leather, leashed to a coldhearted woman with a whip?

I fast-forwarded through some of the other raw tapes, the interview with Anya. But it just didn't connect for me. All those people in masks didn't help either. For all Anya's lofty talk about her crowd being more honest about love and pain and rules than most people, how trust is important in these relationships, they certainly had their own hypocrisies, the masks, the code words, the fact that Anya couldn't trust her boyfriends beyond the length of a leash.

Anya said she'd been at the club the night Kanengiser, whom she claimed not to know, was killed. Said she'd been with Charles, as I recalled. But a man who couldn't be trusted to mean "no" and "stop" when he said them couldn't be trusted to tell the truth about where his mistress had been two nights before—especially a man who walked around on all fours like a dog to win her approval.

Now I had a new theory. Maybe Kanengiser had been walking on the wild side and got mixed up with Anya. Maybe he was one of her Werners. Maybe she found out he had a lot of other women. Maybe she got mad. Anya didn't strike me as the kind of woman who knew how to handle rejection or loss of control.

I could imagine Anya removing the handcuffs from her purse, and some change and a matchbook falling out. She took no note of it, since her hands were full, gun in one, cuffs in another. Maybe she was talking, or Kanengiser was pleading with her. And so she had unwittingly left a clue behind.

But how could I get her to admit it? She'd already denied knowing him at least twice. She had her slavering alibi.

And where was this diary, this little black book? Would Anya be in it?

Unfortunately, I did not have the time, or the authority, to look into it any further. Jerry had left a memo for me on my desk.

"Do it as an unsolved murder," Jerry wrote. "If by some miracle it gets solved before we go to air, we'll update it on cam with a reader. So don't say anything in the script about whether it is solved or not. Just the circumstances of the death, the handcuffs, the matchbook, then straight to the undercover tape Tamayo got at Anya's. You got all those people at Anya's . . . use some of them . . ." Blah blah blah. "Gotta get this on the air tomorrow!"

Jerry wanted a script for a five-minute report faxed to him by lunchtime. When I called him, he told me "absolutely" to include the Joey Pinks story, as a corollary unsolved murder, and to speculate about the black book, but that he wanted that script by lunchtime and the edited piece on his desk by the time he came in Monday morning regardless.

"I can't do this," I thought. Five minutes doesn't sound like a lot, but writing a five-minute report takes a lot of time and work. Of course, it didn't matter what I wrote anyway, since Jerry would just change it all and fax it back. So I pounded out a script, faxed it, waited for the changes, and then took the tapes and the script to edit.

I didn't stay for the edit. The shots were logged and the script was straightforward and, frankly, I couldn't bear to hear my voice over this story or see any more of the videotape. For me, the story is over, I thought. Let go. Move on.

After dropping off the tapes and script, I wandered into the newsroom and was surprised to see Louis Levin.

"What are you doing here?"

"I'm banking days so I can take two extra vacation days next month," he said. "We're ordering pizza for lunch. You want in on it?"

"No thanks."

"I heard about the dead ex-con. Pretty scary."

"I'm not scared. I think he wanted to tell me something

about this story I've been working on, but someone got to him before he could tell me. *Quel dommage.*"

"Why was he coming to you?"

"Well, I'm the reporter on the story . . ."

"Why didn't he go to *Hard Copy* or *Backstreet Affair* and get paid for his efforts?"

"I don't know . . ."

"Weird," he said.

I was still trying to puzzle that one out when Louis said, "Did you hear about Fennell?"

"What?"

"He was missing, on a bender everyone figured. But they found him at Saint Vincent's Hospital. He got kneecapped the other night."

"Oh my God."

"Got him in his artificial knee. Guess he should have been nicer to that last Steven Seagal movie, huh?"

"Oh, then he wasn't badly hurt."

"Well, the knee is destroyed. He has to have a new one made. Fennell himself was actually hurt because he was pretty drunk and when the knee collapsed, he fell into a railing, broke his jaw, and was knocked unconscious. Apparently, while he was lying there, someone robbed him, took his ID, all his money."

I didn't laugh. "Where did it happen?"

"Downtown somewhere. He was coming out of a bar."

He must have stopped off for a drink somewhere after he left me.

"Did he see the guy?"

"No. This is one sneaky sniper," he said. "You know the story about that knee, right?"

"No."

"Well, I hear he lost part of that leg to mobsters in Hollywood in the sixties," Louis said.

According to Louis, the male "talent" were so jumpy now that the sound of a car backfiring—or any similar sharp, loud noise—was enough to make a roomful of anchormen hit the deck immediately. Reb had been seen in the parking garage examining the underside of his Jeep with something that looked like an oversize dental instrument, a large metal pole with a round mirror on the end, and both he and Kerwin had asked for permission to carry sidearms at work.

"Anyway, I'm glad you're here," Louis said. "I have treats galore for you, little girl. Wanna see what I did with your obit?"

He pulled it out of his drawer and popped it into the tape player at his desk.

ANN keeps obits on file for various famous people and ANN's own on-air personalities, of which I am one. They're now updated four times a year, and the updated script is stored in the computer, so that if someone famous dies unexpectedly, the script can be scanned to make sure it is up to date while the tape is run to playback to air as soon as possible.

The problem is, the script in the computer doesn't match the taped obit of Robin Jean Hudson, girl reporter. Louis and I had enlisted people in graphics and in effects to make a fake obit that showed me, dressed like a vamp in a stunning red dress and matching high heels, in a bunch of different historical scenes, à la *Zelig* or *Forrest Gump*. If I died suddenly, the world would see me advising Kennedy, climbing Mount Everest, filling in for Judge Ito, and skating around Madison Square Garden with the Stanley Cup.

"Looks the same to me," I said as I watched.

"It's coming up," he said. "Remember when Kim Il Sung died? The footage of all the thousands of grief-stricken Koreans prostrate before billboard-size photos of the Great Leader?"

"You put my picture up instead of Kim Il Sung's! It's brilliant, Louis. I can't wait until I die. Thanks. Have you heard anything about the reshuffle, by the way?"

"Everyone knows Joanne is going to Paris and Claire is

going to Washington, Rappaport to *Perspective,* Madri to PR. Other than that, anything could happen. Sure you don't want pizza?"

"No, as soon as that stupid tape is on Jerry's desk, I'm going home," I said.

"Take this with you," he said, handing me a clipping.

"You *are* full of treats today."

"It's about a guy in England who can't turn his television off because it makes his monkey crazy. The monkey goes ballistic and starts tearing people's hair out."

"I know people like that."

" 'It makes my monkey crazy,' I like that phrase," Louis said.

He yelled at an indolent PA who was leaning on a pod flirting with a writer. "Hey, don't lean on the furniture," he said. "It makes my monkey crazy."

"That doesn't make sense," I said.

"It makes more sense than 'It gets my goat,' " Louis reasoned.

"If the viewing public knew what high-caliber philosophical questions occupy the minds of the omnipotent news media . . ."

"The viewing public," Louis said, "makes my monkey crazy."

I didn't go straight home. Because I was feeling badly about Fennell, I took a detour to Saint Vincent's.

Before I went up I bought a huge floral basket. I was still glad I hadn't kissed the pig, but I did feel bad that he'd been shot and I wanted to pay my regards, out of respect for him as a professional, if not for him as a man.

Fennell saw me and said something through his broken, wired jaw. It sounded like "Uunnh. Ee khet arr arrerz."

Poor Fennell. His face was swollen and bruised and encased in a wire grid.

"I can't understand you," I said, putting the floral basket down on his bedside table.

His eyes grew wide. He wanted something from me. Suddenly, he reached up and grabbed me by the coat lapels, pulling me back down toward his face. I thought he was going to try to kiss me again, maybe try to tongue me through the wire grid, but he didn't. Instead, he sneezed all over me.

Then he screamed in pain from having to sneeze through a broken, wired jaw. Then he sneezed again. Followed by yet another scream of pain.

"Aiii ayyeryic!" he managed to shriek between sneezes and cries of agony.

Sneeze, scream. The nurse came in.

"Omigod," she said, rushing over. "Who brought these in here?"

"I did."

"He's allergic to flowers," she said, and whisked the offending bouquet away.

"I'm so sorry, Fennell," I said. Who knew a basket of flowers could be such an object of pain and menace?

He groped for a pen and paper and wrote: "It's all your fault."

It wasn't all my fault, but I decided to humor him, seeing as I'd just inadvertently inflicted pain upon him.

"I am really really sorry, Fennell. Really. God. It's awful."

He scribbled something on the pad.

"That perfume you wear smells like cat piss," he wrote.

17

"Did you hear about Fennell?" Tamayo asked me as soon as I got in Monday morning.

"Yes."

"Did you know he had a prosthetic knee?"

"No."

"Did you hear a creak creak when you and he—"

"I only went out with him once and we didn't have sex."

"Have you ever had a legless man?" she asked.

"No." Pause. "Why? Have you?"

"No. Not yet."

I couldn't keep up with the range of romantic options in her life. I had thought she was kidding around when she asked me once, in a voice thick with nostalgia and primal longing, if I'd ever had a glassblower. I thought she was kidding, until she showed me a picture of him, blowing a blue glass globe.

"If I met the right man, and he had no legs, it wouldn't bother me," I said.

"I think it might turn me on," Tamayo said. "Oh, Mike called twice."

"I'll call him later," I lied. I was avoiding him because I

wasn't sure how to deal with sleeping with him Sunday morning. I'm notoriously bad at aftermaths.

"Jerry wants you to work up a new series on Satan now that the Kanengiser story is over."

"The Kanengiser story isn't over."

"I mean, now that it's over for *us*."

"Yeah, it's over for us," I said. But I couldn't quite let go. "I just wanna make another call to Anya. Ask her about a few loose ends, like Joey Pinks, a black book—"

"Oh, that reminds me! Mistress Anya called. She wants you to call her back. Boy, did she sound pissed off."

"She always sounds pissed off," I said, dialing. "It's her bread and butter . . ."

When Anya came to the phone, she didn't bother with formalities like "Hello."

"I ought to sue you," was the first thing she said: You'd be surprised how many conversations I've had that began this way.

"Why?" I asked. "What happened?"

"About two a.m., after you left my club, an elderly woman came in with two very large men in suits and demanded to see the manager, and when I came to her, she asked me about you."

Aunt Maureen.

"She caused a scene."

That was certainly saying something, because it would be hard to cause a scene in a scene like that one. But Aunt Mo did it. All those sinners in one place, overripe for salvation— Aunt Mo was like Jesus with the money changers. After getting no information about me, she and her two fundamentalist Christian henchmen had stood in the dungeon room loudly exhorting people to "put some clothes on and go home to your families for heaven's sake!"

Then she gave her testimony.

I had to laugh. That's one thing about my Aunt Maureen, she takes a stand. I would expect no less from her. Another thing about my Aunt Maureen, she believes what she says. Yes, she's bigoted and fascistic and mean and has the power to reduce me to a quivering mass of low self-esteem.

But she's also a tough, big-mouthed broad who stands up for what she believes in. For that, you gotta respect her. She's no hypocrite, except in one way: Aunt Maureen has constantly preached the docility and submission of the female of the species. "Nice girls," she repeatedly told me, "should be seen, not heard."

Aunt Mo was never docile, never submissive, and she knew how to make herself heard.

"Sorry about that," I said to Anya.

"I almost called the cops on her," she said.

"I wanted to ask you about Joey Pinks," I interrupted, trying to sneak it in.

"I told you, I don't know him," she said, and hung up.

Aw hell. I might as well meet Aunt Mo, see if I can undo some of the damage, I thought. If she saw me, maybe she'd see I wasn't moonlighting as a call girl/witch/dominatrix/sex slave. Maybe I could explain I was researching a story.

So I called her hotel and left a message.

And she didn't call me back.

I called her again.

Again, she didn't call me back.

I called her three more times, at different times of the day. She never did call me back.

I didn't need the Empire State Building to fall on me. Aunt Maureen was now avoiding me.

But why?

As it turned out, I didn't have much time to think about it that day. I got off the phone and heard people come into the outer office.

"Our humble abode," Jerry Spurdle said.

He wasn't alone.

"We've offered Jerry new offices, but he says he's happy

with this. Doesn't need much. Wastes no resources," Georgia
Jack Jackson was saying to someone.

My door opened.

"This is the reporter's office," Jerry said, and Jack Jackson
and Dave Kona, the supercilious pip-squeak who was after my
job, came in.

"Miss Hudson," Jack said, smiling. "You still work here?"

Was he kidding? It was hard to tell with Jack. Even given
the fact Jackson never watched the crap we put on the air, I
figured he'd know I still worked there. This was a bad sign.

"Yes sir," I said.

This was only the fourth time the Great Man had spoken
to me. The first time was when I was a young newswriter and
still smoked, and he wandered into the newsroom after midnight and caught me smoking at my typewriter.

"Did they change the rules about smoking in the newsroom?" he asked.

"No sir," I said.

"Then don't smoke," he said, and strode away.

Once, he saw me in the hallway and said, "Hello, sweetheart." Yet another time, he complimented me on my dress
at a company shindig, just before I dropped a plate of lasagna
down the front of it. What a fine impression I'd been making.

"Robin is the reporter working on the Kanengiser story,"
Jerry said. "I should say she *was* working on it."

"Jerry and I have been talking about some interesting
changes in your unit," Jack said, slapping his right arm around
Jerry's shoulder paternally. For some reason, he seemed to
have genuine affection for Jerry.

"Oh yes?" I said.

"The research shows viewers are getting turned off by so
much sex and sensationalism, that they want a little more
'good news,' " Jackson said. "Jerry's completely in sync with
me on this one. Has some ideas about blind tap dancers, a
free clinic on Twenty-fourth Street, some welfare mothers who
. . . What did they do?"

"They formed a baby-sitting cooperative with the help of a social worker so they could all go back to school," Jerry said, avoiding my eyes.

Actually, there was more to it than that. They shared a group house, shared all the chores, pooled their food aid, and bought healthy foods in bulk. Three of the six women in the experiment were off welfare, and two others were just about to get their GEDs. I know, because I wrote up the story proposal.

"Maybe you can come up with a few ideas too, Robin," Jerry said. Our eyes locked. He was challenging me to say something.

Oh, what I wouldn't have given just then for an eighteen-pound turtle named Henri.

Around five p.m., when I was reeling from my topsy-turvy day, Mike wandered in, holding a videotape.

Okay, I thought. I'll just act like nothing happened Sunday morning, make a joke about it if he brings it up. It isn't that I didn't like the guy, you understand. It's just I didn't want him to assume I expected more from him and for him to then get defensive about it. My third date with Howard Gollis, he abruptly gave me a completely unsolicited speech about what a freedom-loving guy he was and how he wasn't ready to see anyone exclusively. Well, I hadn't asked him to. And that had been before our ill-fated attempt at sex.

"Hello, Robin," Mike said. "That was fun the other night, wasn't it?"

He smiled in a very nice way.

"Yeah," I said.

He said no more about it.

"Sorry I didn't get this to you sooner, but I had to stop off at security."

"Why?"

"Oh, someone took a shot at me last night. Would have

got me, but I hit the sidewalk in time to duck the shot. Sixth sense, you know, from all the wars."

"That's odd. Do they think it's the sniper?"

"Yeah. Unlike Reb, I recovered the bullet, so once they finish the ballistics testing, they'll know for sure."

"Did you see the guy?"

"Fleetingly. A flash of green, and then all I saw was the gray of the sidewalk."

"I thought he only shot at people who were on the air. Hmm. Maybe it *is* someone with a grudge against the company and maybe it is connected . . . but then . . . How would Anya's figure into it? See, Mike. This is what I mean. There are too many guns around, and too many of the wrong people have them."

"I'm glad I have one. I only wish I'd got a shot off at the guy who shot at me. Let's look at the tape," he said, clicking the remote control and starting the video.

"I saw the tape yesterday and you're right. Charles was twitchy. But I don't think it's—"

"I took shots of two different shoots, then did a split image of the two times we shot 'Charles.'"

I looked at the monitor. The second Charles was a little longer in the torso and a bit wider around the waist than the first Charles, but not so much that you would notice without seeing them side by side.

"See the front right paw . . . hand, on the first Charles," Mike said, freezing the frame and zooming in.

There was a thick red scar on his very white hand, one conspicuously absent from the second Charles. I hadn't noticed it before.

"This is it," I said. "This is the connection between Kanengiser and Anya's."

"How so?"

"Because that first Charles, I bet his real name is Joey Pinks. That's the guy the cops found, dead, with my address on him and that OTB slip. Joey Pinks had a scar on his hand like that."

"Holy mother," Mike said.

"Now it's a story," I said.

"Yeah," Mike said. "We should go back and talk to Anya again. Confront her with this tape. Get it on camera."

"You're right."

"What are you going to tell her?"

"I'll lie," I said. "I'll say the video is fucked and we need to shoot her one more time, and this time, we'll give her more time."

"Okay," Mike said. "Beep me when it's set."

Anya was brusque with me on the phone, and reluctant to "trust" us to do a proper job if we came back.

"How do I know you won't be dragging loudmouthed do-gooders around with you?" she asked.

It took a lot of bullshitting to get her to agree, but finally, she did, which made me wonder: If she was the killer, would she have agreed at all? Of course, in her world, things were out of kilter. Maybe this was part of her cover. How the hell did I know?

"Seven p.m.," she said.

That was a bad time. It meant Mike and Jim would be on overtime, and I couldn't authorize overtime, only Jerry could. But I didn't know where Jerry was and I had no choice.

"Seven p.m.," I said.

"What are you going to do?" Tamayo said to me, obviously amused by my situation.

"What am I going to do? I finally get a break in this stupid story, which, incidentally, I didn't even want to do, and Jerry says it's over. Then he takes credit for the stories I researched on the blind tap-dancing troupe and the welfare mothers . . ."

I stopped myself. One of the best pieces of advice I know comes, funnily enough, from Brenda Starr, the glamorous red-headed woman reporter from the comic strip. I once cut out a panel in which Brenda is leaving a movie theater weeping after some painful thing in her personal life, and she says, "Reporters don't have time to dawdle over their own grief. Our lives are devoted to telling the stories of other people's misfortune."

Fuck it, I thought. I beeped Mike. When he called back, I told him I couldn't reach Jerry so we couldn't go ambush Anya.

"Let's do it anyway," Mike said.

"I can't authorize the overtime, Mike."

"Just a second." When he came back on, he said, "Jim and I, we'll do it off the clock."

These are words you never hear from New York crews. But then, Mike was a maverick, and Jim, well, Jim idolized Mike.

"God bless you and all your ancestors, Mike. One other thing."

"Yes, my queen," Mike said.

"Bring your gun."

18

The club was closed Sundays and Mondays and nobody answered our knocks and hollers at the front, so we went around to the back. The door was open.

"She's expecting us," I said, leading the way up the back staircase, which was narrow and painted blood red. By the time we got to the fourth floor, I was panting. Anya's office door was open, but the lights were out. I knocked. There was no answer.

"This is weird," Jim whispered. Mike had his trigger-hand in his pocket, holding his gun.

Suddenly, my beeper went off. We all jumped and then a shot rang out. Mike had shot a hole in the pocket of his jacket.

"Jesus, calm down, Mike," I said.

"Sssh," he said.

The hamburger shift was just starting up next door and, except for the low, distant grumbling of their machines, it was very quiet. You'd think, if there was someone else present, they would have reacted to the gunshot.

Jim and Mike looked at me, questioning. I shrugged, and pushed the door open.

"Anya," I said. She was sitting in shadow at her desk.
She didn't answer. I reached in and turned on the light.
Anya was looking straight ahead.
She was handcuffed to her chair.
Her chest was covered with blood.
"Oh my God."
"What is it?" Mike said, pushing past me into the room.
"I think . . . she's dead."
"Sssh," Mike said. "Hear that?"

Jim and I strained our ears. We heard nothing, but Mike
really did have a sixth sense, the senses of a wild animal, because a moment later we heard footsteps coming up the back
staircase.

"Jim, put the camera on the desk and start rolling," Mike
said. "Then get behind the desk. You too, Robin."

I crouched behind the desk and pulled out my hot glue gun
to cover Mike. The footsteps got closer. Mike was behind the
door, holding his gun. The footsteps came to the doorway and
stopped.

"Anya?" said a woman's voice.

"I have a gun on you. Come in with your hands in the air,"
Mike said.

A moment later he said, "She's unarmed."

Jim and I came out from behind the desk.

It was Carlotta, and she'd just seen Anya dead at her
desk.

"What did you do?" she said.

"We didn't kill her," I said. I could imagine what she
thought, seeing Mike with his gun and Anya dead in the chair,
as if she'd just stumbled upon a mad news crew. "She was
dead when we got here."

Carlotta sighed deeply and sat down. "It has to do with
Joey, doesn't it?" she said.

Jim called the cops and I got Carlotta a seltzer from the mini-
bar in Anya's office.

"Should we close her eyes?" Mike asked. Anya was still sitting in her chair staring ahead.

"I don't think we should touch her. Wait for the cops," I said. I turned to Carlotta. "Are you going to be okay?"

"Yes yes," she said, shortly.

"Why did you come by just now? The club is closed tonight, isn't it?"

"She wanted me here for your interview. Because Charles wasn't available today . . ."

"The second Charles."

"Yes."

"The first Charles, that was Joey Pinks," I said.

"Yes," Carlotta said.

"He's dead, you know."

"He is?"

"Anya didn't know that?"

"No. She was looking for him. She thought he'd contacted you."

"I think he was trying to tell me something when he was killed. So he left her?"

"Yes, shortly after you interviewed them the first time."

"Why didn't she tell us?"

"She didn't want to," she said.

"Why? What was she hiding?"

Carlotta looked up. "She was hiding Joey. He skipped out on his parole in California . . . he'd been in jail for forgery . . . she didn't want to give him away to the police and she didn't want him giving himself away by getting involved in this murder investigation. So he ran away. Anya hoped he'd come back soon."

"He tried to kill his mother. That's what he did time for. The forgery thing too, but . . ."

"Oh my God."

"Anya didn't know that?"

"I don't think so."

"Why did she harbor a fugitive? Why did she risk herself for Joey Pinks?"

"She loved him," she said, surprised, as though it were self-evident. "She loved taking care of him. He was a sweetheart, a real sweetheart, at least, that's the Joey we knew. He tried to kill his mother?"

"Yes."

"Holy shit."

"What was the connection to Kanengiser?"

"I'm not completely sure, but I think it may have had something to do with Joey's brother, or half-brother, Vern. Joey came out here looking for Vern and couldn't find him at first. He was hanging around the S&M clubs looking for him, and that's when he met Anya."

"Did he find Vern?"

"Yeah. Anya was afraid Joey had done some work for him, forgery, before Joey skipped out on parole in California. . . . Anya had met him. Vern."

"Did you meet him?"

"No."

"So you don't know what he looks like?"

"No."

"What do you know about Vern? What did Anya say about him."

"Well, he'd moved here, to New York, a few months ago, and Joey came out about a month ago. Hadn't seen his brother in some time, I gathered."

"Do you know Vern's last name? If he was a half-brother, he might not have the same last name."

"Half-brother or stepbrother. I don't know his last name. I'm trying to remember if Anya said anything else about him. No, I don't think so."

"Who is the second Charles?"

"Oh, that's someone else's slave. He just filled in when you were filming. He's actually a veterinarian from Staten Island."

"Anya borrowed a slave. Wow. Did Anya mention a little black book?"

"No." She gazed sadly up at me, and suddenly this bitch-in-training looked scared and vulnerable. "I'm going to get into trouble, as an accessory after the fact or something like that, aren't I?"

There was a stampede of footsteps coming up the stairs. The cops had arrived, Bigger and Ferber and a bunch of uniforms.

"Trouble just follows you around," Detective Richard Bigger said to me.

"I follow it around."

"Don't be too sure of that."

"I'll handle it," Ferber said, pulling me away from my crew. "Let's go somewhere where we can talk."

We ducked into one of the rec rooms.

"What is it?" I asked.

"Have a seat," he said.

I looked around. There was one leather chair, a hard bench, and a spanking horse in the room.

"I don't think so. I don't know who or what has touched this furniture."

Ferber smiled. "We beeped you. Did you hear us?"

"You're the one who beeped me! Why?"

"We got the ballistics report back on some of these shootings. The bullets removed from the doctor, Fennell Corker's knee, and Joey Pinks, they match, as does the bullet"—he checked his notes—"turned in by Kerwin Shutz. We've got another bullet your security office sent over today that looks like it might match too."

Mike's bullet.

"So there's a link between the ANN sniper, Kanengiser, and Pinks. Looks like this woman is the third murder victim," he said.

"I don't get it," I said. "What's the link between all these people?"

"Robin, the link we find is you," he said.

At first, I thought I'd heard him wrong. "Me?"

"Yes."

"That's ludicrous . . ."

"Reb Ryan was shot at the night after he went out with you. Fennell Corker was shot at the night he went out with you. Dillon Flinder was seen leaving a bar, walking arm in arm with you, the night he was shot at. Dr. Kanengiser was killed the night he was supposed to examine you." He referred to his notes. "Your cameraman Mike was shot at after being out with you."

"I never went out with Kerwin."

"That's funny. He says you did go out."

"Well, we didn't. Dillon and I hang out a lot, but we don't date. So sure, you can make a connection between anything if you try hard enough . . . ," I said. "They probably all had take-out from Tycoon Donut. Or something else. Like all these men, except Joey Pinks, worked in the JBS building. Maybe it's someone with a grudge against Jack Jackson. It's not like there aren't a lot of disgruntled and/or demoted employees or former employees running around."

"Yeah, we thought of that. Still, it seems a big coincidence, in light of your cameraman being shot at . . ."

"But I didn't date Dr. Kanengiser. The others in the JBS building were shot at; he was killed."

"Er, you didn't date Dr. Kanengiser, but since he was a gynecologist, the killer may have assumed he saw you . . . touched . . ."

"We never got that far. Jerry beeped me and the examination ended . . . prematurely."

"But the killer wouldn't know that."

I thought about this. Reb had been shot at but wasn't hurt. Like a warning shot. Fennell had kissed me, and he had got it in the knee. Dillon . . . Kanengiser . . . Mike . . . well, it made some sense. And Joey Pinks had wanted to tell *me* something about it. He could have gone to *Backstreet Affair* and received money for his knowledge, but he had come to find me . . . because I was involved? He had died because he knew who the killer was, maybe his own brother. The family that slays together . . . Anya had known who the killer was too, and now she was dead.

"You know, nobody knew I went out with Reb," I said. "Not that I know of. Well, a couple of close friends . . ."

"You might have been followed and the sniper saw you with Reb."

"Possible but doubtful."

The date had been very covert, conducted like a CIA operation.

"Did you have it written down somewhere?"

"Yeah, I did. In my old Filofax calendar. It was in my old purse, which was stolen at ANN about a month ago."

"That could be the diary you were talking about."

That would mean it had been no accident my bag was stolen.

"Who else was in your Filofax?"

"Max Guffy. I did a pre-interview with him one evening at Guffy Funeral Services."

"Is that all?"

"This blind date, Gary Grivett. But he lives in Minneapolis, so I expect he's okay. And Howard Gollis. Oh God. I *did* have Kerwin in my Filofax. We met a couple of times to discuss some vigilante videotape I shot that he wanted to use in his show," I said. "I didn't want to give it to him."

This was a lot to handle. Had Herman Kanengiser been killed not because of his human failings, not because he was a priapic misogynist or a liar or a fraud, but because of me?

Damn. Why did I have to be so irresistible?

Back at my office, Ferber and I went through my fan mail, which I kept, in no particular order, in a cardboard file box. Pete Huculak hovered over us and watched. Unlike many people at ANN, I didn't get bags and bags of fan mail. I got a few letters a week.

"These are part of a flurry of letters I got after someone placed an ad under my name in the pen pal pages of *Prison Life* magazine. I never did find out who," I said, handing Ferber a stack of letters.

"Suspicious," Pete said.

"Well, actually, most of them are critiques of my reporting and the stories I do, or story ideas. Not at all threatening. I get the nuttiest letters from outside the penal system. A considerable number of them from masochists for some reason. But no Verns."

The further you are from most people, the better they look. The television screen adds a lot of distance, with a paradoxical illusion of warmth and closeness, so that you feel you know the people you see, you identify with them, or at least with their television personae.

My ex-husband Burke likened this to Carl Jung's observation of the "bush-soul," wherein primitive people identified with the soul of something in nature. One man might feel he was sharing his soul with a tiger, another with a tree, a rock, a waterfall, an elephant, et cetera. (I think I share mine with an eighteen-pound turtle named Henri, but anyway . . .) He called the obsessive fan phenomenon the "celebrity soul" syndrome, wherein people identify too strongly with a famous figure and think that person knows their innermost thoughts and desires and is speaking directly to them, and them alone.

Hey, I'm no Jodie Foster. Ninety-nine point nine percent of the American population probably doesn't even know my name. So it is especially sad to me that some guy out there identifies with me this way. I mean, if you're going to go to all that trouble to be obsessed with someone, write them many letters, call them at home and hang up on them, even physically stalk them, you ought to aim a little higher, stalk Joanne Armoire or Diane Sawyer. "Hard work without ambition yields few fruits," my father used to say. But hell, Lorena Bobbitt gets adoring letters from men obsessed with her, so why not me?

(And recently I was reading that Ed Sullivan had groupies, which baffles me completely.)

Especially scary to me was that this underachieving stalker would kill because of his twisted affection for me, or for my television persona.

Ferber was sorting the letters into piles by category: "obsessive love"—this included the masochist faction, led by would-be footlicker Elroy—"death threats," and "other," which covered unfocused rantings about freemasons, Jews, blacks, Mexicans, extraterrestrials, and missives from all those people who claimed to be delivering messages from God, Satan, or dead world leaders.

"I'll take these," Ferber said, scooping up a bunch of letters. "See what we can find out from them, if anything." He turned to Pete. "Her security is arranged, right?"

"I'm sending my best men to look out for her," Pete said.

"You don't have to talk about me in the third person. Can I say something here?"

They both looked at me.

"This guy isn't threatening me, okay? Maybe you should put security on Reb, and Fennell, and Mike, in case he decides to do some follow-up work."

"We have security arrangements for them too," Pete said. "Don't worry. We need to give our ladies extra protection. Hector and Franco will be parked outside your building tonight, guarding you in shifts."

I had a feeling this sexist strategy was going to cost us. At the very least, I questioned the wisdom of leaving those two alone in my nutty neighborhood. Would they be safe? But who was I to argue with professional law-enforcement people?

My mind was churning with possibilities and anxieties, but then my eye caught on a photograph Mike had given me, which I'd taped to my computer. In the mountains of Pakistan, on the Karakoram highway to China, they have signs that say, WARNING—SLIDE AREA and then RELAX, SLIDE AREA OVER. As the road gets closer to China, the signs become more economical, even Zen. The photo showed a plain triangular white road sign that said, simply, RELAX.

19

I had worked hard to keep myself out of the tabloids in the last year and a half. I'm not one of those boldface mentions you read about in the columns being squired around by actors and moguls. When I get into the columns, it's usually because I've done something embarrassing. But even during the death series fiasco, I had managed to keep it quiet, keep it out of the "TV Ticker" column of the *New York Post*. I'd been lucky for a long time.

But in the morning, there, on the front of the *News-Journal,* was my face, with the big black words, FEMME FATALE?

Below, it asked: DID YOU DATE THIS WOMAN?

They hated me at the *News-Journal*.

It was almost all there in the story. Kanengiser, Reb, Fennell, Pinks, Anya. A gynecologist, a dominatrix, an attempted mother-killer, and two famous television personalities. Two dead, one wounded, the other scared shitless, et cetera, and all, the paper said, because of their contact with me. It was made for the tabloids.

Who had leaked all this?

"We decided to make all of this public," Detective Richard

Bigger was quoted as saying, "in hopes of saving the lives of other men who may have been in contact, even innocently, with Ms. Hudson."

They also dredged up the old Griff murder case, as well as my live, on-air belch and a few other incidents I really wanted to put behind me.

Was I ever going to escape my past?

By the afternoon, men all over the city had publicly disassociated themselves from me. There were jokes on Democracy Wall and in the Rumor File, and someone at ANN graphics had run up T-shirts with DON'T SHOOT . . . on the front and I NEVER DATED ROBIN HUDSON on the back. I saw four or five people wearing them just in the cafeteria. Admittedly, they were pretty funny T-shirts. Har har.

Well, I would probably never get another date as long as this nut was loose. The problem with nuts is, they're so unpredictable and can be so hard to detect. I mean, there are guys like Hank, who stalks Dillon Flinder backward, who are obviously nutty. Then there are those nice quiet types who live next door for years and end up having a freezer full of dead drifters.

Around three p.m., a press release was issued by Max Guffy, which someone thoughtfully, and anonymously, faxed to me.

"Not only did I not date Robin Hudson," he wrote. "I found her grossly offensive."

That was rather overstating it, I thought.

No, I hadn't dated Max Guffy. I had, however, thought about dating him when we met for our pre-interview, before I blew it all with a slip of the tongue.

There's always that one question I should never ask, that one anecdote I shouldn't tell, that one comment I shouldn't make, but I can't seem to stop myself, like the cannibalism question I asked the plane-crash survivor a couple of years ago.

With Max Guffy, avant-garde undertaker, I never should have told the Lazarus-sex story.

The notorious Romanian Lazarus-sex story, which ran on one of the European wire services, never made our air, although it was probably the most widely reported story within the network for a week or so. It was one of those stories that isn't suitable, as anchorman Sawyer Lash would mis-say, "for *any* members of your family."

As the story goes, a funeral home attendant had sex with a young female corpse, freshly dead, and the shock of it brought her back to life.

Imagine the attendant's horror. He's having sex with a dead woman who suddenly opens her eyes.

Now, imagine her horror. She wakes up after being unconscious to find a strange man is having sex with her on an examining table in a strange room.

("Imagine that guy's ego now, standing around the bar, bragging," my neighbor Sally had said. " 'I can bring dead women back to life.' ")

In any event, the girl's family didn't press charges, despite the vileness of the crime, because they got their Olga back. That's what I call a blessing in disguise.

("The Lord moves in mysterious ways," said my piggish boss Jerry Spurdle when he heard this tale.)

I asked Guffy what he thought about that, if it was possible to bring someone back to life that way. People at ANN were torn over that story, and it was endlessly discussed as some sort of extreme metaphor for the gender wars. A few argued the moral implications, as if it wasn't completely black and white and they could actually build a defense, the "might be okay if it's a matter of life and death" necrophilia defense. The rest of us argued the veracity, since the story came from Romania, a country so far into its id it brought us vampires, torchlight mobs, and Nicolae Ceaușescu. But some people swore by it, so I figured I'd settle a few bar bets by asking an authority like Max Guffy. Remember, Guffy and I had had a little vodka, he'd told some morbid jokes, and I was feeling very comfortable by this point.

But Max Guffy got very defensive and angry, launching a rant about stereotypes, rigorous screening and supervision, double-teaming so the bodies were never alone, how such sensationalist crap preyed on the public's fears and helped make people uncomfortable with death.

Then, red-faced, spitting mad, he asked me to leave.

Before you rush to judge me, consider that Max Guffy specialized in offbeat funerals, funerals as performance art, as comedy, as a reflection of the individuality of the dead guy. In his spare time, he also authored pseudonymous humor books about death.

Understand also that the man was proud of the *New Yorker* article that had said he was giving death a raucous eroticism. I was just a little blunter. It's not like I asked him if *he* ever did it with a dead person. I mean, hey, anyone who can stage a Mummenschanz funeral with a straight face and then write a humor book called *101 Uses for a Dead Clown* can take a story about necrophilia.

(Make that 102 uses.)

In retrospect, I probably shouldn't have told a necrophilia story to a mortician, but how often does one get the chance to tell a necrophilia story with a happy ending?

People called me all day. My ex-husband Burke called from Washington, where he was now a big-shot reporter at the State Department.

"Holden," he said, using one of his nicer pet names for me. "Take care of yourself. I assume you're armed to the teeth with corkscrews and electrolysis needles . . ."

"A hot glue gun and pepper spray," I said.

"And you still grow the poison ivy in your window boxes."

"Yeah," I said. "But I'm not really in any danger. Men who've been involved with me are in danger."

"That's always been true of you," he said. He was not properly sympathetic. What had once been a passionate love affair between me and Burke had dwindled down to an occasional phone call, an occasional dinner, a few shared memories, some joshing. We were like war buddies who get together every year to recall the battles they shared.

He laughed.

"What's so funny?"

"Don't tell me your legendary sense of humor in the face of everything has deserted you? I was laughing thinking how funny it would be if this stalker actually met you and discovered he didn't like you."

"You've always known how to flatter me, Burke."

"You take care of yourself, seriously. I'm laughing, Holden, but this guy has killed people, so be careful. I mean it. You have some protection, security?"

"Yes, I've got our top security men looking after me," I said. I was being sarcastic. Hector and Franco did not make me feel safer. I was sure they could both be lured away from their posts by a fast-talker on a snipe hunt.

"You be careful too, Burke."

"I will." Burke is smart and good-looking and has a lot of obsessed women fans. He receives Fabioesque quantities of fan mail.

Dillon called. "I'd take a bullet for you any day," he said.

"That's sweet. Kind of," I said.

Even Eric E-mailed me from Moscow. "Don't take *any* unnecessary chances," he said. "Keep your sweet head down."

I had a steady stream of visitors as well. Jerry, thank God, was in meetings, which took precedence over li'l ol' me, so he would have to wait to harass me about this. But Dave Kona came in to express his concern. I couldn't help noticing the way he sized up my office.

Louis brought me some funny stories, and Phil the janitor brought me a flower.

"You're a lot like me, Robin," Phil said. "Life throws you into craziness. But you're too silly to die too, I think."

Ferber called me twice. Once to tell me he couldn't find

Howard Gollis, and once to tell me ballistics had matched the bullet Mike recovered.

Then Mike came in.

"I'll be happy to stay at your place tonight," he said. "Just to keep you company."

"Thank you, but it's really not that big a deal. This isn't someone who wants to hurt me, just men who are seen with me," I said. "Don't put yourself at risk. Be careful. This guy might take another shot."

"Girl, I've been in much tougher spots than this one," he said.

After he left, Tamayo came in. "You've seen the latest papers?" she said, sympathetically, and put the evening papers down on my desk.

"I'm doomed," I said. "This was the last thing I needed right now, what with the reshuffle and the cutbacks and some nut out there shooting at any man who whistles my way . . . and my Aunt Maureen is in town, she's bound to see the papers and . . ."

"Oh, someone called about your aunt," Tamayo said.

"Who?"

"Where did I put that message? Just a second."

She came back a moment later. It was a message from Aunt Mo's roommate, Mrs. Sadler.

"I'm sorry to bother you," Mrs. Sadler said when I called her back. "But your aunt didn't come back to the hotel yesterday. I woke up this morning and her bed was made. Did she stay over at your home?"

"No. Are you sure she didn't come in after you were sleeping and then get up early to pray or something?"

"I don't think so. She was acting very strange when she left last night."

"Did she say where she was going?"

"I'm not sure. She got a call and said she had to go out. But she'd been reading your diary . . ."

My diary is kept on my home computer. To read my diary, she would have to break into my apartment, boot up my computer, access the software, load the relevant floppy disk, and find the relevant files, of which there are many, all locked. Then she would have to guess all the passwords, not an easy task, some of them in obscure languages, some of them made-up words, or she would have to find my secret password file in a separate subdirectory and then guess the password for the locked password file, *tushnob,* a Pushtu word for toilet I learned from Mike.

That's a hell of an accident for a woman who can't set the clock on her VCR.

"Diary?"

"I think it was your diary . . ."

"My Filofax," I said.

She began to cry. "Oh dear, I never should have let her go out yesterday."

"Why did she?"

"Your boyfriend called her and she went to see him."

"Hold on," I said. "I'll be right over."

I collected Hector and we went over together. I had to take Hector with me since it would have been impossible to sneak out of the office without him seeing me. Even if he hadn't been parked right outside the door of Special Reports, guarding me like I was a vault full of money, someone would have seen me on the vast network of in-house video cameras.

On the way, I called Ferber from the car phone.

When we got to the Gotham Manor Hotel, which is owned by Paul Mangecet Hotels, Inc., the lobby was full of smiling Christians, milling about after some sort of symposium. I could tell they were Christians because they smiled so much and because they all had adhesive name tags with crosses on them.

Just as I was about to raise my hand to knock on Mrs.

Sadler's door, it opened. I guessed she'd been watching for me through the peephole.

"Thank heavens you're here," she said, ushering me into the chintzy, twin-bedded room.

"Tell me about the diary," I began.

"One of your neighbors ran into a man outside your building who gave her the diary," she said.

"That would be Joey Pinks," I said. "He gave it to Mrs. Ramirez and she gave it to Aunt Maureen?" I was thinking out loud.

"That sounds right."

"What did the man tell Mrs. Ramirez, my neighbor? Did Aunt Mo say?"

"No."

Not that it mattered. Mrs. Ramirez put her own spin on things. For that matter, she made stuff up out of whole cloth.

"Did she say anything about this ex-boyfriend?"

"Oh, I am sure she said 'boyfriend,' not 'ex-boyfriend.' And other than that, she said nothing."

"It doesn't sound like Aunt Maureen to be so reticent," I said.

"Well, we didn't speak much . . . we weren't . . ."

I watched her struggling for the Christian thing to say.

"You weren't friends," I helped.

"No, we weren't."

"How did you come to be roommates?"

"Well, er, I . . . nobody else wanted . . . oh dear."

"Nobody else wanted to room with Aunt Maureen."

"Well, yes," said Mrs. Sadler, apparently the group martyr.

Boy, even the other right-wing Christians didn't like being around Aunt Maureen very much. Poor Aunt Mo. It was like being the last kid chosen for softball, in a way.

Poor Aunt Mo. I had no doubt the shooter had her. I didn't hold out much hope for her. A madman alone in a room with a gun and my bigmouthed Aunt Maureen? It would be awful hard not to kill her.

If only I'd seen her. Maybe she would have given me the Filofax and we could have given it to the cops and the shooter wouldn't have come after her . . .

As traumatic a figure as she cut in my life, she was my aunt and blood is thicker . . . and stickier . . . than water. And, to be fair, there had been times when I was glad she was my aunt. Now that she was missing, I started remembering other times, other events. Episodes flashed before me all day and well into the night as I lay in my bed, inconsolable by rain forest singers or purring cats. Like the time I was cornered by a group of menacing older boys in the playground, and Aunt Mo saw out her kitchen window and came out with God's Little Helper. She just went nuts with those boys, like a samurai, swatting them every which way until they scattered.

After Dad died, it was Aunt Mo who came to stay with us, and took care of us in those crucial first weeks without him. It was Aunt Mo who insisted I have a tenth birthday party, three months after my Dad died, and, because my mother was too shell-shocked to handle it, Aunt Mo came to town and threw a pretty good party for me. That day was the first happy one I had after Dad died. In high school, when I didn't have enough money for a new dress for the junior prom, it was Aunt Mo who sent me a nice check, unasked. Sure it came with a long letter about the sin of vanity and scriptural prohibitions against fornication, but it's the check that counts.

It could even be said that, in her inimitable way, Aunt Mo had been a positive influence in my life. For example, her attempts to get custody of me had made me work hard to keep it together for me and Mom and keep Aunt Mo at bay. I learned to cook, and at age ten I was cooking all our meals and doing all the housework, making sure Mom signed the checks for the bills and took her medication. Now, I rarely cook and I hate to clean. I did enough of that crap by age twenty-one to last me my entire life, and when my Aunt Minnie was widowed and moved in with us, I took the opportunity to ditch Chuck Turner and get out of Ferrous, Minnesota.

But the point is, rebelling against Aunt Mo made me a lot more independent. Granted, my life wasn't anywhere near perfect, but I made my own living. I could take care of myself.

Poor Aunt Mo. Alone in this big, wicked city, with nobody to take care of her. Was she even still alive? It was impossible to sleep, waiting for the phone to ring or the buzzer to sound, expecting, fearing the voice that said, "We found your aunt's body at a Staten Island landfill," hoping and praying for the voice that said, "We found your aunt and she's alive."

I needed a drink. Shortly after midnight I called down to Sally, asked her if I could borrow a cup of vodka to help me sleep. She not only had a premium vodka at hand, she brought it up to me and did a tarot, which foretold wonderful things in my future. Before she left, she promised to burn a candle for me and assured me I had every reason to be optimistic. My aunt was missing, my job was in jeopardy, and someone was shooting at men who went out with me. Yeah, I was feeling really optimistic.

Who was this guy? Was it Joey Pinks's half-brother Vern? Had Joey done forgery work for him? What would he need forged? What kind of things did people get forged, anyway, stuff like Social Security cards, green cards, maybe letters of reference? I wasn't sure.

Green cards. Why did that stick with me? I knew a few people with green cards. Mike had one, because he'd been married to an American. Tamayo, she had dual citizenship, so she probably had an American passport. Phil was British . . .

Phil would have to have one to work at ANN. Or a work visa. It bothered me, because Phil had been in the freight elevator the evening Kanengiser was killed. He'd gone up to a floor in the twenties. Could have been twenty-seven. It would have been easy for him to steal my handbag . . . and then steal a few more to cover it up. Who would suspect him, a cheerful, philosophical senior citizen?

But no, that's not right, I thought. The vodka was addling me. I mean, what was I thinking? That I was being stalked by a seventy-ish British handyman? He was too old to be Joey Pinks's half-brother. Besides, Phil had been out with the flu that day. If he'd lied about the flu and come back to the building to kill Kanengiser, he'd hardly strike up a conversation with Hymie from the newsstand.

But he was on that tape.

However, the tapes, while time-coded, were not date-coded. Someone must have replaced the right tape with a tape from another day . . .

Maybe it was someone who had worked in U.S. Army Intelligence, who was able to sneak in somehow and change the tapes. Someone like Reb Ryan.

Reb Ryan wasn't his real name. He'd changed it years before, Mike said. Maybe his real name was Vern.

Reb was clearly nuts. He knew how to take a beating, he had a masochistic desire to be in war zones, and he enjoyed drinking his own urine.

Yeah, I had dated Reb. But so had the younger, prettier, beestung-lipped Bianca. I had to be realistic here. If I were Reb, would I be obsessed with me, or with Bianca? As attractive as I think I am, Bianca was indisputably one of the most beautiful women to grace ANN's air.

Maybe he was upset that Bianca had ditched him for Pete. Maybe he had picked a fight with Dillon at Keggers because Dillon had gone to Bianca's table and shamelessly flirted with her, not because Dillon had walked out with me.

After talking to Pete and tracking a promo the night of the bar fight, Reb would have had plenty of time to get over to Dillon's building and take a shot.

My mind was racing. Or maybe it wasn't Reb.

Someone in security could have replaced that tape.

Pete controlled security and he could switch the tapes. How

much did we know about him anyway? Some second-rate celebrity bodyguard who had won Jack Jackson's trust during a drunken moment. Maybe he was brother Vern, with forged identification as Pete Huculak. There were probably a lot of men who would whip themselves silly just to hear Bianca say their names through those acclaimed lips. Pete could be one of them. He was known to be jealous. They practically lived together, so he would know her schedule, and if she didn't tell him about the guys she dated, he could have picked it up from the company grapevine.

My Filofax, though . . .

Well, we hadn't seen the thing. It might not be my Filofax. It could be Kanengiser's mythical black book after all . . .

Now I had a new theory. Joey Pinks had come to me because he knew me from interviewing Anya and he didn't know Bianca at all, or he couldn't get close to Bianca because he'd risk running into Pete, or Pete's deputy Hector. To warn her, he had tried to go through me.

Maybe I'm not so irresistible, I thought.

Aunt Maureen must have seen something, or Pete must have seen her . . .

My phone rang. It was Hector calling from the car phone downstairs, where he and Franco were "guarding" me.

"We found your aunt. She's alive. Wanna go see her?"

I didn't even bother to get dressed. I grabbed my purse, threw a coat on over my pajamas, and rushed downstairs to the company car.

"Okay, let's go," I said chirpily, sliding into the front seat.

There was a flash of white over my face, I heard a loud pop, and everything went dark.

20

When I came to, my head was covered in a leather mask, and I was standing against a wall, my feet and hands chained. I felt queasy, maybe from the ether or chloroform or whatever I'd been knocked out with. I looked around, but the mask impaired my peripheral vision. It was a big room, bare, with rough wood floors. The windows were bricked up, so I couldn't tell if it was day or night. But the bricking and the fact that the only light in the room was strung in from elsewhere—indicating pirated electricity—told me we were in a condemned or abandoned building, or a squat.

Was there anything in this room that would make a good weapon? Not really. There was a broken-down sofa missing its arms, and a queen-size bed. There were two doors.

I looked at myself. My hands were linked with a foot-long chain, as were my feet, allowing me to move with limited flexibility. I was hooked up to a retractable harness attached to the wall, with wire cables attached to my arms, like marionette strings. The cables went to the ceiling, rather like trolley cables, to a track, like the tracks used in track lighting.

With a little effort, I could move away from the wall and

walk within a ten-foot circumference. I made it, with some strain, to one of the doors and opened it. Down the hallway, I could see a sliver of another room and part of a table, with my purse on it.

I tried wriggling out of my restraints, but no amount of struggling could free me. I was pretty well secured. And I was getting really angry.

"Robin, is that you?" a voice called from another room.

I heard mechanical motion. One of the doors opened—the door to the attached bathroom—and a zaftig woman harnessed in black leather came out. Like me, she was masked and hooked up like a trolley. But I recognized the voice.

It was Aunt Mo.

"You're alive!"

"Of course I am," she said.

"Where are we?"

"Dear, I don't know. But it's an empty place. I've tried screaming and nobody has heard me."

"Aunt Mo, have you seen the guy who kidnapped us?"

"Yes."

"Can you describe him?"

"Tall, protruding forehead . . ."

God, it could be Hector, Howard Gollis, Pete Huculak, the ex-con on the subway train with the Aryan Nations tattoo. It could be any number of men I passed every day in the streets or in the hallways of ANN.

"Can't you be more specific?"

"Didn't see his hair color. He wore a hat of some kind, a hunting cap . . . my eyes aren't what they used to be . . . I'm doing the best I can, you know? I came to New York to enjoy a nice conference, see how my niece was doing, see a few shows. I end up kidnapped. . . . He was wearing a security guard uniform."

"Hector?" It happened so fast I couldn't be sure.

"Hector? Is that his name? He told me his name was Elroy Vern."

"Elroy Vern? Elroy? Where is he now?"

"He went out. He said he'd be gone a few hours but I don't know how long ago that was."

"Has he hurt you?"

"He hasn't touched me, except to put me into this contraption."

Was Hector really Elroy Vern? It made a little sense, and lately things had been so senseless that a little went a long way. Using his position in security, Hector must have switched the tapes from the freight elevator, so nobody would see he'd gone up to twenty-seven the night Kanengiser was murdered. He had been able to switch tapes, because he worked in security. He had been able to steal my Filofax and keep tabs on me, because he worked in security.

"What else did Elroy Vern say?"

"Oh, not very much. He says he was 'away' for five years and he watched you on television in that time and wrote you letters. He came here to find you."

"Away where? Where was he?"

"Judging by the time I've spent with him," Aunt Mo said, "I'd guess a mental hospital."

"What else did he say?"

"Not much. Sometimes he just won't talk at all. He just stares at a photograph of you."

"We have to get out of here, Aunt Mo."

"I've tried to get out of this thingamajiggy, but I haven't been able to."

"Is it day or night?"

"Day," she said. "I think."

"Aunt Mo, how did you get the Filofax? How did you end up involved in this?"

"Your neighbor, Dulcinia Ramirez, met a man outside your building, and he had this book for you and a message . . . Didn't you get my message? I left messages all about this on your answering machine."

"You did?" Oops. Those must have been the messages I

fast-forwarded through. "I guess my machine screwed up. I didn't get the message. What was it?"

"According to Dulcinia, your pimp was hurting your boyfriends and this man she met thought he might hurt you too. I tried to warn you. I tried to help you. But you just ignored me."

"Why didn't you let my boss know when you saw him? He could have warned me."

"I certainly didn't want to tell your employer all these terrible things about you. I wanted to talk to you personally."

"Now tell me about this so-called boyfriend of mine who called you up."

"Well, he called me at the hotel and said he was very, very concerned about you. I said I was concerned too, but that you wouldn't listen to me. We agreed to meet. That's when he knocked me out and abducted me. I'd seen him before."

"Where?"

"One night, I saw him outside your apartment building."

"What night was that?"

"I hardly know what day it is now, dear. It was a few days ago. There were several strange men outside your building that night. A young man shouting about a blindfold . . ."

Howard Gollis.

". . . an older man, middle-aged with hair plugs."

Fennell Corker.

"And Hector," I said. "Or Elroy Vern."

She nodded. "Now, tell me how you managed to get us into this mess," Aunt Mo said.

It was so like her to assume that it was something I'd done that started this whole ball rolling, that at its root, the responsibility for all this lay with me.

So I gave her the whole story and tried to impress upon her that it wasn't me at fault, it was just my bad luck. But Aunt Mo didn't hear a word of it. When I was done, she said, "Robin, this is where sin and abandon lead . . ."

It was very disorienting to hear her voice coming out of that outfit.

"I don't need a lecture right now, Aunt Mo. All that stuff you heard about me, and saw, it's not true. I was researching a story. I was being stalked by a crazy man. There was nothing I could do, really, to prevent this."

"You could have prevented this a long time ago, by making different choices with your life," Aunt Mo said. "If you'd married Chuck Turner and stayed in Minnesota, instead of running off to New York and going into television, I daresay we wouldn't be sitting here dressed like minions of the devil and being held hostage by a crazy person."

She trolleyed closer to me and put her hands over mine. "You know, dear, we may die here. So I want you to think seriously about some things. It's not too late for you to be born again," she said. "Do it for me, so if we die, I'll die knowing you're going to be in heaven."

Aunt Mo, she just never gives up. On one hand, it was really sweet of her to think of me. On the other, I saw this as a last-ditch effort to win our lifelong battle of wills.

I thought about how, when I was little, Aunt Mo had said to me, "Don't you want to go to heaven?" I paused, thought about it, and asked, suspiciously, "Are you going to be there?"

That's the thing. If she's right, then heaven is going to be full of people like her. Frankly, the idea of spending eternity with Aunt Mo, Pat Robertson, Jerry Falwell, Oliver North, Paul Mangecet, and Phyllis Schlafly is, well, hell.

"I can't do that for you, Aunt Mo," I said. "Can we talk about something else, other than how I've fu— . . . fouled up my life and yours?"

"You are so stubborn. Just have to spite me and try to pick a fight . . ."

"I'm not picking a fight. Why is it, if ever I disagree with you, I'm picking a fight? I'm merely defending myself."

"Defending yourself? Against whom?"

"Against you."

"I'm not your enemy! I'm on your side!"

This is a confrontation I have played out in my head a thousand and one times. Never in a million years would I have pictured it happening like this, however. Here we are, dressed like something out of an Anne Rice novel, pushing each other's buttons again, screaming at each other.

"What did I ever do but help you, or try to help you?" she asked.

"You found constant fault with me and you embarrassed the hell out of me—"

"Well, I had to get the hell out of you somehow."

"This isn't the time or place to discuss this . . ."

"Name one time I embarrassed you."

"What about the time I was fifteen and I came in with a boy I liked and you grabbed my face and started talking about my acne . . ."

"You're still holding a grudge about that?" Aunt Maureen said to me.

"There are so many times. You always saw only the worst in me, Aunt Mo," I said. "Whenever I was feeling weak, you were there to make me feel weaker."

"Well, your parents praised you to the heavens, and I didn't want you to get a swelled head. Your mother and father thought you could do anything. Your father thought you could be the first woman president of the United States and your mother . . . your mother thinks you're an English princess royal. She thinks you should be a queen. I felt they were feeding you false expectations of what a woman could expect in this world. I felt you'd be happier if you'd submit your will to God and accept your fate, accept your place as a woman. Look at you. You're not happy now."

"I'm happy sometimes. We shouldn't be arguing right now," I said. It's funny how she and I can get going and lose perspective. Still, I was glad I had had it out with her, glad I'd stood up to her at last.

"No, we shouldn't," she said.

We sat in silence for a while. Whenever we'd been together before, we'd only argued, or rather, Aunt Mo had berated me and I'd listened sullenly. We didn't know how to relate to each other in any other fashion. Every conversation we'd ever had, it seemed, had degenerated quickly into a battle. Small talk wasn't really appropriate at this juncture.

For a few long minutes, we sat there, staring at each other. "Did you know your father was a miracle baby?" she said.

"What's that?"

"Our mother had four daughters, and she and father wanted a boy, but the doctor told her she couldn't conceive any more children. But then she had your dad. A miracle baby. He was a cute baby too. When he was little, he used to follow me around like a puppy dog. And did he get into trouble! He was so curious and full of mischief."

She told a story about when she was a teenager and one of her young suitors came to call, and Dad hid in the back of the suitor's automobile and spied on them their whole date. It was hard to imagine my dad as a kid, even harder to imagine Aunt Mo as a teenager who "sparked" with suitors in the parlor.

I remembered a photograph of Aunt Mo when she was about seventeen, in my father's family photo album. In it, she had her hair done in a very glamorous 1940s fashion—I think they call it a finger wave. Even then, she had looked like Mussolini, but a young Mussolini with the hairstyle of Veronica Lake. She was wearing shorts and a striped T-shirt and leaning on the hood of a car, almost flirtatious. There was a young man in the picture, just back from the war. It wasn't Uncle Archie.

Dad always said Aunt Mo had never been young, she was born an old woman, but I knew from that picture that there had been a glimmer of youth there, however briefly.

I asked her about the photo.

"Oh my," she said. "Oh my oh my."

"Who was he?"

"Truman Dirk. I almost married him."

"Wow. Why didn't you?"

"He was shell-shocked, from World War II. He fought in the forest of Ardennes during the Battle of the Bulge and it changed him. Oh, he could be wonderful though. He had a charm sometimes, a joy . . . but then something would set him off and he'd drink, he'd get violent . . ."

"I'm sorry."

"Oh it was hard. That's when I turned to the church, to give me the strength to go on. I really loved him," she said. "But he wouldn't have been a good husband or a good father for my children. Archie, he was a good provider and a good father to Raymond."

I would dispute that, since Uncle Archie had spent most of his free time alone in the attic making cribbage boards out of firewood, when he should have been guiding his young son toward manhood. But maybe poor Raymond had been better off not spending a lot of time with his dad. Who knew? After all these years, nobody knew much about Uncle Archie.

"How come you didn't have more kids, Aunt Mo?"

"Female problems," she said. "I miscarried five times before I had Raymond, my miracle baby, and the doctor advised me not to have any after Raymond."

"I didn't know. I'm sorry."

"It was my faith that got me through that too. And your Uncle Archie. It wasn't easy for him."

I guess not. Back then, before the Pill, the only way you could be sure *not* to get pregnant was to abstain. Made me think that maybe, when Uncle Archie was up there alone in the attic, he had more than cribbage on his mind.

"I think that's why I took an extra interest in you. I thought of you as the daughter I never had," she said. "What always got me through, Robin, was my faith. I just wanted you to have that same faith to help you through life, because life is hard."

"I envy you your faith, Aunt Mo," I said softly. How comforting to have all the philosophy you want in one convenient book, and not have to pick it up willy-nilly from all over the known universe and then cobble it together.

"I really do," I went on. "But I'm just built differently. Blind faith just doesn't work with me."

"Your father used to say almost the same thing to me. It's funny. I never realized how much you remind me of your father."

I saw something of my father in her too. Like my father, she was tenacious, opinionated, and fiercely devoted to her own vision.

"Let's read the Bible, shall we?" Aunt Mo said. "It will give us strength."

She picked up a huge family Bible, the size of the *Complete Pelican Shakespeare* in hardcover, from behind the bed. I hadn't noticed it before.

"He let you keep your Bible?" I said.

"Yes. And he made me tea."

"You carry that big Bible around with you everywhere?"

"Yes."

"But it's so heavy."

"I like feeling the weight of it," she said. "It makes me aware always that God is with me. Now, I think this occasion calls for the Old Testament, when the Hebrews were in bondage to the pharaoh . . ."

"Aunt Mo, we have to get out of here."

"How do we do that?"

"I don't know yet."

"Well, in the meantime, why don't we pray for courage and inspiration," Aunt Mo said, opening her Bible to Exodus and reading from it.

"I'm sorry, Aunt Mo, but would you mind reading that to yourself? I'm trying to think."

"The Bible will set you free," Aunt Mo said, absently.

I almost didn't hear her. I was thinking about Elroy, wondering what he'd do to me, to Aunt Mo, to himself. Would he shave his legs with a rusty razor, then sit in an acid bath while we listened to his screams? Would he then lick my feet? Or would he go nuts and just shoot us?

"What did you say?"

"I said, the Bible will set you free."

"Let me hold that Bible."

It was heavy. Five pounds, maybe more.

"Aunt Mo, we can stay here and behave ourselves and hope this nut lets us loose. Or we can do something. But it's risky, either way."

"Let me take the risk," she said. "I'm elderly, if I die, I know I'm going to heaven. But if you die . . ."

"We'll both be at risk, Aunt Mo," I said. "Now, one of us will have to have her hands free. It will have to be you, I think. He'll be less suspicious of you, because you're an elderly Christian lady."

I outlined the rudiments of a plan and we discussed it. Before we had it nailed down, we heard a door opening in another room, and then heavy boots. He was back.

It wasn't Hector.

It was Franco.

21

Franco was standing in the doorway, wearing his uniform and a hunting cap with ear flaps, which explained how Aunt Mo had missed those hairy ears in her description.

But how had he . . . ? Well, of course. During Hector's shift, Franco must have called him from a nearby pay phone, had him call me. When I got into the car with Hector, Franco shot Hector and knocked me out. Franco could have taken my bag very easily. Franco could very easily switch the freight elevator tapes in security. Franco was not named Franco, and so he needed fake ID to work at ANN. That's where Joey Pinks would have come in.

Franco had flown below my radar.

"Elroy," I said.

Elroy said nothing for a long time. After untying my mask and removing it, he gave us each a paper bag from McDonald's, then sat down on the armless sofa, peeled a nicotine patch off his arm, and lit a cigarette. Then he just stared at me.

"Are you going to let us go?" I asked.

Stupid question, but it was worth a shot, anyway.

"No," he said.

"Are you going to keep us?"

"Yes," he said.

"For how long?"

He shrugged, continued to stare.

"What do you want from me?" I asked.

"I just want to make you happy," he said.

You know, you pray for a man who will see all your finest qualities, and none of your worst ones. A man who will look on you adoringly, treat you like a queen.

Be careful what you pray for . . .

"I would be so much happier if you'd let me go," I said. "I can't be happy like this."

"I know her," Aunt Mo said. "She's telling the truth."

"Shut up!" he said, suddenly angry. He pulled out his gun and pointed it at Aunt Maureen. "*You* shut up! I wasn't talking to you."

Crazy people. They are so unpredictable.

"She's tired," I explained. "And she's been in leather for a long time. Can't she just take a shower? It would make her feel so much better. She's elderly. Please."

"Eat first," he said.

I did eat, but I also took careful mental notes about Elroy. He had keys on his trouser loops. Presumably one of those keys fit the lock on the chains around my hands and feet. He had a gun holster. Black scuffed shoes.

"Okay," he said to Aunt Mo, suddenly sweet now. He unhooked her from her harness, unchained her, and took her at gunpoint to the bathroom. "Knock when you're ready to come out. Take your time."

When he heard the shower going, he came back, reholstered his gun, and sat at my feet. The Bible was just out of reach.

"We're alone," he said, kneeling at my feet, which he began to massage.

Hurry up, Aunt Mo, I thought. It was disgusting. Not that I wouldn't like it if someone else were doing it. He looked up at me, and I smiled politely, pretended I was enjoying it. I just knew at any moment he was going to start sucking on my toes and licking my feet.

He had it all set up now. He could make me spank him. He had my aunt as a hostage, he had me in harness, and he had a gun. By now, the cops had to know who Joey's half-brother Vern was. Maybe they had prints. Maybe they had a photo. Still, all Franco had to do was cover those ears and he could move pretty easily around a big city like New York without detection. The *New York Post* says there are seventy thousand fugitives from justice—most of them felons—hiding out in New York.

They might not find us for months. Years. A happy three-some, me, Aunt Mo, and Norman Bates. I have died. I have gone to hell.

"You have beautiful feet," Franco said.

I have size ten feet, extra wide. You know, I always wanted a man who would not only overlook my physical flaws, but fall in love with them . . .

I was trying to figure out how I was supposed to react to all this. You know that old joke? A masochist and a sadist are sitting on a bench. The masochist says, "Hurt me," and the sadist says, "No"? Did he want me to beat him? I'd beat him all right. Did he go both ways, S *and* M? By killing Kanengiser and shooting at all those others, he'd demonstrated the same corollary violent streak Joey Pinks had. Would he try to beat me?

Before he could suck my toes, Aunt Mo knocked. He took his gun out. When he went to let her out, I inched closer to the Bible, and pulled it toward me.

"You're dressed?" Elroy asked before letting Aunt Mo out. "Yes."

She came out and looked at me.

"Back to the wall," he said, taking her by the arm back to her harness. It took both hands to hook her back up, so he reholstered his gun. His back was to me. I stood very slowly and raised the Bible. Just as he was about to lock her padlock, I brought the Bible down on his head.

At the same time, Aunt Mo punched him right in the balls. She nailed him good three or four times, while I grabbed his gun and held it on him. Aunt Mo threw off her chains and went for his keys.

Once she unshackled me, she said, "Give me the gun, dear. I'm trained in firearms."

It didn't surprise me in the least that Aunt Mo knew her way around a firearm. I gave her the gun.

Aunt Mo put the gun right to his head, and said, "Up against the wall, you son of a bee."

"Son of a bee" is about as profane as Aunt Mo gets. Even in times of crisis she'd never say "bitch."

Except, perhaps, with her body language.

"Didn't anyone teach you that thou shalt not kill? That murder is a mortal sin?" she said.

That's Aunt Mo. Misses no opportunity to give a stern lecture and witness for the Lord.

"Thou shalt not kill!" she said again.

"I'm sorry, I'm sorry," Elroy wept. "I love her. I love her. I'm worthless!"

"I could blow you away right now," she said. "You know what keeps me from blowing you away right now?"

Unfortunately for Elroy, Aunt Mo wasn't the real forgiving type of Christian.

"W-what?"

"Because it's a sin, you blithering idiot! Didn't you hear a thing I said? Murder is a mortal sin."

Jeez, give this woman an action movie.

Once I was free of my harness, I chained Elroy's hands. There was nothing to hook the harness onto, though—he was not wearing the convenient angel-of-death black leather number Aunt Mo and I had on, and he wouldn't fit into mine or hers.

"Keep the gun on him," I said. "I'll look for a telephone."

"Look for our clothes too, dear," she said.

There was no phone in the other room. I noticed an electricity cable coming in through a crack in a locked, painted window. A quick check of drawers and the closet produced no rope, no clothes, but quite a few guns. I saw my purse on the table. Next to it was my glue gun. Elroy had apparently examined it, determined it to be useless, and put it aside.

I had an idea.

It took fifteen minutes and a whole big glue cartridge, and Aunt Maureen had to sit on him while the adhesive set, but we managed to glue him to the broken-down sofa. Just to be on the safe side, I hit him several more times with the Bible and knocked him out. Once I got started hitting him, I could hardly stop. I was angry. He wanted punishment, I'd give him punishment. It was Aunt Maureen who stopped me from bludgeoning him to death with the Bible.

"He's out," she said.

"We'll have to leave like this since I can't find our clothes. Let's grab our handbags and get out of here. Find a phone. Call the cops."

Beyond this makeshift squat was nothing but a decrepit warehouse. A long hallway led to an exit. It was deadly quiet, until we opened the door and rats scattered.

"Oh good Lord," Aunt Mo said. "That stairway does not look safe."

"Come on, Aunt Mo," I said.

"I can't. I . . . you don't know this, dear, but I'm terrified of rats. I . . . I . . ."

Suddenly, a door opened behind us. I turned. There was a flash of chintz and a gunshot.

It was Elroy, weaving down the hallway, stuck to a sofa, his hands chained, waving one of his other guns.

Aunt Mo was through that door and down that stairwell like God himself pushed her. We had got down one flight when we heard him come into the stairwell above and thunder down. He was a strong boy. It couldn't have been easy to come down those stairs with a sofa stuck to his back. And after that thorough thumping I gave him too.

We came out on the street. I didn't even have time to take note of where we were. It was somewhere on the Lower East Side, judging by the bombed-out-looking buildings. I grabbed Aunt Mo by the arm and we ran down the street.

"He's behind us," Aunt Mo said.

We were being chased by a man with a sofa on his back. Two women in black leather, being chased by a man with a sofa on his back.

"Can you run faster?" I asked her. We were almost at the corner.

"Surely someone will see this and call the police," she said.

"Not necessarily, Aunt Mo. We're downtown."

Elroy took a shot, and Aunt Mo wheeled around and shot back at him, just as I yanked her around the corner, almost giving her whiplash.

We were on Avenue C and Third Street now. Passersby stopped and glanced at us.

"Call the police, call the police!" Aunt Mo screamed.

Nobody made any move to call the police.

Elroy came around the corner shooting. Bystanders hit the sidewalks and covered their heads.

I pulled Aunt Mo into a little Korean grocery. As soon as the guy behind the counter saw us, he whipped out a gun.

"Lock the door," Aunt Mo said. I did. She turned to the man behind the counter. "Call the police!"

I saw a dark-haired woman slip into the back. She'd be calling the police, I expected. A young man in front of the beer cooler had his hands up.

"Get outta my store," the man behind the counter said. "I shoot you!"

"Don't shoot! We're not trying to rob you," I said, huffing to catch my breath.

Elroy was banging on the glass door.

"He's trying to kill us," I said.

"Holy shit," said the Korean man. He started screaming in Korean.

The door broke and Elroy came flying through in a shower of shattered glass, roaring like the crazy person he was and waving a gun.

A shot was fired.

Elroy's body slumped and fell to the ground under the sofa.

We looked up. The Korean man put his rifle down on the counter.

"You saw," he said. "It was self-defense. You're witnesses."

Aunt Mo and I were both, by this time, hysterical and having trouble getting out an intelligible story, and the store owners, the Lees, were pretty hysterical too. You can imagine this poor Mr. Lee's shock. One minute, he's organizing the ginseng-extract display by his cash register, and the next a man with a sofa glued to his back comes flying through his door brandishing a gun.

When Bigger and Ferber arrived, we were almost coherent. In fact, Detective Richard Bigger and Aunt Mo bonded, and she was able to get out her version of the story, which was riddled with inaccuracies about me that I felt it necessary to dispute point by point. This forced Bigger to split us up, banishing me to an orange crate by the steel beer refrigerator.

I sat down and Detective Mack Ferber put a hand under my right elbow to steady me. It's a funny thing, but my elbows are big erogenous zones for me and I got a thrill when he did that. He smelled good, too, like clean cotton and soap.

"Tell me everything," he said.

I did. Then I made him tell me everything he knew.

Just as Aunt Maureen had theorized, Elroy Vern had spent the last five years in a series of mental institutions in three states. He'd been committed by his mother shortly before her other son, Joey, tried to kill her.

"Elroy wanted to watch ANN all the time," the administrator in one institution had said. "Sometimes he became disruptive when other patients wanted to turn the channel in the rec room."

Just like Louis Levin's monkey, I thought.

A fellow patient had said, "All he talked about was this reporter, a redhead, like his mother when she was young."

Diagnosed as a paranoid schizophrenic with extreme sadistic and extreme masochistic tendencies, Elroy Vern had been shuttled about to several hospitals. Then, due to government cutbacks and institutional overcrowding, he had been medicated and released. With forged papers from Joey, he had made his way east and applied for work at ANN, where Pete took a liking to him.

("I was impressed by his obedience," Pete said later.)

The cops recovered my Filofax from Elroy Vern's squat in the abandoned building, which he kept in addition to a legitimate address, a small efficiency in Queens with an answering machine and nothing else. The Filofax was mine all right. The only change that had been made were the red X's through the names of men who had come in contact with me.

Hector was an innocent party, Ferber told me, and he was now in a coma after taking a bullet in his neck and then being dumped on Avenue D when Elroy was making his getaway. Poor Hector.

Several hours later, when I got to the office, Jerry Spurdle's first comment was, "See, I told you that doctor's murder had something to do with S&M. Didn't I tell you I had a hunch—"

"Shut up," I said.

"If you'd just have listened to me—" he said.

"Shut the *fuck* up!" I said. "You *fucking, stupid asshole.*"

Jerry and I had argued plenty in the past, before my ill-advised good attitude change, but he'd never heard this tone of voice from me before. This was the tone of voice of a woman one step away from an eighteen-pound turtle.

For a moment, Jerry just stood there, stunned.

I knew my ass was fried for yelling at him this way. But for some reason, saving this sorry job didn't seem so important anymore.

Suddenly, Jerry smiled at me. His usual smarmy smile.

"You are going to be so sorry you called me that," he said, and walked away.

22

"**W**ell, my prayer partners will certainly have a lot to pray for when I get back," Aunt Maureen said.

We were standing at LaGuardia Airport, outside the metal detectors before her gate. We'd had breakfast together, tried to clear up a few remaining discrepancies between her version of events and mine. Although she had finally accepted my explanation for why she ended up in leather and chains being chased by a man in a sofa, she still believed I was living a dangerous and sinful life, and that I would have been happier, safer, and heaven-bound if I'd stayed in Ferrous, Minnesota, and married Chuck Turner.

"Are you convinced yet? Are you ready to thank the Lord for saving your life and give your life to the Lord in payment?"

When Aunt Mo put it that way, I almost felt like I had no choice. But then I remembered that, by Aunt Maureen's uncompromising Old Testament standards, all the great guys would be in hell. Doubt suddenly clouded my faith.

"No," I said. "Not the way you want me to, anyway."

I was grateful and all, but I had to stand my ground. It's just the way I am.

Other happy Christians were streaming past us.

"Well, I had to try. Do I have a few stories to tell the girls on the book-banning committee when I get back! Thank you for seeing me off," Aunt Maureen said. "Take care of yourself now, and *be good.*"

"Yes, Aunt Mo."

"It's a shame you can't see your way to the light after this experience but—"

"Have a safe trip, Aunt Mo," I said. In truth, I just wanted to get her on the plane and get the hell out of there. Otherwise, I was going to be late for my lunch with McGravy and Jerry.

"Just tell me, are you happy, living in this city, doing the work you do, living the life you live? Really?"

"More or less," I said.

There are a lot of things that make me happy, when I think about it. My cat makes me happy, and my friends make me happy. Even my friends' successes make me happy, when you get right down to it.

Funny, interesting men make me happy too, sometimes. The wall full of hieroglyphs makes me happy. New York City makes me happy, mostly.

Playing practical jokes on Jerry Spurdle and making him suffer, that makes me really happy.

"I'll be praying for you."

"Thanks, Aunt Mo."

"Do you know who Philo T. Farnsworth is?" Aunt Mo asked.

"The inventor of television."

"Do you know what he said about television?"

I shook my head.

"He said: 'Television is a gift of God, and God will hold those who utilize his divine instrument accountable to him.' Remember that, dear."

McGravy and Jerry were already there when I got to Cafe Napoli. Jerry, in fact, had already ordered.

"Sorry I'm late," I said. "I had to see my aunt off, make sure nothing else bad happened to her."

"Nishe lady your aunt," Jerry said, with his mouth full of pasta.

"Robin," McGravy said. "Jerry and I wanted to let you in on the upcoming changes. As you know, the company is undergoing a lot of changes at the moment . . ."

While Bob spoke, Jerry chowed down on his veal, a healthy chunk of which he shoved into his mouth in one lengthy piece. Apparently he hasn't yet mastered the manipulation of cutlery, so he eats his food like one of those animals that swallows its prey live and whole. He takes a huge chunk of food and stuffs half of it into his mouth and the other half hangs out as he slowly chews, swallows, and pulls more of the overhang into his mouth until it's all absorbed.

"Yes?"

"I know you have your heart set on remaking a career in general news," McGravy began.

"Ain't gonna happen," said Jerry, talking with his mouth full.

"What is it, Bob. I can take it. I'm a big girl."

I was feeling pretty damn lucky to be alive, I must say, and the idea of losing my job was no longer as frightening as it had been.

"Okay. Jerry's going to Berlin for a year. We'd like you to take over the Special Reports unit. I know you wanted out of Special Reports, but this could be a blessing in disguise."

"I'll be head of the Special Reports unit?"

"At least for a year. Then we'll see where Jerry is, where you are."

"I get to run the show?"

"You shtill haf to get ratingsh . . . ," Jerry said, through a mouthful of partially masticated meat.

"And Jerry will be a half a world away, more or less?"

"There may be a few mandated series," Bob said. "And you will have to keep the ratings up. But you will have a lot of leeway. And you'll report to me. It isn't general news . . ."

"It's a blessing in disguise, all right," I said to Bob. "I'll take it."

Special Reports unit for a year? Sure. Even if they still expected me to do UFO stories, I could do them my way. Maybe I would do more good series like the one on vigilantism. Maybe I still had a career in news.

"Will I be reporting as well?"

"You could do a few series, just the ones you want to do," McGravy said. "We're assigning another reporter to work with you."

"Oh no, not . . ."

"Dave Kona."

The supercilious pip-squeak.

"Bob, he doesn't respect me. He'll be insubordinate—"

"Welcome to management," Jerry said. "Now, wasn't I right? Aren't you sorry you called me an asshole?"

It was fucking stupid asshole, to be precise, I thought. But I didn't say it. I wasn't sorry either.

So Jerry's off to Berlin, Madri's gone to PR, Sawyer Lash is getting another shot at daytime programming as co-anchor of *Gotham Salon*, Dave Kona is coming to work for me, and Claire Thibodeaux has gone to D.C., her last name intact.

Speaking of Claire, about a week after my promotion, a gift arrived from her. Wrapped in tissue inside a black enamel box was a small statue of Saint Clare of Assisi, with this note:

> *Dear Robin,*
>
> *Congratulations on your promotion!*
>
> *Did you know: In the Roman Catholic religion the patron saint of television is Clare of Assisi, the founder of a penitential order of nuns in 12th-century Italy. Her designation as the patron saint of television alludes to an incident during her last illness when, on her deathbed, she miraculously heard and saw the Christmas Mass in the basilica of San*

*Francesco on the far side of Assisi. A woman who has taken
a vow of poverty and a satellite downlink rolled into one.
ANN's perfect woman."*

Love, Claire

In the media blizzard over the following few days, it came
out that Howard Gollis, comic-artist-writer, was the brains
behind Chaos Reigns, the guerrilla art group. Not a group
really. Just him and a friend with a pickup truck. So the guillotine wasn't random but was, along with his car alarm concert, a special form of guerrilla art designed to harass
ex-girlfriends. The day before I was kidnapped, he'd gone on
the road to do stand-up at a bunch of clubs in Pennsylvania.
When contacted by police, he told them he'd been shot at one
night after seeing me, but didn't connect the two events.

He no longer calls.

Gary Grivett also had been shot at after seeing me. The
report had been stuck at the precinct level and was never
connected with the Manhattan South investigation, until now.

"I thought it was just one of those New York things," Grivett said to the *News-Journal.* "I had no idea it was because of
Robin."

As it turned out, Kanengiser hadn't kept a black book. Like
me, he had kept everything in a locked computer file, having
learned not to leave a paper trail after ex-wife Hannah Qualls
found his old black book. The file contained names, addresses,
phone numbers, and sexual details, along with personal information about the women he was sleeping with so he could
print out a cheat sheet and avoid making the mistakes he had
made with Susi Bure.

Bianca broke down one night at Keggers and confessed to
Claire and me that Kanengiser had treated her for a case of
vaginal warts. To her, it was some kind of big-deal dark secret.

Hector recovered from his injuries, just a few brain cells
shy of where he was before. Now, he has the sympathy of the
newsroom. He's kind of a hero. Like Forrest Gump.

My super died, alas. He was very old. But there was an opening for a super, and I mentioned it to Phil. He loved the idea, and since he moved in the water pressure is great and the elevator works again. Everyone likes him, even Mrs. Ramirez. I like to imagine she has a crush on him—to her, he's a younger man—that they have some torrid December-November romance going on. But it seems a long shot. Phil had me over for tea and "biscuits" in his basement apartment in our building. He had it done up quite nicely. We showed each other our scrapbooks. It turns out he really did survive Rommel and plane crashes and he really did save people's lives when he was a fireman in Liverpool. His first wife was an American girl he met in London just after the war. That's how he got his green card.

And I finally found out what Wim Young, the mysterious guitar-playing man, did for a living.

One night, I ran into him on the stoop and this time he smiled at me and spoke.

"Saw you on the news," he said.

I no longer feared him, so I chatted him up a bit. He asked me if I wanted to go get something to eat. As we were walking down the dark, deserted street, it suddenly struck me where I had seen this guy before.

America's Most Wanted.

I could see the episode so clearly. He was the guy who killed his girlfriend *and* his boyfriend after robbing them both blind.

Talk about jumping from the frying pan into the fire, I thought. I escaped Elroy, only to land in the clutches of some other killer. This is a new nightmare. I was about to become a future episode on a real crime show. I could see the mediocre actors reenacting it, hear the narrator: ". . . On the night of April eighteenth, reporter Hudson met a man outside her apartment building . . ."

We were walking down Avenue A, he was talking about having been in Florida recently—which is where the crimes took place—and I abruptly turned and screamed my lungs out, right in his face.

It turned out this guy was the *actor* who *played* the bad guy on *America's Most Wanted*, in a segment shot on location in Miami. So what he was seeing was not the classic response of a threatened woman, but a nut, who, in the middle of a civilized conversation, started screaming like a banshee when she heard the word "Florida."

Damn shame. He's good-looking and interesting and close by. I still see him sometimes, on his way out at night to meet friends or go to the theater. But he hasn't asked me to go anywhere since then. Our eye contact has gone from amazing to wary. He thinks I'm a crazy person.

But, as Aunt Maureen might say, were she a better sort of Christian, when God closes a door, he/she opens a window. Two days after I gave the guitar-playing man tinnitus, Mike asked me to a movie. I know he's one of those devilish Irishmen, and he's a gypsy, and he has the blood of twenty-seven Pakistani dogs on his soul. I know he's in news and I vowed not to get mixed up with any more newshounds, but what the hell. Ya takes yer chances or ya don't get laid. We could have a lot of laughs together.

I'm having dinner with my ex-husband next time he comes to New York. I mean, I'd never marry him again even if he wanted to marry me again, and he doesn't, believe me. But he's single, I'm single, and there's still chemistry there, so who knows what might happen?

You never know. You know?

I'm supposed to go watch Detective Mack Ferber's softball team play, and Eric's coming back to New York on home leave in the summer. The guy upstairs might get to know me better, and decide I'm not too crazy. I don't have to make my mind up right this minute.

So this is the dark side: I'm not Diane Sawyer or Joanne Armoire or Claire Thibodeaux and I never will be. I'm a middle-aged woman in a youth-obsessed culture whose on-air prime is in the checkered past. I'm divorced, with no steady boyfriend, and friends who flit in and out of my life. I live in a bad neighborhood in a crazy city and a crazy world where people go along all nice and peaceful, and then suddenly beat their husbands to death with an eighteen-pound turtle. And someday, I'm going to die.

But there is a bright side: I'm not Aunt Maureen, or Anya, or Cecile Le Doc, and I never will be. For that matter, I'm not Diane Sawyer. Her life looks good to me, from here, but all lives have their sorrows and, not knowing what hers are, I'm not sure I'd want to trade.

True, I live in a bad neighborhood. But it is a bad beautiful neighborhood and I live in an interesting downtown building that, thanks to Mrs. Ramirez's spying and my poison ivy, is peculiarly safe.

My on-air days may be numbered, but I am now the boss, which definitely has its downside, given my staffing—an absentminded anarchic comedian and a supercilious pip-squeak reporter. But I have more control. My friends flit in and out, but that keeps us all fresh and interested in each other and independent. No steady boyfriend, true, but on the other hand, I'm a Free Woman and I get to sleep with any attractive, interested man I choose to sleep with. I suspect this is one of those freedoms it is better to have than to use, but maybe not. I'll get back to you on it.

And, duh, someday I'm going to die.

But I'm not dead yet.

ARTICHOKE

Acknowledgments

Just when I'm out of money and ready to sign up as a paid human trial subject for medical experiments to finance my writing career, someone shows up to help. Just when I'm convinced the world is a sucky place, that life's a bitch and so am I, the fax machine rings and a hilarious true story culled from a wire service comes rolling through from some good soul.

I would be a really big asshole if I didn't mention these people. At the risk of sounding like Cloris Leachman, the author wishes to thank those who generously shared their hearts, homes, refrigerators, expense accounts, time, insights, newsroom legends, wire stories, inspirational stories, money, and party invitations:

Mom, Dad, Bill Dorman (Spasiba), Jennifer Hayter, Emerson Macintosh, and my whole damn family for being the funniest people I've ever met; my agent, Russell Galen, and my editor, Caroline White, for all their hard work and for many other things, including reassurances at critical crazy points that all their other writers are crazier than me; Debbie Yautz; Laura, Juris, and Melanie at Soho Press for making me become a better writer; General Publishing, Helen Metella, Mark Nixon at Book Company Southgate, Snoop Sisters, Sleuth, Wayne Kral, Bonnie Claeson, and Prodigy MBC.

Thanks also, in no particular order, to: Bill of IMC, Katherine Neville, Nancy Pickard, Janine Turner; Andrea Peyser, who did the S&M field work with me; Grant Perry, "a previous special reporter now in our London bureau"; Chris P. for the Romanian-necrophilia wire story, Harris Salat and Lisa Napoli for keeping me up-to-date on TV technology and lingo, amazing and anarchic Tamayo Otsuki, Steve Herman and Ito for hosting my book party at the Morg; Diana and Jake, Jesse, Bruce Gillette, David and Mary Helen, Nance, Lisa Schiffren, Paul Mougey, Siv Svendsen, Peter and John Holm, Baard and the rest of the Norwegians, Steven and Kathrine, Lynn Willis, Marianne Hallett, Eva Valenta, Elaine, Dana, Susan, Scott, Squadron, Cheryl, Nicki, Mark, Joanna L., Maggi O'Connell, the Chelsea, and the very understanding men and women in the credit collections department at American Express.

If I've left anyone out, I apologize and will make it up to you somehow.

Thanks for everything.